Vendetta

Sherryl D. Hancock

PRESS

Published by Vulpine Press in the United Kingdom in 2017

ISBN 978-1-83919-241-8

Cover by Armend Meha
Cover photo credit: Tirzah D. Hancock

www.vulpine-press.com

Acknowledgements

As always to my wonderful wife without whom I wouldn't have been able to understand love and know that it's real.

To victims of molestation, you can get through this. I did.

Chapter 1

Cody crawled out of bed on a Sunday morning, knowing she needed to get going. Glancing over her shoulder her eyes scanned the naked woman lying on the rumpled bed. She was a hot one; Cody knew for sure she had some scratches down her back for the experience. She moved her neck around stretching it, and heard it pop a couple of times. She walked into the master bathroom, closed the door, and turned on her music.

Turning to look in the mirror, she saw long, bloody claw marks. Whistling lowly to herself, she grinned. *Wanna play rough, ya gotta pay,* she thought to herself. Getting into the shower, she stood under the spray, letting it soak her back, feeling the water hitting the scratches. Somehow, it actually felt good. She stood with her arms braced spread eagle, her hands on the shower wall, head bowed. She sensed the other person in the room before she even stepped into view.

"Not the smartest thing to do," Cody said, without raising her head.

"What?" the woman, who'd been sleeping minutes before, asked as she stepped into the shower behind Cody.

"Sneaking up on a cop," Cody said evenly.

"I wasn't trying to sneak up on you, Cody," the woman said, sliding her hand around Cody's slim waist, her tone chiding.

Cody shook her head slowly, not responding.

The woman positioned herself between Cody and the wall. Cody's hazel eyes, that looked green at that point, stared back into the woman's blue eyes. Leaning down, she captured her lips with hers, her kiss hungry and strong. Minutes later the woman was screaming in her orgasm, scratching new marks onto Cody's back, even as Cody thought *Oh shit!* Her mothers would definitely hear that which meant she'd hear about it too.

Predictably, after the woman left, Cody couldn't even remember her name. Lyric knocked on the bathroom door and opened it at Cody's bidding.

"Jesus, Code, could you at least keep them down to a few decibels in the morning?" Lyric said, although her grin was rather prideful.

She'd already been chastised by her wife for being proud that her daughter made a woman scream that loudly.

As she got a look at Cody's back, she saw the scratches. "And could you ever pick one that doesn't have nails? Christ, you're gonna get an infection," she said, winking at her daughter in the mirror.

Cody grinned, knowing that Lyric was giving her a hard time out of a sense of duty, not any real ire.

"You headed back undercover this morning?" Lyric asked, leaning on the bathroom counter as Cody finished getting ready.

"Yeah, gotta hit the office first though. I need to check a few things."

"Any progress?"

Cody shrugged. "Still kind of establishing myself at this point."

Lyric nodded, knowing how the job of an undercover agent went, having been one herself.

"Well, at least stick around long enough to have breakfast with us. You know your mom needs to see your face for a while," Lyric said, grinning.

"I know," Cody said, smiling fondly. "I'll be out in a few."

Cody and Lyric both worked for the TRaCE task force. TRaCE stood for Tax Recovery and Criminal Enforcement. While it sounded benign, the task force was responsible for the disruption of multiple human trafficking endeavors in the Los Angeles area. At thirty-seven, Lyric was a supervising agent for the task force, having been an undercover agent for years prior to that. At twenty-two years old, Cody had been an undercover agent for a year. Her youthful looks made it easy for her to pass as an underage woman that would be targeted for human trafficking.

There was no doubt in Lyric's mind that Cody was excellent at her job. The girl had a very quick mind, and was able to process not only mass amounts of information to come up with logical conclusions quickly, but she was also what Lyric called, "fast on her feet." Cody was able to adjust quickly to situations to be what someone wanted her to be. It didn't worry Lyric any less though, because there was no way not to worry about someone so young being put into such dangerous situations, let alone a person you loved.

Many of the modern human trafficking rings were run by gangs. Gangs in and of themselves were dangerous commodities. Add to that the nature of human trafficking and what it meant for a young woman caught in it; it was the stuff nightmares were made of for any parent. The concern was double for Savanna Falco, who not only had a daughter in danger constantly, but a wife as well. It took a strong woman to deal with two very dynamic women who put themselves in dangerous situations for a living.

Not that Savanna would have it any other way; she loved her "girls" endlessly and wouldn't want to live any other way. At the age of thirty-six, Savanna was a board-certified psychiatrist, with a doctorate in psychology and a medical degree. She worked with both teens and adults. Her passion, however, was helping LGBT teens through a group home she ran.

Savanna had always known she was gay. Her father, who'd raised her from the age of two, was a gay man. She'd never thought for a moment that she might be straight; in fact the idea of being straight had always seemed absolutely foreign to her. The idea of having sex with men had sickened her, as she assumed the idea of having sex with a person of the same sex horrified a straight person. To her heterosexuality seemed like the anomaly, not homosexuality.

She'd been quite the conundrum for a number of her teachers over the years, but the precocious redhead had always maintained her staunch ideal that homosexuality was as normal as breathing. It had been for that reason she'd focused on helping young people struggling with their sexuality. It had also been the shortage of group homes open to gay youths that had her borrowing money from her father, a successful interior designer, to buy a home and get it made legal for a group home. She maintained a private practice as well, and pulled in good money annually from that source.

"How many prospective scars is she sporting now?" Savanna asked when Lyric emerged from the other side of the house, where the second master suite was located.

"Really wanna know?" Lyric asked, raising an eyebrow at her wife.

"No," Savanna said, shaking her head and rolling her eyes. "That girl is going to stress me to death, I can feel it… Did she even know this one's name?"

Lyric looked heavenward. "Didn't even bother to ask, babe, there's no point. It isn't like she'll be back, they never are."

"Isn't she eventually going to run out of women in Los Angeles?" Savanna asked.

"There are other counties, Mom," Cody said, grinning as she walked into the kitchen.

"Could you maybe see one more than once?" Savanna asked.

Cody shrugged. "They bore me after the first night."

Savanna looked over at Lyric, her look deadpan. "Oh, my God, she's you," she said simply.

Lyric did her best to subdue the grin, but she wasn't successful, and her wife narrowed her eyes at her. She held up her hands surrendering.

"Not my fault," she said.

Cody grinned, having heard a number of times how hard core a player Lyric had been when she'd met her mom. The problem had been that, at the time, Lyric dated men.

"You don't understand," Savanna said patiently to the third police officer she'd talked to that morning. "She's missing."

"Ma'am, she's a runaway, that's probably what she did," the officer said, looking distinctly uncomfortable.

"Aren't you the police?" Savanna practically screamed. "Isn't running away illegal? What the fuck is wrong with you people?"

"Uh, ma'am," a woman's voice said from behind her.

Savanna turned, setting her eyes on Lyric Falco for the first time. What she saw was a woman in her late twenties, with white blond hair with dark roots worn a couple inches past her shoulders and cut in layers. She stood at five foot eight, with beautiful blue eyes, and the long lean body type that Savanna always fell for. On top of that, this woman was dressed in blue jeans, with black leather chaps, Harley Davidson boots, a blue denim shirt with the Harley Davidson logo, and a thick black leather band watch. She smelled of motorcycle grease and gasoline... a heavenly smell to Savanna who immediately thought, butch... nice...

"Hi," Savanna said, momentarily forgetting her ire with the police department. Her light gold-brown eyes, framed with dark lashes, sparkled with interest as she smiled.

Without even being conscious of it, she flipped back her rich red hair that fell to just at her waist.

"You seem a bit upset," the woman said, nodding toward the young man who'd been trying to help Savanna.

The young man disappeared immediately.

"Special Agent Lyric Falco," she said, extending her hand to Savanna.

"Savanna Henning," Savanna said, taking the woman's hand and feeling the slight callouses of a motorcycle rider.

"Come with me, Ms. Henning," Lyric said, leading the way to her desk.

"Special Agent?" Savanna queried. "You aren't a police officer?"

"No, ma'am. I work for the Department of Justice, but rest assured, I'm a sworn peace officer," she said, sitting down and gesturing for Savanna to take a seat in the chair next to her desk.

"Please call me Savanna," Savanna said then. "I'm only twenty-nine, hopefully not much older than you," she said, her tone indeed hopeful.

Lyric's look flickered with amusement. "I'm thirty, ma'am," she said.

"Oh," Savanna said, oddly pleased by that news. "I never would have guessed."

Lyric nodded. "What can I do for you, ma'am?" she asked, looking officious.

Savanna was taken back for a moment, suddenly remembering that she'd been a screaming nut a minute before, and this woman probably still thought she was.

Sighing, she began the story again. "I'm doing my residency in a group home," she said. "And one of the girls who is usually very reliable hasn't shown up for three days in a row, and I'm really worried about her. Everyone here seems to think that just because she's been a runaway before, that she doesn't matter to anyone now..." Savanna's voice trailed off as she looked around at the people in the station.

Lyric nodded, pulling out her pen and jotting down a note on a pad in front of her.

"What's the girl's name?" she asked.

"Cody," Savanna said. "Cody Wyatt."

"Okay, can you give me a description?"

"She's about five foot five, dark hair that's cut short, and hazel eyes."

"She's Caucasian?"

"Yes," Savanna said, nodding.

"What was she wearing the last time you saw her?"

"A black hoodie, blue jeans, and white sneakers."

"And you said it's been three days?"

"Yes, but she's always in by curfew," Savanna said. "The fact that she's not is really worrisome."

"Why?" Lyric asked gently, unlike the previous officers who'd treated her like she was some kind of overwrought parent.

"Cody is only thirteen," Savanna said, "and she didn't grow up in LA like a lot of the kids at the home. She's from the Midwest somewhere. She doesn't have the street smarts the other girls do… I'm really worried about her Agent Falco."

Lyric nodded, her look contemplative. "I understand, ma'am."

"Please stop calling me ma'am," Savanna said, smiling. "I'm younger than you, for God's sake."

Lyric grinned, her blue eyes sparkling in the first real show of humor. "Got it," she said, nodding. "I can do some checking," she said, then. "Some local areas where the kids tend to gather, see if anyone's seen her…"

"That would be wonderful," Savanna said, reaching her hand out to touch Lyric's in her joy that someone was finally listening to her.

Lyric's look flickered with mild surprise at the intimate gesture, but then she put her hand over Savanna's and patted it gently.

"Give me your contact information," Lyric told her then, pushing the pad toward her, and holding out the pen.

As she wrote down her information, Savanna glanced at the notes Lyric had taken.

"You can read this?" she asked Lyric, her eyes taking in the characters that were far from any kind of English she'd ever read.

Lyric grinned. "Yep," she said, "I tend to take notes in Italian," she said. "Weird habit I picked up from my dad and brothers."

"Oh," Savanna nodded. "You're Italian?"

"Falco?" Lyric queried, raising a dark eyebrow.

"I guess I could have guessed that one, huh?" Savanna asked, smiling.

"Most people could, yes," Lyric said, her lips curled in a sardonic smile.

"I guess I'm a little slow on the uptake," Savanna said, staring back at Lyric's eyes, they were such a bright pretty blue...

"Well," Lyric said, moving to stand dismissively. "I'll get back to you by the end of the day with anything I can find out."

Savanna stood with a stab of disappointment, but she nodded. "Thank you so much Agent Falco, you have no idea how much I appreciate your help."

"Happy to help, ma—"

"Ah!" Savanna interrupted her holding up her hand.

Lyric grinned, nodding. "Sorry."

"You're forgiven," Savanna said. "This time."

"Duly noted," Lyric replied.

It was later that evening when Savanna got a call from Lyric.

"Ms. Henning, this is Agent Falco," Lyric said, identifying herself. "I wanted to let you know that none of my contacts have seen Cody Wyatt, but I will be taking a look myself tonight on my rounds. I will update you if I find anything."

"Thank you so much, Agent Falco," Savanna said, smiling at her end.

That night as Lyric drove through the various areas where the teens tended to circulate, especially the runaways, she didn't see the girl. Later, however, when she was driving on the outskirts of town she saw a lone figure walking down the street. As she drew closer she saw a black hoodie, and white sneakers. She pulled over and she got out of the car.

Walking towards the slight girl, she saw her glance quickly over her shoulder.

"Cody?" Lyric queried.

She turned around then, looking at Lyric suspiciously.

"How do you know my name?" she asked, fear in her eyes.

Lyric lifted the side of her jacket, exposing her badge that was clipped to her belt.

"It's okay," she told the girl, who tensed at the sight of the badge, rather than relaxing. "You're not in any trouble…"

"I'm not?" the girl asked, looking suspicious.

"No," Lyric said, taking a couple more steps to get closer. "Are you okay?" she asked then.

Cody's look said 'Why do you care?' and it bothered Lyric that she was not only so suspicious of the police, but that she didn't think that cops cared about her well-being.

Cody Wyatt took in the pained look on the cop's face, what did that mean?

"I'm fine," Cody said, her tone indicating that it was automatic.

Lyric nodded. "So where are you headed?" she asked.

Once again, the girl hesitated.

"I was going to offer you a ride," Lyric told her gently.

Cody's eyes went to the expensive-looking black sports car that Lyric had driven up in.

"What kind of cop drives a car like that?" she asked, her tone suspicious again.

Lyric chuckled. "The kind of cop that has a family full of Italians that won't drive anything but Italian cars."

Cody looked back at her for a long moment, trying to decide what to do at this point.

"Come on, Cody," Lyric said. "It's fuckin' cold out here."

Cody looked shocked at the cuss word, but grinned, nodding.

Lyric walked back her car, opened the passenger door for the girl, and waited for her. Cody got into the car, looking around at the interior. It was a really nice car, but she could tell it was old and restored. It smelled of leather and car polish.

Lyric got into the car on the driver's side, glancing over at Cody as she did and seeing that the girl was trying to get her bearings. She started the car with a satisfying roar. She saw Cody's eyes widen slightly and grinned over at her.

"Just love that feeling of power..." Lyric said in a dreamy tone.

Cody grinned. "What kind of car is this?"

As Lyric put the car into gear, she grinned. "It's a 1962 Ferrari SI 250 GTO," she said. "And I restored most of it myself."

"Wow..." Cody enthused, forgetting for a moment that this was a cop and she was supposed to be suspicious and wary of cops.

Lyric smiled. "A lot of time spent on this baby," she said affectionately.

"Definitely worth it though, right?" Cody asked.

"Oh yeah..." Lyric said. "Every morning when I turn her over..."

In that moment Cody decided she liked this cop. She seemed really genuine, like she wasn't trying to bullshit her.

"So where ya goin', Code?" Lyric asked, shortening her name in a way no one ever had before. Cody tried not to like it.

"Back to the group home," Cody said, her tone tentative. "If they'll let me back in," she added with a grimace.

Lyric nodded, looking circumspect.

"Well, it was Savanna Henning that sent me looking for you, so I'm betting she'll make an exception for you this time."

Cody couldn't hide the shock on her face.

"She was looking for me?" she couldn't help but ask.

Lyric nodded. "She was worried about you," she told the girl, knowing that she was surprising the kid.

"Why?" Cody asked, unable to fathom the reason.

Lyric looked over at her. "Because that's what people do for other people, Code."

Cody blinked a couple of times, obviously trying to process that statement. Finally, she shook her head, blowing her breath out. "Not where I'm from."

"Welcome to LA," Lyric said, winking at the girl, making her smile.

Savanna answered the door to the home, shocked to see Lyric standing on the front porch with Cody next to her. Savanna smiled with relief at Cody, seeing that the girl looked unharmed. She stepped out onto the porch and hugged a shocked Cody.

"Oh my God, Cody, you had me scared to death!" Savanna said.

Savanna pulled back and looked down at the girl. "Are you okay?" she asked her.

"I'm fine," Cody said, nodding. "Is it okay to come back? I know I missed curfew…"

"Go inside," Savanna said, smiling and nodding at the girl.

Cody went inside, turning to flip a wave to Lyric, who smiled back.

Savanna looked at Lyric then, taking in the jeans, combat style boots, black collared shirt and leather biker style jacket, once again thinking the woman was just plain hot. She smiled at Lyric.

"Thank you so much for this," she said, unable to adequately express how happy she was that Cody was back and unhurt. "You can't imagine how worried I was about her."

Lyric shook her head. "You're gonna need to develop thicker skin, doc..." she said, her tone chiding. "These kids... they do their own thing, and sometimes they don't even know when people are worried about them, or care." She shook her head ruefully. "You're gonna stress yourself into an early grave if you worry about all of them this much."

Savanna pressed her lips together. She knew what Lyric meant, and she'd heard it before, but hearing it from the hot cop made Savanna really want to believe that Lyric actually cared about her health. She knew it was ridiculous, but she was really hung up on this woman and it made no sense at all.

"I don't, really," Savanna said. "Cody's special. I can't put my finger on it, but that girl has been through the wringer... I don't know her whole story yet, but I'm going to get it out of her if it's the last thing I do," she said, sounding determined.

Lyric looked back at the redhead, smiling, she liked that Savanna was as dedicated to these kids as she was. Lyric saw a lot of throw away kids in her line of work, and a lot of very jaded social workers that were supposed to help them. Someone like Savanna caring about one girl, any of them, was a great thing, and a welcome change. That had been the reason Lyric had stepped in to help when Savanna had been raging at the department. In Savanna, Lyric heard someone that actually cared and she didn't want that kind of extraordinary thing to just be passed over.

"You go, Doc..." Lyric said with an amused her grin.

Savanna looked back at Lyric, knowing she was making fun of her, but she could see that Lyric had respect in her eyes. She liked that. Now if she could just get a different look out of her...

Cody had just walked back into the group home, going back to her undercover assignment. Once there she assumed her cover persona, appearing withdrawn and shy, with her *don't make eye contact* expression. Her hair was green where the bleach blond usually was, and she wore dark makeup on her eyes. Regardless of the wild-looking exterior, she appeared introverted and didn't really talk to anyone. It was her style to disappear into the group, not stand out. Her wild hair and makeup wasn't even close to the wildest-looking kid in the place. She'd had to assume the colors to fit into this particular home.

She sat down in one of the chairs in the living room, a good place from which to observe the goings on in the house. There were other teens in the room, but none of them paid her any attention. She noted that the dark-haired girl who'd been at the home a little less time than her, had a rather haunted look to her suddenly. Taking mental note of that, Cody watched her as she moved around the room. Narrowing her eyes, she noted that the girl was moving stiffly. Getting up, Cody walked by her, accidentally bumping into her shoulder.

"Sorry," Cody muttered, not noticing any kind of pain reaction from the girl.

The girl just nodded, and continued on her way. Cody picked up a book from a shelf and made her way back to her seat, noting the girl now sitting on the couch. She picked up a pen as she walked by the end table in the room and sat down. Her chair was right next to where the other girl sat on the couch. As she pretended to read, she wiggled the pen back and forth, then accidentally dropped it. She watched as the girl grimaced as she leaned down to pick it up. That told Cody that she had something going on internally, which raised a major red flag to her. She made a mental note to keep tabs on her and try to trail her when she left the house again.

"Thanks," she said to the girl as she handed back the pen.

The girl nodded, not looking at her.

The front door opened, and Cody heard people talking in the foyer. Curious and always wanting to keep tabs on the comings and goings of people in the house, she got up and walked in that direction. She could hear a woman's voice and John, the guy that ran the house, making introductions. She heard the name McKenna, and she thought she heard the last name Tucker, which was the same as John's last name. *Wife?* she thought immediately. He did wear a wedding ring.

She rounded the corner she almost bumped into someone. As she got a look at the person, she found herself staring into the most incredible gray-green eyes she'd ever encountered. There was a moment where she literally could not tear her eyes away from the other woman's eyes; she felt a visceral jolt go through her. Suddenly realizing that she was completely out of character, she shook her head to try to clear it, moving out of the woman's way mumbling an apology with her head down.

"It's okay," the woman said gently. "No harm, no foul."

Cody nodded, dying to look into those eyes again, and check out the rest of the face they belonged to, but knowing she shouldn't. It took everything she had to slink out of the area without looking up again.

Outside in the backyard, Cody looked around to make sure no one was around. She paced back and forth to walk off the excess energy her body was exploding with suddenly. What the hell was wrong with her? She couldn't figure it out. She wanted desperately to smoke to settle her jangling nerves, and wondered if she dared. No one really knew her in the house; they wouldn't know that Cody Wyatt didn't smoke… But Cody Falco most certainly did and desperately needed a cigarette right then. For once, she broke one of her rules, breaking cover to do something her undercover persona wouldn't do.

Reaching into the inner pocket of the old beat up bomber jacket she wore, she pulled out a cigarette and an old beat up lighter. She made sure that anything she wore or carried on her when she was undercover fit her cover, so the lighter was a cheap bic; she just prayed it would still light.

Putting the cigarette into her mouth with hands that were disconcertingly shaking, she flicked the lighter and thanked the Gods when it lit. She touched it to the tip of the cigarette and inhaled deeply, feeling her nerves settle almost immediately. As she blew the smoke back out, she moved to lean a hip against the retaining wall in the yard. It wasn't really much of a backyard, there was the dirt and a retaining wall with a half-dead ice plant going up a slight hill and then the fence. There was no grass to speak of, but it was at least a place to escape to at moments like this.

"Is everything okay?" asked a voice from above her.

Cody opened her eyes and looked up to the stairs that led down from the house. It was the woman from the foyer, and this time Cody got a full view. All she could think was, *Holy fucking shit!* The woman was beautiful, almost model perfect. She had long wavy honey blond hair, a perfect heart-shaped face with disgustingly perfect skin, and from what Cody could observe from her position below, a petite body that had curves in exactly the right places. Once again her pulse was racing, and this time she didn't have the luxury of an opportunity to pace it off.

Dropping her gaze, once again, she nodded, kicking at the dirt with pronounced disinterest in the newcomer. Furtively, she took another long drag off her cigarette, willing the smoke to smooth her ragged nerves. She was hoping the woman would go away, but she had no luck there. She descended the stairs, far too gracefully as far as Cody was concerned and walked over to where Cody stood. She leaned against the retaining wall, facing Cody and looked around the backyard.

"I can see that this will need to be one of my first projects…" she said, her voice held a sigh.

When Cody didn't respond, she put her hand out to her. "Hi, I'm McKenna Tucker," she said.

Cody raised her eyes long enough to look at the woman, and then nodded. "Cody," she said quietly.

"Hi Cody," McKenna said.

McKenna refrained from asking if the girl was old enough to smoke, knowing that she really couldn't be. Since the smoking age was now twenty-one and if she was twenty-one then she wouldn't be at the group home. She waited to see if Cody would say anything else and when Cody didn't, she tried to think of another way to engage the girl. John had told her that Cody was newer to the house, and that she didn't seem to really socialize with the other residents.

"So, I'm gonna be hanging around," McKenna informed her. "Kind of doing an internship for my degree."

Cody nodded, keeping her eyes down. She found she could think better when she wasn't looking at the woman. And what she was thinking at that point was, *Why are you telling me this?*

"I'm hoping you and I can talk a bit," McKenna said then.

18

That had Cody's head snapping up. "Why?" she asked, her look purposely fearful.

McKenna was surprised by the sudden reaction from the girl; she held her hands up in a stilling gesture.

"Nothing bad," McKenna said her tone soothing. "John has just told me that you don't really socialize with any of the other kids… I thought maybe you could use someone to talk to."

Cody narrowed her eyes slightly, she'd heard someone say that before, years ago. She let the wariness come into her eyes, because Cody Wyatt wouldn't trust anyone, least of all someone like McKenna Tucker.

McKenna looked back at the girl thinking, *Someone so young shouldn't look so wary.* It made her heart ache a bit. John was right about this girl; she seemed like a scared rabbit, ready to run away at the first sign of danger. The last thing McKenna wanted was to make the girl run, so she made herself back off.

She shrugged nonchalantly. "Just sayin'," she said, then looked around the yard again, smiling and shaking her head. "This yard is pathetic." Cody knew McKenna was trying to back off at that point. The words, *Don't scare the mark* echoed in her head. Cody sensed that she was the mark, and felt a stab of disappointment. McKenna was part of this… *Damnit.*

"I just don't know what to tell her," Savanna said to Lyric that night while they were eating dinner.

"Well, exactly how did she ask it?" Lyric queried.

"She said, and I quote, 'Can I be gay if I just like rainbows a really lot?' "

Lyric laughed out loud at that point, shaking her head. "You got me babe," she said, shaking her head. "I think that's the first time I've ever heard that one…"

"Me too!" Savanna said. "I just don't get why they all want to come to my house!"

"Well, I do," Lyric said, smiling.

Savanna tilted her head. "Why?"

"Because you draw everyone in, babe… Just like you did me," Lyric said.

"I didn't draw you in, Lyric," Savanna said. "I drew you out."

Lyric inclined her head. "Okay, true. But, babe, you get people, and you get these kids, just like you did, Cody. They want someone who gets them, gay or straight."

Savanna pressed her lips together in consternation. "But there are so many LGBT kids that need more, you know?"

"I know, honey," Lyric said. "And that's why you have to stand by the rule that you only take LGBT kids. I'm just trying to tell you why you get so many requests."

Savanna looked back at Lyric, thinking that she'd been damned lucky when fate had put this woman in her path. It hadn't been easy, but when she'd finally claimed Lyric's heart, she'd known she'd found her soul mate. In the seven years they'd been together, Lyric had been the steadfast rock that Savanna needed to do the work she did. She did her best to be that for Lyric as well. To her it was funny that Lyric said she drew people in, when in truth, it was Lyric that did. She'd drawn Cody in from the first day she met her.

"Are you working today?" Cody asked Lyric, looking over at her as Lyric drove.

"No, I'm off today, why?" Lyric asked.

"So you're off and you thought you'd spend time with some kid?" Cody asked, her tone cynical.

Lyric looked over at the girl. "You don't want to hang out with me?"

Cody clasped her hands together in her lap. "It's not that…"

"But you don't trust any adult that's too nice to you," Lyric deduced easily.

Cody nodded, looking down at her hands.

Lyric nodded. "That's actually probably pretty smart," she said. "But I think you probably already feel like you can trust me, don't you?"

Cody chewed on the inside of her cheek, then she nodded.

"Code," Lyric said, her tone patient. "If you don't trust me, it's okay," she said, "I just think that you could use someone to talk to is all."

"Why do you think that?" Cody asked.

"Because Savanna says you really don't talk to anyone there at the home, including her."

"What are you expecting me to talk about?" Cody asked suspiciously.

"I'm not expecting you to talk about anything," Lyric said. "I'm just letting you know that if you do want to talk about anything, I'll listen, okay?"

Cody nodded, taking a deep breath and expelling it slowly.

They were both silent for a while and Lyric turned her stereo up to fill the silence. "Fast Times" by Billy Squire was on. Lyric sang the words as she always did with her music. Cody watched her, listening to the words and the music itself. She liked the words, when it talked about not needing to be told how to run their lives.

"What is that song?" Cody asked when it ended.

"It's from that eighties movie Fast Times at Ridgemont High," Lyric said, "It's called Fast Times."

Cody nodded. "I like it."

"I can get you a copy," Lyric said, nodding.

"Wouldn't have any way to listen to it," Cody said, shrugging.

"Oh," Lyric said, realizing that she hadn't thought about that part. "Well, I could fix that, if you want."

"How?" Cody asked, looking perplexed.

"Pretty simple, really," Lyric said. "I've got at least one old Nano laying around."

"Nano?" Cody asked.

"Yeah, iPod," Lyric said, looking over at Cody, seeing the blank look on her face. "Never heard of it?"

"I've heard of them," Cody said, "but they're like major expensive."

"Not really," Lyric said. "I have a few, and I'm always listening to music."

Cody nodded, wondering if she'd ever be in a place in her life where she could have anything she wanted.

"So, I could give you one if you want," Lyric said.

Cody looked back at her, once again looking suspicious.

"Code," Lyric said, "I'm not trying to play you here, okay? I just can't even fathom not having music with me all the time."

"How come?" Cody asked.

Lyric looked considering. "I dunno, I guess I just like having that friend with me all the time, you know?"

"Friend?" Cody asked, surprised by word choice.

"Yeah," Lyric said, grinning. "That one friend you can always count on, the one that makes you feel better, or screams her head off with you, tells you a story or lets you cry on her shoulder?"

"Music does all that for you?" Cody asked.

"Oh yeah," Lyric said, stopping at a red light and reaching over to hit a couple of buttons on the stereo to change CDs. "Listen to this," she said, hitting play.

The song "Manhattan Project" by Rush began. Cody listened to the lyrics. She liked one of the last verses and the chorus. She particularly liked the part that talked about the pilot who had dropped the atomic bomb on Japan flying out of the shock waves.

As the song ended, Cody nodded.

"That's about the bomb, right?" Cody asked.

"Yep," Lyric said, nodding.

"I like that part about the pilot," Cody said. "It's like you're there..."

"Exactly!" Lyric said. "And that's what I love about music. It's like books, only with sound."

Cody bit her lip, nodding.

"What else do you listen to?" Cody asked.

"I'm mostly into rock," Lyric said, once again hitting buttons. "This album is awesome," she said, hitting pause. "It's by a band called Queensrÿche, ever hear of them?"

Cody shook her head.

"Well, this album's called Operation Mindcrime," Lyric said. "It's this whole cool story about this revolutionary group that's trying to overthrow the government, and they use this kid that's addicted to heroin and get him to kill key people for them… It's wild."

Cody's eyes widened at Lyric's description, then she nodded. "I want to hear it," she said, smiling.

Lyric laughed, hitting play on the CD player. They spent the next half an hour listening to the songs from the album and discussing what certain lyrics meant. Lyric found that Cody was really sharp and had insights into things that someone her age usually wouldn't. She really did like the girl, and she could sense that Cody really needed someone to take an interest in her.

When Lyric pulled into the parking lot of the area Costco, Cody looked over at her.

"Gotta shop for my family," Lyric said and pointed to the list on the floor near Cody's feet. "You mind?" she asked.

"No," Cody said, shaking her head. "You have a big family?" She asked.

"Well, no, it's my dad and three big brothers, but they eat a lot, so…" she said, grinning as she gestured to the land of bulk foods.

"Your mom doesn't shop?" Cody asked.

"My mom died giving birth to me," Lyric said. "It's always just been me, my dad, and my brothers."

"Oh," Cody said, nodding.

"What about you?" Lyric asked as she parked. "Big family, small family?"

Cody didn't say anything for a long moment, then shrugged. "My dad got killed in a drunk driving accident, he was the drunk," she said, her tone even. "It was just me, my brother and my mom for a couple of years and it was okay. But then my mom married this other guy…" Her voice trailed off as she looked out the window.

Lyric nodded. "You didn't like him?"

"He was a Baptist preacher," Cody said, her lips curled in disgust.

"Aw," Lyric said, nodding. "Yeah, I get the whole messing up of the family dynamic," she said. "I always freaked out when my dad tried to start dating again. I'd do some insane thing and get myself hurt, and suddenly there'd be no girlfriend anymore…" she said, looking at her hands on the steering wheel. "I feel bad now, 'cause my dad's retired and he's alone…" Her voice trailed off as she shook her head.

Cody looked over at Lyric, surprised by what she'd just said. She'd never had an adult talk to her like she was another adult before. At fourteen, Cody felt like she'd seen more life than a lot of people twice her age, but everyone always tried to treat her like a kid. Lyric didn't do that, she was really cool. Cody knew that she was growing very attached to the cop and it could spell trouble, but at that moment in time she enjoyed the kinship she was feeling.

They walked into the store and Cody noticed that Lyric received a lot of looks from people. She had a way of carrying herself with a level on comfort that she couldn't even begin to imagine ever having. Cody didn't know if it was the cop thing, or just an overall confidence about herself, but she knew she wanted to be like that someday. She wanted to be confident, to be strong and brave, like Lyric seemed to be.

Lyric walked through the electronics section, playing with various gadgets. Cody wandered over to the iPod display, looking at the one on display, playing with the buttons.

"Ah-ha," Lyric said, grinning as she walked up. "There ya are."

"This thing's pretty cool," Cody said, sounding awed.

"This is a cool color," Lyric said, picking up the purple one.

"Yeah, that's my favorite color," Cody said.

Lyric looked over at her, seeing the way that she was looking at the display. She picked up the box marked for the purple 16 gig Nano and stuck it in the cart.

"Come on," she said, and turned and walked away.

Cody had to rush to catch up. "What are you doing?" she asked, as Lyric continued toward the food area of the store.

"Shopping," Lyric said, grinning.

"I mean with that," Cody said, indicating the box in the cart.

"Buying it," Lyric said.

"For you, right?" Cody said.

"No, I already have two and an iTouch, I don't need another one," Lyric said.

Cody looked back at her, her look becoming afraid. Lyric stopped and turned to Cody. "I'm buying it for you, okay?" she said.

"But you said…" Cody began, her voice trailing off.

"I know what I said, Code," Lyric said. "But this is the latest model, it's a 16 gig, so it'll hold more songs, and it's a cool color…" she said, grinning as her voice trailed off.

"But, that's like three hundred bucks!" Cody exclaimed, surprising people walking by them. "I've never even seen that kind of money!" Cody said.

"Well, then it's a good thing I'm not asking you to buy it, huh?" Lyric said, winking at the girl and then turning to continue on her way.

A while later in the car, Cody sat with the box on her lap, looking at it almost reverently.

"You really didn't have to buy this for me," she said quietly.

"I wanted to, okay?" Lyric said.

"Why?" Cody asked plaintively.

Lyric looked back at her for a long moment. "Because you need a friend," she said, smiling.

Chapter 2

Lyric and Savanna awoke to sounds of a woman screaming in pleasure.

"Seriously?" Savanna muttered, glancing at the clock. "It's four in the morning, are those two ever going to go to sleep?"

Lyric chuckled, turning over and pulling her wife close.

"That's youth for you, they can go all night long…" she said, nuzzling her wife's neck from behind.

"Yeah, well, she keeps this up she's gonna be old before her time," Savanna said, shaking her head.

"She does seem to be rather dedicated lately," Lyric said.

Savanna turned over looking at her wife. "*Dedicated*?" she repeated.

"To debauchery," Lyric said. "Almost fixated on it."

Savanna looked back at Lyric, her eyes narrowed slightly. "What are you sensing?" she asked.

Lyric's lips twitched. "I think I need to talk to her," she said simply.

"Good," Savanna said, nodding.

Later that morning, Cody wandered out into the backyard where Lyric sat drinking coffee and reading the paper. Lyric glanced up, her blue eyes bright in the morning sunlight. Cody looked tired, and Lyric noticed that her hands were shaking when she reached for a cigarette.

"Overdoing it a bit, aren't ya?" Lyric said, as she went back to looking at the paper.

Cody shrugged as she sat down. "Live fast, die young, right?" she said, grinning.

"Don't let your mother hear you say that," Lyric said, narrowing her eyes at her daughter.

"It's what you used to say," Cody said.

"Not to you," Lyric said pointedly.

"No, to Grandpa," Cody responded.

"Just to irritate the shit out of him," Lyric said, grinning.

"And Uncle JJ," Cody added.

Lyric narrowed her eyes at Cody, her look assessing this time. "Why are you so on edge suddenly?" she asked.

Cody looked back at her mother, her lips twitching. "Why do you say that?"

"Code," Lyric said. "I know you, and you're pushing really hard right now, I'm just asking why."

Cody look contemplative as she took a long drag on her cigarette, she knew she could get away with not answering Lyric's question. That was the cool thing about Lyric, she never pushed too hard, just enough.

"Right now it's nothing, really," Cody said.

Lyric nodded slowly, her eyes narrowing again slightly.

"But you know if you need to talk…" Lyric said.

"I know, Mom, I know," Cody said, nodding.

"Just be careful, Codes, holding too tight can break things, ya know?" Lyric said.

Cody looked back at Lyric, her mother always had a way of putting things in a way that made sense to her. It was one of the things she'd always loved about her.

Two nights later, Cody was back at the group home. She was almost asleep in her room when she suddenly noticed the complete absence of sound, other than the wind howling outside. She noted that the house was completely dark and silent. Then she saw a light in the hallway as she sat up.

"Cody?" McKenna queried from the hallway. "You okay?"

"Yeah," Cody replied. "What happened?"

"Power went out," McKenna said. "The whole block is out."

"Oh," Cody said, thinking about who else was in the house.

McKenna must have been thinking along the same lines because she said. "I think we're the only ones here tonight," she said as she walked into Cody's room carrying a candle and the flashlight she was using. "Mind if I hang in here with you?" she asked.

Cody shook her head thinking, *Probably not the best idea, but what am I supposed to say?* McKenna lit the candle and set it on the nightstand. Cody shifted to the other side of the bed, as McKenna sat down on the bed.

Cody noticed that McKenna was wearing a pink thermal long-sleeved shirt and cotton blue and pink paisley pajama pants. Cody was wearing a black tank top and sweatpants. McKenna eyed the chain around Cody's neck, but she couldn't see what was suspended from it. The differences between them were immense. There was a crack of thunder outside and rain began pouring down.

"Hope this isn't the part where we find out the house has leaks," McKenna said, grinning as she looked around at the ceiling.

Cody nodded, sitting with her knees up to her chest, her arms wrapped around them.

"You don't talk a lot, do you?" McKenna asked, looking at her.

Cody shrugged. "Not a lot to say I guess," she said.

"Maybe if I ask questions, I can get you to talk," McKenna said trying to cajole her.

Cody just looked back at her, her face expressionless.

"Tough crowd," McKenna muttered under her breath.

Cody smiled slightly at that.

"Ah-ha!" McKenna exclaimed softly. "At least I got you to smile." She winked. "So where are you from, Cody?"

Cody looked back at her for a long moment. "Wyoming," she said.

"Way over there?" McKenna asked, surprised.

Cody nodded.

"And how long have you been in LA?"

"Since I was fourteen," Cody said.

"That long?" McKenna said. "Three years, right?"

Cody nodded.

"Why did you come here?" McKenna asked. "To become a movie star?" she asked, chuckling softly.

Cody gave her a censorious look. "No," she said simply.

McKenna suppressed a grin at the look the girl was giving her.

"You could do that," Cody said, surprising her.

"Do what?" McKenna asked.

"Be a movie star," Cody said, her tone soft.

McKenna laughed softly. "Well, thank you for the compliment, but I don't think so," she said, shaking her head.

"Why?" Cody asked.

"I don't think I'm pretty enough or talented enough," McKenna said.

Cody looked back at her for a long moment, knowing she needed to shut up, but feeling some insane need to push this.

"I don't know about the talent part," she said, "but definitely pretty enough."

McKenna looked back at Cody, feeling a rush of fondness for this girl. It bothered her that she was so closed up. She just wanted to make her smile and relax for a minute. She wished she knew how to make that happen.

"Well, thank you, Cody, that is really sweet of you to say," McKenna said. "I just think we may need to have your vision checked now," she added, winking at Cody.

Cody surprised her by chuckling and smiling a little, her eyes softening just slightly. McKenna suddenly felt completely breathless for a moment; she didn't understand it, nor did she understand the stab of disappointment when Cody lowered her face to rub it against her knee in sudden discomfort. They were both silent for a few minutes, listening to the storm outside.

"So, what do you want to do when you grow up, Cody?" McKenna asked, wanting to get the girl engaged in conversation again.

Cody looked back at McKenna for a long moment, having to tamp down on the urge to raise an eyebrow at the woman. She knew McKenna was trying really hard to draw her out, and felt bad for her, so she played along.

"Dunno," she said, shrugging. "I just want to make money."

McKenna nodded. "Have you applied for any jobs?" Cody chewed on the inside of her cheek. "Actually, John had said he thought he could find a way for me to make some money," she said, her look hopeful.

McKenna looked surprised at that statement. "Really?" she said. "He hasn't said anything to me about that, but… I guess I'll have to ask him."

Cody nodded.

McKenna leaned her head against the headboard of the bed, still facing Cody. "You really have to be careful out there though," she said, her tone cautioning.

"What do you mean?" Cody asked.

"I mean, there are a lot of people out there who will try to use you," McKenna said.

Cody looked blankly back at McKenna.

McKenna reached her hand out, touching Cody's knee. "I mean, for their own purposes or profits."

"You mean pimps," Cody said, her tone matter-of-fact.

"Yes," McKenna said, nodding. "I mean pimps."

"I already know about that stuff," Cody told her, looking direct.

"You do?" McKenna asked, feeling sick for some reason at that thought.

Cody looked back at her, seeing the pained look in her gray-green eyes, and for some reason pleased by it. "You don't live on the streets of LA for long without knowing about that."

McKenna looked at Cody for a long moment, almost not wanting to ask the next question, but knowing she needed to ask.

"Cody, have you… done that?" she asked, hoping against hope that the girl said no.

That hoped was dashed a moment later when Cody nodded looking away. McKenna winced, hating the idea that someone had taken advantage of this girl. She'd known going into this area of study that she was going to deal with stuff like this on a regular basis. She just had no idea how it would feel when it was a girl like Cody.

"When did you do that?" She asked Cody then.

Cody looked back at her like she was afraid to answer.

"It's okay to tell me, Cody, I'm not going to get you into trouble, I promise," McKenna said.

Cody blinked a couple of times. "Not since I came here," she said.

McKenna nodded, looking relieved. "Good, okay," she said. "I don't suppose I could get you to promise me that you won't do that again, could I?"

Cody looked back at McKenna. In her head she was trying to reconcile what the woman was saying. She didn't want her to prostitute herself? That would go completely against the whole point of the sex trafficking operation that Cody was sure was going on in that house, or at the very least supplying girls for the operation.

McKenna wasn't sure what Cody was thinking, maybe trying to decide whether or not to lie and promise something she had no intention of honoring. Part of McKenna thought she should probably take it back, but the other part, the part she wasn't sure she understood at the moment, wanted to force the girl to promise her that she'd never sell her body for sex ever again.

It was that part that made her kneel face-to-face with Cody, taking her face in her hands, and staring right into Cody's eyes in the flickering candlelight.

"Please Cody?" she whispered, her tone so earnest that Cody felt a stab of guilt for making this poor woman think she'd ever do that kind of thing again.

She blinked a couple of times, trying to figure out what was going on. It didn't add up, and that bothered her. McKenna mistook her pensive look as hesitation and in desperation, moved closer to Cody, wanting to get through to the girl. Cody averted her eyes until McKenna moved closer still and then Cody's eyes connected with hers and once again, suddenly McKenna felt that breathless sensation come over her. And then she saw the heat in Cody's eyes; it was unmistakable. And the realization slid through McKenna making her almost gasp in surprise.

Pressing her lips together, McKenna moved back, terrified that she'd be crazy enough to act on what she'd just felt. Cody looked away and turned to sit on the edge of the bed, with her back to McKenna. What McKenna couldn't see was that Cody was closing her eyes, doing her damnedest to will away the virulent reaction to the desire she'd seen in McKenna's eyes moments before. She knew she was playing with fire here, and she knew she'd be smart to get the hell out of there that second.

"Cody," McKenna said, feeling horrible and her voice reflecting just that. "I'm so sorry. I didn't mean to make you uncomfortable."

"It's okay," Cody said, her voice coming out as a ragged whisper.

"No," McKenna said, wanting to touch the girl's shoulder, but afraid to make any more physical contact when her emotions were in such turmoil. "It's not okay," she said. "I'm just really afraid for you, that's all." She hoped that she sounded sincere.

Because it was true, the idea of this girl, or any girl, put in the position of having to sell their body to men to survive was absolutely horrifying to her.

Cody turned around, looking back at McKenna, seeing how shaken she was and feeling bad that caused it. Cody knew that McKenna was freaking out because she thought she was feeling hot for an underage girl. She couldn't change that at this point in time, but she could do something.

"I promise," she told McKenna, her look direct and her voice strong.

McKenna smiled sadly and she nodded. "Thank you."

Cody nodded, her look solemn.

There was the sound of the door opening downstairs then, and someone was calling out to McKenna. She got off the bed and went out to the stairs.

"Hi," she said to the person, "I'm coming." Cody heard McKenna walk down the stairs. She got off the bed, walked over to the doorway, and stood leaning on the doorjamb, listening to see if she could hear the conversation. She couldn't really hear anything. She looked across the hall and saw that the office was open; it was usually closed. She heard the door to the basement open. She walked back to her nightstand, opened the drawer, and pulled out a small flashlight and her cell phone that she kept concealed in a book.

After waiting a couple of extra moments at the doorway to make sure there was no sound downstairs, she walked out onto the landing, then into the office. She picked the lock on the file drawer. Looking hurriedly through some files, she pulled out papers, transfer paperwork for different girls. She took pictures of some, noticing McKenna's signature on them. She pulled out other papers, financial transactions, taking pictures of those, as well as the signature information for the bank that was contained in the file. She carefully put the papers back, making sure nothing was disturbed or out of place. After closing the drawer and relocking it, she went back to her bedroom. She put her phone back in the hollowed out book, and put the flashlight away.

She lay back down on the bed and stared at the ceiling, watching as the flickering candlelight created dancing shadows all around her. She let her mind explore what could have happened. What could have happened if she'd given in to the insane desire to kiss McKenna. She let herself think about what it would have felt like to feel those hands not on her face, but on her body. She closed her eyes and felt the desire slide through her. She wanted this girl like she'd never wanted anyone before. It was that old cliché of wanting something you couldn't have.

Blowing her breath out slowly, she let the gnawing feeling of regret have its way for a while, knowing she was being almost sadistic at this point. It was the only way she knew how to handle desire sometimes, just letting it eat away at her.

It was the reason she'd been "on edge" as Lyric had described it. For all the times she made women come screaming for her, she rarely if ever allowed the same for herself. It was a troubling situation at times, but she simply would not allow anyone to see that level of vulnerability in her. In fact, very few women had ever seen that side of Cody; it was something she kept to herself and refused to examine too closely. She knew it was something Savanna would want to discuss with her at length; Cody just couldn't see that happening. What she could do was talk to Lyric. She resigned to do just that the following weekend when she went home.

Things between Lyric and Savanna became much more casual as Lyric came by the house regularly to talk to Cody and check in with both of them. Savanna often made a point of making Lyric coffee or at least offering to do so. Lyric told Savanna that she drank coffee that tended to be outrageously strong, espresso level, as that was what her father and brothers always drank, so she'd picked up the habit.

Savanna had discovered that Lyric had three big brothers and that her father was her only living parent. Lyric was part of a law enforcement family, a large Italian family that went back generations all the way to Sicily. In fact, the car that Lyric drove had been in her family for years. Lyric had been given the car by her father, because he had known she'd take the time to restore it as she had.

There were other conversations that weren't as benign, however. One such conversation happened after Lyric had spent another afternoon with Cody. Cody had just gone upstairs, and Savanna handed Lyric a bottle of water. As Lyric twisted the cap of the bottle off, she canted her head slightly.

"So, can I ask you a question?" she said.

"Of course," Savanna said as she led the way out to the back patio where they tended to sit and talk.

"Why didn't you tell me that you're gay?" Lyric asked in an even tone.

"Well..." Savanna said, taken back by the question. She needed a moment to gather her thoughts and in truth try to figure out for herself why she hadn't told Lyric that piece of information.

Finally, Savanna shook her head. "I don't know, really," she said honestly.

Lyric nodded slowly. "You know I'm not, right?" she asked then, looking directly at Savanna.

Savanna looked back at her for a long moment, wanting to argue, if for no other reason than that she really wanted Lyric to be gay. But it wasn't a surprise to her that Lyric didn't think she was gay.

Lyric could see the conflict in Savanna's eyes and figured it was simply the confusion that most people had with her sexuality. They assumed because she was more of a tomboy with the use of little or no makeup and didn't wear things like dresses, that she must be gay.

"Don't worry about it," Lyric said, waving away Savanna's discomfit. "Lots of people think I am."

A look flickered across Savanna's face that Lyric didn't understand, even as she nodded. "I'm sorry, I hope that doesn't bother you," Savanna said then.

"That you're gay, or that you thought I was?" Lyric asked.

"Either, both," Savanna said.

"No, neither of those bothers me," Lyric responded, smiling. "Who people sleep with is none of my business or concern. All I care about is what kind of people they are, and you're a good person. So the rest..." She shrugged as she let her voice trail off.

Savanna nodded again. "I have to tell you," she said, smiling, "that you're amazing with Cody. She's come so far out of her shell in the last couple of months and I know that's because she's been spending time with you."

"Well," Lyric said, "I think she needs someone to talk to. And I think the psychiatrist in the house," she said, giving Savanna a pointed look, "probably intimidates her a bit."

"But the cop doesn't?" Savanna asked, grinning.

"Touché," Lyric said, inclining her head with a grin of her own.

"She's very fond of you," Savanna said. "You've made a real connection with her. And that's something no one else here seems to have been able to accomplish, including the psychiatrist," she said with a wink.

Lyric nodded. "Well, I'm glad," she said honestly. "She's really a good kid. I just think there was some seriously bad shit at home that sent her running."

Savanna nodded. "What have you been able to get out of her about her home life?"

"Well, her stepdad is a Baptist minister," Lyric said. "And Cody thinks she might be gay."

"Wait, what?" Savanna said, her shock evident.

"I said that Cody thinks she might be gay," Lyric said. "She asked me how she'd know for sure... I actually suggested she might want to talk to you, since I'd just been informed that you were gay..." she said, her voice trailing off as she gave Savanna a mock annoyed look.

"Okay, okay," Savanna said, rolling her eyes. "I get it, I should have told you. Sheesh! It really isn't the first thing that comes out of my mouth you know... 'Hi, I'm Savanna, I'm gay and oh yeah a board-certified psychiatrist with honors who's studied for twelve years to get where I am, blah, blah, blah...' "

Lyric was laughing by the end of her diatribe.

"Point taken, doc," Lyric said, still smiling as she held up her hands in surrender.

"Good," Savanna said, giving her a foul look. "Now, back to Cody. Did she say why she thought she might be gay?"

Lyric shook her head. "I'm not sure she really knows why she thinks it, but there's definitely something deep in there related to sex, I just can't seem to get her to talk about it."

Savanna nodded, her mind working through the problem. "Think she might have been abused at home?"

"Sexually?" Lyric asked.

"Yeah," Savanna said, her look somber.

Lyric thought about it for a long moment, then nodded. "It would explain a few things. And definitely be the reason she ran."

"Yeah…" Savanna said, nodding and grimacing.

She shook her head, her look mournful. "As long as I practice, I will never understand the perversion of molesting a young girl… Why do men to that?" she asked, sounding appalled.

Lyric looked back at her for a long moment. She really couldn't argue the point in men's favor. The fact was that a very large percentage of molestations were committed by men. It was simply a fact.

"Have you ever been with a man?" Lyric asked, not sure why she wanted to know.

Savanna shook her head vehemently.

Lyric nodded. "Well I lived with four of them most of my life, and I can tell you that they're not all like that."

"I know that," Savanna said, her voice softer. "I guess I just see it so much more in this line of work, you know? Sometimes it's hard to keep perspective."

"Well, you should come to dinner at my dad's house sometime. I'll introduce you to four of the best men I know," Lyric said, smiling.

"I might take you up on that," Savanna said, smiling too.

"I hope you will," Lyric replied.

"Mom?" Cody queried.

"Mmm?" Lyric murmured, turning her head from reading the paper.

Cody chewed on the inside of her cheek, a sure sign that she needed to talk. Lyric nodded and picked up her coffee as she stood up.

"Come on," she said, nodding toward the backyard.

Cody stood up and walked toward the back door. Lyric leaned over to kiss Savanna on the lips before following Cody out. Savanna smiled fondly as she watched her girls. Lyric and Cody had always been extremely close; it never bothered her when Cody wanted to talk to Lyric alone. She understood their relationship, and knew that Lyric would share anything with her that she felt she needed to know.

"What's up, Code?' Lyric asked, when Cody sat down and immediately lit a cigarette.

Lyric moved to sit in the chair next to Cody, stretching her jean-clad legs out comfortably, and crossing them at the ankles. She was wearing her usual Saturday morning outfit, faded, tattered jeans, and a DOJ t-shirt, and her feet were bare.

Cody blew her breath out. "I'm kinda…" she began, trailing off, not sure what to say.

Lyric narrowed her eyes slightly, canting her head. "Just say it, don't worry about it making sense, we'll make sense of it, okay?"

Cody nodded, drawing in a deep breath. Lyric always knew what to say.

"I'm screwed," Cody said. "I'm really, really screwed right now and I have no idea what to do, or how to handle it… It's just not something I know how to handle. I can't sleep, she's in my head all the time, and she may be a suspect, and what the fuck am I doing? It's so crazy, and I know it and I know it's stupid and I know I'm putting my case in danger, and it doesn't matter because I just want… So much, everything and nothing at the same time… I don't know what to do here and I'm just holding on so tight and you said things break when you do that, and I'm worried that I'm breaking, Mom…" The last was said with a tremulous voice.

Lyric grimaced. She got up from her chair to squat down in front of her daughter, taking her in her arms and hugging her like she had when she was fourteen. Cody started crying and Lyric's heart broke a little for her. She knew there were things that Cody had never dealt with from her childhood; it was the thing that worried Savanna constantly. It came out at times, in the way Cody went through women like socks and in the songs she focused on at points in time. Other times it came out in Cody stepping up her drinking or smoking or the amounts of calls Lyric got from other officers telling her that Cody was doing 120 on the freeway on her Ninja.

After a few minutes, Cody calmed down, and Lyric pulled her chair closer so she could sit with her hands on Cody's knees, keeping the connection.

"Okay," Lyric said. "Let's take this one thing at a time. Who are we talking about?"

Cody blew her breath out. "The wife of the guy that runs the group home that I'm working."

Lyric nodded. "Okay, so that's what you mean by her maybe being a suspect?"

"Yeah," Cody said nodding.

Lyric turned the idea over in her head. "How bad does it look?" she asked.

Cody took a long drag on her cigarette, blowing it out a full minute later, which told Lyric that her nerves were really shot.

"There's definitely a trafficking connection there," Cody said.

"Okay, and how involved do you think this woman is?" Lyric asked.

Cody shook her head. "I don't know for sure, but I think that he's just using her as kind of a front, you know?"

"Why do you think that?" Lyric asked her tone even.

"Because the other night I baited her, and not only did she not go for it, she actually went the other way."

"Explain," Lyric said.

Cody shifted in her chair, a sign that it was making her uncomfortable to talk about this, but Lyric knew she needed to stick with it so Cody could think it all the way through. Lyric waited for the answer.

"I basically told her that I had been prostituting before I'd come to their house, and she wanted me to promise that I wouldn't do it ever again."

Lyric's brows furrowed. "Okay, yeah, I see what you mean there. Why do that if that's what you want someone to do in reality..." Then she looked at Cody. "Did she mean it? Do you believe her?"

Cody looked pensive, carefully navigating her way around her sexual feelings for McKenna to look at what she felt in her gut. Finally, she nodded.

Lyric nodded too, seeing that Cody was doing her very best to be completely honest not only with Lyric, but also with herself.

"Do you have any evidence to back that up?" Lyric asked then.

"I might," Cody said.

"Explain," Lyric said again with a slight grin.

"I found some documents that have her signature on them, resident transfers and things, but there's also a bank signature document, and the signatures don't look exact…"

"So you think hubby might be forging her signature?" Lyric asked.

"Yeah," Cody said, nodding, "I do."

Lyric nodded. "Okay, so you get those documents to QD for review," Lyric said, talking about the Questioned Documents section of the Bureau of Forensic Services with the Department of Justice.

"Right, that was my plan," Cody said.

Lyric blew her breath out. "So… Let's talk about the rest of it…" she said, her tone softer now, knowing that this was going to be the harder conversation.

Cody pressed her lips together, part of her wanting to say forget about it, but the part of her that knew how insidious suppressing things could be to a person pushed her forward.

"I want her, Mom." Cody said, her tone reflecting the confusion that desire was causing.

Lyric looked thoughtful. "Is it mutual?" she asked.

Cody blinked a couple of times, looking pensive. "There was definitely a moment the other night where I knew she wanted me."

Lyric nodded again. "But she didn't act on it, right?" he clarified.

"Right," Cody said, knowing that her mother was thinking like a cop at that moment.

"Good, okay," Lyric said, looking relieved. "So, do you want to tell me any of the rest of it?" she asked her tone gentle.

Cody swallowed convulsively a couple of times and reached for another cigarette. Lyric waited patiently. When she could see that Cody was having a hard time approaching the subject, she leaned forward, tilting her head to get under Cody's gaze.

"You know that no matter what it is, you can talk to me about it, don't you?" Lyric said.

Cody sucked in her breath, her eyes glazing with tears again, but then she nodded.

"And that no matter what it is, I'm going to love you exactly the same." Cody swallowed convulsively again, biting the inside of her cheek.

"Oh babe…" Lyric said, shaking her head. "You need to look at that ring, right there," she said, pointing to the platinum band that Cody wore on her left ring finger. "That ring means that we're a family no matter what. There is nothing you can do or say that can ever change how much we love you."

Cody looked at the ring on her finger, remembering the day Lyric had given it to her.

It was Lyric and Savanna's wedding day. A fourteen-year-old Cody was acting as Lyric's best 'man'. As they stood in the anteroom waiting for the wedding to begin, Lyric had tossed Cody a small velvet box.

"What's this?" Cody asked, when she opened it she saw that it was a band. "Is this for Savanna?"

"No, it's for you," Lyric said. "We got the word this morning that your adoption is legal as of today."

Cody looked at Lyric, her eyes wide. "I'm your daughter now?" she breathed.

Lyric smiled warmly, nodding. Cody threw her arms around Lyric, in tears immediately. She had been so amazed that these two women had been willing to take her into their home, their lives, and their hearts.

"So where do I wear this?" Cody asked.

"Wherever you want," Lyric told her.

Cody had put it on her left ring finger. The only time it left her finger was when she was undercover, and then it was on a platinum chain that was long enough to keep it low on her chest near her heart. She always had it with her, always.

Looking over at Lyric now, she felt so grateful to have her support.

"When you said that you want everything and nothing," Lyric said, "what did you mean? From her?"

Cody considered the question for a moment. "I guess I meant that part of me wants everything, and the other part of me wants nothing from her… Is that crazy?"

Lyric grinned. "Well, that's your mother's department," she said. "But the part that wants everything… What is everything to you?"

"Letting her see me, the real me, all of the real me," Cody said.

"And why does that scare you?" Lyric asked.

"Because no one has ever seen that." Lyric nodded slowly. "There's a lot in your past that you really haven't dealt with, Code," she said, her voice soft. "But are you talking about emotionally, sexually or both?"

"Both, I guess," Cody said.

Lyric narrowed her eyes. "In terms of sexually, what are we talking about here, specifically?"

Cody chewed on the inside of her cheek, shifting in her chair again.

"I know this is tough," Lyric said. "But I need to understand, Cody, or I can't be of any help at all."

Cody nodded, drawing in a deep breath.

"I know you have sex, Code," Lyric said, grinning. "'Cause your mom and I hear it most of the time... Or... Are we talking like all the mushy stuff, spooning, and whatnot or...?" Her voice trailed off, her tone questioning.

"Well, I don't do any of that either," Cody said matter-of-factly.

"Either?" Lyric asked.

"I don't usually... You know..." Cody said.

"Finish?" Lyric asked.

"Yeah," Cody said, grateful that Lyric was helping her navigate this extremely uncomfortable conversation. She couldn't even begin to imagine talking to Savanna about this kind of thing.

Lyric blinked a couple of times. "So the reason we only hear them screaming is because you don't... finish?"

"Right," Cody said.

Lyric looked back at her for a long moment, then blew her breath out shaking her head. "You've got to have nerves of steel…" she said, her tone astounded.

"What do you mean?" Cody asked, looking perplexed by the comment.

"Well, it might be a little bit of TMI, but when Savanna goes over, it usually puts me over too."

Cody looked considering. "Well, I'm not saying that their screaming and stuff never does anything for me," she clarified. "But… just never there totally."

"You're probably killing egos all over the city," Lyric muttered, grinning in spite of herself. "Do they ever try to… help?" Lyric asked, trying to put things as delicately as possible.

"I don't let them." Cody said.

"Why?" Lyric asked, sensing that they were getting to the heart of the matter now.

Cody hesitated, fully aware that what she was about to say was really screwed up and jaded, which was why she rarely even thought about it, let alone said it out loud.

"I don't want anyone to see that part of me."

Lyric's chin came up slightly as she considered the ramifications of what her daughter was saying. Intimacy issues were always a factor in sexually abused women. Lyric had wanted to believe that Cody didn't have any of those, because she was so prolific with women. She realized in that moment she'd been sorely mistaken.

"And you think you might want to let this woman, what is her name?" Lyric asked, feeling strange about calling her 'this woman' when she obviously held such an attraction for her daughter.

"McKenna," Cody supplied.

"So you think you want McKenna to see that?" she asked.

"Something inside me thinks so," Cody said.

"Is that something your libido, or your heart?" Lyric asked.

Cody looked back at her, then blew her breath out, shaking her head. "I don't have any idea."

Lyric nodded, seeing the problem. And there was even more to the problem than just whether or not Cody simply wanted to lay the girl or love the girl.

"You do realize," Lyric said, her look bleak, "that when she finds out who you really are and that you've been…"

"Playing her," Cody supplied.

"Yeah," Lyric said, nodding. "That she might hate the very thought of you."

Cody grimaced. "Yeah."

"And that's where the problem is, isn't it?" Lyric asked.

Cody nodded, looking mournful.

Lyric shook her head. "Babe, the very best that you can do is not to put her in the position of breaking the law with you. And the next best thing you can do is clear her as a suspect. Then you just gotta pray that she's willing to listen to your side of it when everything is said and done." Then another thought occurred. "Or do you want off the case?"

Cody looked back at her for a long moment, never having considered the last question. She thought about it for a few long minutes, then she shook her head, looking resigned.

"No, anybody else may not care about her, and might just railroad her to make the case; I don't want to have that happen," Cody said, her voice full of conviction.

Lyric looked relieved. "That's my girl…" she said, very proud of her daughter in that moment.

Cody stared back at the man, knowing there was no way out. Gritting her teeth, she closed her eyes and just waited for it to be over. In her head, she sang the words to Linkin Park's "Crawling" wincing as pain shot through her body, but refusing to open her eyes. She would not look at his face. She would not see that horrible contorted mask that came over their faces when they finished what they were doing to her. She would not have another image of that contorted face burned into her head. She pictured Lyric's face when she smiled at her, wishing she was there, wishing she was anywhere but this cold, dirty hotel room.

After it was over, Cody curled up into a ball, pulling her knees up to her chest but refusing to cry. She wouldn't give them that kind of satisfaction. Monsters, they were all monsters… She was caught in a spider's web of fear and threats of violence. They didn't know who Lyric was, but they'd told her that they'd slit her throat and let Cody watch her die if she ever told her about this "game." Cody couldn't take that chance, not with Lyric. Lyric and Savanna were the only people in the world that seemed to care about her at all. She wouldn't put them in any danger. She could take whatever they did to her, as long as she had Lyric and Savanna as her friends.

One of the lesser gang members shoved at her a while later.

"Get up!" he snapped. "Get out of here, coño!" he said, laughing raucously calling her a "cunt" in Spanish.

Cody got up off the filthy mattress and moved to straighten her clothes as she hastened out of the room. She didn't make eye contact with anyone, lest they change their minds about her leaving at that point. Rushing out to the street she took gasping breaths to try to remain calm until she was away from there. She walked quickly down the street, feeling the sickening slick feeling between her legs and wanting to throw up. Knowing she couldn't take the time to wipe away the filth, she forced her mind somewhere else. She reached into the ripped lining of her cheap jacket and touched her iPod and headphones, holding onto them until she knew it was safe for her to pull them out. Putting the headphones in her ears, she found the song she wanted, hit play and cranked the sound all the way up. Linkin Park's "Crawling" blasted in her ears and she sang the words silently as she continued down the street.

By the time she reached the backyard of the group home, she felt calm enough to take the chance of running into anyone inside. Had to act normal, like she'd just been breaking the rules, not doing anything horrible and shameful... She climbed up the backstairs, moving to stand on the railing and pulling herself up onto the low eves of the roof. Standing on the roof, she looked down, thinking if she fell maybe she wouldn't have to think about any of this anymore. She shook her head firmly at herself. No, Lyric told her that she needed to have goals. She had them, she would get through this and she would find a way to get back at these people who'd hurt her so much... That was her goal... She'd get them all...

Her bedroom window was still open slightly. She wasn't sure it still would be after three days, was that all it had been? Pushing it open, she climbed quietly inside. Taking off her clothes and doing her best to clean up, she put on the DOJ t-shirt Lyric had given her and her threadbare sweatpants, crawled in bed, turned her iPod on again and fell asleep with Mike Shinoda screaming in her ears and tears on her cheeks.

In another part of the house, Lyric was doing everything she could to try to calm Savanna down. It was difficult to do, since she was freaking out herself. Cody had left the house three days before and had disappeared. She'd done it before, and Lyric told herself that the girl would come back, like she always did, but there was always that fear, that worry... What if she got the call about a body found, and they'd connected the body to her, and could she come down to make an identification...

"You're worried too," Savanna said, her look knowing.

"I'm worried," Lyric said, nodding. "But she always comes back, we know this."

Savanna shook her head, tears in her eyes. "What if she doesn't this time? What if she can't this time? Oh God, Lyric..." she said, her voice breaking as she reached for Lyric.

Lyric took Savanna in her arms, closing her eyes as she did her best to hold back her own tears. Part of her knowing that no matter how many times she told Savanna that Cody would be back, she didn't know if it was true. She'd seen it too many times, way too many times. It made her sick to think of what could have happened to the girl.

Where the fuck was she? Why didn't she call? Why didn't she just come back? What the fuck was going on? Lyric gritted her teeth. No matter how close she'd gotten to the teen, she still hadn't been able to get to that part of her, to find out where she disappeared to every so often. She staunchly refused to talk about it, becoming absolutely petrified with fear whenever Lyric tried to push her. It would force Lyric to back off, lest the girl runaway completely.

"Miss Savanna?" A girl queried from the doorway to the sitting room.

"What is it Sara?" Savanna asked, turning and reaching up to wipe at her tears as she did.

"She's back," Sara said.

"What!" Savanna asked, turning to look at Lyric who just shrugged, shaking her head.

They both stood and followed Sara who took them to Cody's door. Opening the door, Savanna looked into Cody's room and there she was, asleep with her headphones in her ears and her DOJ t-shirt on, something she wore almost constantly in the house. Savanna blew her breath out, weak with relief.

"Thank you, Sara," Savanna said, hugging the girl.

"No prob," Sara said, glad she could help Miss Savanna.

Sara walked away then, and Savanna and Lyric looked at each other. Lyric dropped her head, blowing her breath out loudly.

"Uh-huh," Savanna said, nodding. "So confident, huh Agent Falco? Come on," she said, heading back down the hallway.

At the office door, Savanna pulled out her keys and unlocked the door. Inside, she unlocked a cabinet, reached in and pulled out a bottle of tequila and two glasses. Going past another room, Savanna stuck her head in looking at her second-in-command, Jenna.

"I'm done for the night," she told Jenna. "Cody is back. Keep an ear and eye open, okay?" she said.

"Yes, ma'am," Jenna said, nodding.

Savanna led Lyric down to the staircase at the back of the house, and headed up to the attic area, where she had her bedroom. Lyric followed her up. Savanna walked over to her bed, sat down, and leaned against the headboard. Lyric grinned as she opened the full bottle of tequila and poured some into each of the glasses. She held one glass out to Lyric, waving it back and forth like a lure. Lyric walked over, moving to sit on the bed facing Savanna and took the glass.

"We've earned this over the last three days," Savanna said, holding up her glass.

"Yes, we have," Lyric said, nodding, touching her glass to Savanna's.

They both drained the contents of their glasses, and Savanna obligingly refilled them.

"So how did your date go last week?" Savanna asked Lyric at one point as she was refilling their glasses.

Lyric looked back at her, grinning, and then shrugged. "Same shit, different guy," she said.

"What does that mean, exactly?" Savanna asked, because Lyric tended to use it a lot to describe the men she dated.

From what Savanna gathered, Lyric dated a lot of men, moving from one to the next, never finding exactly what she was looking for. Some of them were too overbearing, some of them were too wussy. Then there were the ones that smelled bad, or the ones that smelled way too much. Then there was the lousy sex.

Only when Savanna specifically asked for details, did Lyric tell her where some of the men had shortcomings in that department. Some of them quite literally had shortcomings, some of them didn't bother with foreplay, others seemed to think that foreplay was talking like pigs before sex... It went on and on and Savanna found it quite telling that Lyric couldn't find a man that she wanted to be with for more than a date or two.

Lyric grinned at Savanna's question. "It basically means that this one, while a lot of talk about how good he was in bed... Yeah... not so much," she said, rolling her eyes.

"What was this guy's problem?" Savanna asked, feeling the tequila in her veins and it making her braver by the minute.

"Where do I start?" Lyric said, rolling her eyes. She moved onto her back, lying across the bed sideways, her glass on her stomach, one knee bent, her foot on the bed. She'd already kicked off her boots.

"Well, you could start with the sex," Savanna said, grinning as she put her foot out to nudge at Lyric's butt. "'Cause we both know that's the part that usually really sucks, but I digress... Tell me where it started to go off the rails..."

"Okay, I think you need to have less of this," Lyric said, reaching to take the half a bottle of tequila out of Savanna's hands. "You're getting awfully mouthy," she said, winking at her.

"Yeah, yeah, yeah," Savanna said, rolling her eyes, and taking the bottle back to pour more tequila into their glasses. "Talk!"

Lyric sighed, looking up at the ceiling. "Well, let's see... He talked endlessly about himself... How awesome he is, how every girl he meets thinks he's hot... Blah, blah, blah, yadda, yadda, yadda... Apparently *the concept of opening doors for women is beyond him... Oh, and picking up the check seems to be far too blasé for this guy too..."*

"Seriously?" Savanna said, her look telling Lyric she thought she was just messing with her now.

"Oh, no, it gets better," Lyric said, grinning. "I put up with all this shit, because he's got a damned nice body, right? And I'm thinking at least I'm gonna get off with this guy..." she said, glancing over at Savanna. "Oh, sorry... too much?" she asked, wincing, thinking that the tequila was loosening her tongue far too well.

"Pfft!" Savanna said, giving her a wry look. "I know what you're looking for with these guys, Lyric, you don't have to candy coat it..."

Lyric looked back at her. "What am I looking for with these guys?" she asked her, curious what she thought.

"You said it yourself, you're looking to get off," Savanna said, her tone a little softer.

Lyric pursed her lips slightly, wondering if that was the vibe she put off to the men too. Maybe that's why they just wanted to get to it every time.

"Okay, stop thinking and tell me the rest..." Savanna said, seeing that Lyric was trying to puzzle out her love life suddenly.

Lyric grinned; Savanna definitely knew how to tell her to get to the point. "So we're back at his place... Total bachelor pad, gag..." she said, rolling her eyes. "So fuckin' obvious, I'm surprised he didn't have mirrors on the ceiling... Anyway!" she said, seeing Savanna shake her head. "He puts on the moves... I've seen them before, its Top Gun meets Ghost... Again, gag... Finally, we're down to it... and... wham bam, and he's done!"

"What?" Savanna said, stunned. "He came without you?"

"He finished the race before I even got my shoes on..." Lyric said, shaking her head ruefully.

"Man..." Savanna said, shaking her head. "You just aren't having any luck these days..."

"I will admit that my luck is definitely in the suckage department these days," Lyric agreed.

Savanna gave her a direct look then. "Maybe you need to change it," she said.

"My luck?" Lyric asked, one eyebrow raised. "If it's that easy..." she started to say, then caught the look on Savanna's face. "Oh," she said then, sighing. "You meant I need to change teams." This wasn't first time Savanna had suggested it, so it didn't surprise her.

What did surprise Lyric, however, was when Savanna set aside her drink and straddled her, looking directly into her eyes, she felt her pulse quicken. But she shook her head, almost trying to shake the feeling away.

"Savanna," she said, her voice sounding almost normal, at least to her anyway. "I'm not gay."

"Uh-huh," Savanna said, shifting slightly to press a little more directly on Lyric's pelvic area and hearing Lyric's quick intake of breath. "Tell me again," she said, her voice somewhat husky suddenly, her eyes staring directly down into Lyric's.

"I'm not gay," Lyric said, her voice a little more ragged this time.

Savanna moved to lean down, pressing her body closer to Lyric's, and putting her lips a breath's width from Lyric's lips. "Tell me again," she said whispered seductively, her eyes still on Lyric's.

"Savanna..." Lyric said breathlessly, her eyes searching Savanna's almost frantically.

"I know," Savanna said, her lips brushing against Lyric's as she spoke. "You're not gay."

She could feel Lyric's heart pounding, and she could feel the tension in Lyric's body as she fought to resist what was happening.

"No..." Lyric said, her voice rasping.

Savanna moved back slightly, putting her hand on Lyric's chest. "Then why is your heart beating so fast?" she asked, her eyes searching Lyric's.

Lyric didn't answer; she simply looked back at Savanna, still not willing to give in.

"And why..." Savanna whispered as she shifted her hand ever so slightly, her thumb brushing over one breast, dangerously close to a nipple. "Why are you laid there hoping I'll touch you... here..." she said as her thumb brushed over a rock-hard nipple.

Lyric gasped and her body jumped in reaction. "Savanna..." she breathed, starting to shake her head again.

"Don't," Savanna ordered. "Don't fucking tell me again that you're not gay..." she said, almost angry now. "Don't try to tell me that you aren't aching so badly right now you could come at any moment..." she said, eliciting a low moan from Lyric's lips.

Once again she lowered her lips to just above Lyric's, moving her hand from Lyric's chest to the bed beside Lyric's head. With her other hand braced on the other side, she levered herself up slightly, causing her to press closer to Lyric. Lyric's eyes closed as she struggled to hold onto her control.

Savanna could see that she wasn't going to get Lyric to admit anything, no matter what. Finally, she just figured "fuck it" and moved her body against Lyric, simulating the motion of lovemaking, her body sliding over Lyric's as she did.

Lyric groaned loudly and came immediately, her hands suddenly grasping desperately at Savanna's waist, as she writhed in ecstasy. Savanna gave a shout of orgasm as well, having made herself incredibly excited in the process of trying to convince Lyric of her own desires. Combined with the sound of Lyric's pleasure, it was more than she could stand and hold out against.

Afterwards, they both lay breathing heavily. Savanna continued to lie over Lyric, refusing to move, lest Lyric move away. Lyric closed her eyes, starting to feel the impact of two sleepless nights and the tequila. A minute later she was asleep, as was Savanna. During the course of the night they both shifted, Lyric shifted them up onto the bed, both lying on their sides, but Savannah kept her hand on Lyric's waist. They were both still fully clothed.

Early the next morning, Lyric stirred. She glanced at the clock on the nightstand; it was four o'clock. She got up carefully, Savanna stirred but didn't wake. Lyric left the room and went downstairs. As she went through the foyer, she picked up her helmet, riding jacket and used her keys locked the house back up as she left. Savanna had given her a key as a safeguard the month before.

Pulling on her jacket, she stuck her hand in her pocket and pulled out her iPod. She plugged the headphones into her ears and hit play, then put the iPod back into her pocket. She climbed onto the Suzuki GSX-R1000 and pulled on her helmet and gloves. She gunned the engine and as a new song on the iPod started, Lyric let off the clutch and took *off quickly. As she drove down the road, the song "Putting Out Fire with Gasoline" played in her ears and she thought, "Yeah, pretty much..."*

It pretty much described the situation at that point. Lyric mulled over what had happened. It had literally been months since she'd been satisfied sexually. Combined with tequila, it was just a disaster waiting to happen. It didn't make her gay. She'd always been a tomboy, and just because Savanna had made her come, it didn't mean she was gay, it meant she'd had too much to drink and had desperately needed to get off. That's all it meant.

Chapter 3

Cody felt like she was hanging on by a very thin string. In the last week, McKenna had cornered her more than once trying to engage her in conversation again. Cody had been bound and determined when she'd come back to the house that she would avoid the woman. For whatever reason, that seemed to mean that fate kept sticking her right in her face.

One afternoon, Cody was sitting in the living room, once again observing one girl acting strangely. The girl continually kept looking around her, like she was expecting someone to jump out and grab her. Cody recognized the behavior, it had been exactly how she'd felt years before. It took every shred of self-control she had to keep herself from taking the girl out of there immediately.

She'd followed the other dark-haired girl the day before, and found that she was indeed meeting gang members from the local Mexican gang, the M-13. From what Cody had been able to see, they were running the same 'game' she'd been through years before. She knew that if they were doing this there were likely to be more girls from other homes or just runaways that were being forced to do their bidding. She needed to get information and she needed to get it fast. She made a mental note to check the M-13's dealings and recent arrests; maybe she could flip one of the members. What she knew for certain, was that she needed to shut this down soon.

Cody had followed the girl into the kitchen, and was just turning to leave when McKenna came around the corner. Keeping her head down, Cody did her best to move around the girl without getting too close.

"Cody?" McKenna queried. "Is everything okay?"

"Yeah," Cody said, nodding, and once again attempting to get out of the kitchen.

McKenna narrowed her eyes, sensing that Cody was trying to get away from her. She felt bad, she knew that the night of the storm things had gone a little crazy. Since then she'd been trying to get Cody back into a conversation, but Cody had been very reluctant.

"Cody, can we go talk somewhere, please?" McKenna asked.

"Why?" Cody asked, her look purposefully confused.

"I just feel like we left things on a bad note," McKenna said, sounding concerned.

Cody shrugged. "It's fine, it's okay."

"What is, Cody?" McKenna asked, trying to get under Cody's eyes so she could get her to look at her. It wasn't too hard to do since Cody was about four inches taller than her.

"What is what?" Cody asked, averting her eyes from McKenna's.

"Jesus, Cody! Stop it!" McKenna said, finally losing her patience.

She reached out and grabbed Cody's hand, and dragged her into the study, shutting the doors behind them. Then she turned to look at Cody, whose head was, as always, down. McKenna looked at the girl for a long time, and waited for her to look at her. It seemed that Cody was better at this than she was.

"For God's sake, Cody, please look at me," McKenna said.

Cody dutifully lifted her head. Her eyes looked almost gold in the sunlight coming through the windows.

"It's not like I'm going to attack you or something," McKenna said, her own concerns coming to bare.

"I didn't think you were," Cody said, not wanting McKenna to think she was afraid of that.

"Then why are you avoiding me?" McKenna asked.

"I'm not," Cody said stubbornly.

"I'm calling bullshit on that one, Cody," McKenna said, her gray-green eyes flashing.

Cody couldn't stop the grin that tugged at her lips, and McKenna saw it. Feeling a little foolish suddenly, McKenna started to grin too.

"Now that we cleared that up," McKenna said, rolling her eyes. "I really am sorry about the other night," she said her tone softer.

"Why are you sorry?" Cody heard herself ask, even as she mentally kicked herself.

McKenna hesitated, not sure how to answer that question.

"I guess because things got a little bit... intense," she said.

Cody narrowed her eyes slightly and nodded. McKenna looked back at Cody. She took in the narrowed eyes, and wondered at that. Then she found herself asking a question she never should have asked.

"Cody, are you gay?" she asked gently, but even as the words came out of her mouth, she wanted to smack herself.

There was a slight shift in Cody's look, but then she nodded slowly, lowering her eyes.

"No," McKenna said, stepping toward Cody, not wanting the girl to feel like she was judging her, or in any way blaming her for the other night. "Please," McKenna said, reaching out her hand to touch Cody's cheek.

Cody raised her eyes to McKenna again, and this time McKenna could read turmoil clearly in them.

"God…" McKenna said, shaking her head and walking over to one of the windows. "I completely suck at this," she said, more to herself than to Cody.

"At what?" Cody asked from behind her.

"This," she said. "Social work, trying to work with girls like you, when I obviously couldn't say the right thing if my life depended on it."

"You say the right thing," Cody said, feeling the need to ease the girl's conscience, even if she knew she should just leave things alone.

McKenna gave a short laugh. "Thank you for saying that Cody, but it's not really your job to comfort me, I'm supposed to be the one comforting you…"

Cody didn't say anything, but went to sit down on the love seat nearby. McKenna turned and saw that she was sitting down, and moved to sit next to her.

"Why do I feel like I always say the wrong thing around you?" McKenna asked, sounding mournful.

Cody pressed her lips together. "You try too hard," she said quietly.

"With you?" McKenna asked.

Cody nodded. "You're a lot more natural with the other girls, I've heard you."

"So what it is about you then?" McKenna asked, again, more to herself than to Cody.

"I make you nervous."

McKenna glanced at her, surprised by the statement, but then she realized that Cody was right. She nodded, looking perplexed.

"But why?" she asked.

Cody shrugged.

McKenna stared back at Cody for a long minute, her mind turning over the problem. "I think you make me nervous because you remind me of my sister…"

"Your sister?" Cody asked.

McKenna nodded. "She was older than me by three years," she said. "She's the reason I wanted to get into this line of work."

"Why?" Cody asked, curious now.

McKenna looked at Cody, unsure if she should really talk about it, but feeling like she needed to at least try to make sense of it to Cody. She didn't want the girl to feel like there was something wrong with her and that was why she made McKenna nervous.

"My sister ran away from home when she was fifteen," McKenna said. "Our parents were a bit on the strict side and she didn't want to play by their rules."

Cody nodded cringing inside, because she was afraid she now knew why McKenna had been so vehement about her not prostituting.

"She ended up on the streets here in LA. We lived down in San Diego then."

"And?" Cody asked, knowing there was more.

"And she sold her body to make money and she ended up on drugs," McKenna said. She swallowed convulsively as the memories came back, all the worry and recriminations her parents had gone through.

"What happened?" Cody finally asked when McKenna didn't continue.

McKenna took a deep breath, attempting to calm herself. She didn't want to say the words, but she knew that Cody needed to hear it. "She ended up getting murdered by one of her johns and they never caught the person," she said the last with a misting of tears in her eyes, which she turned her head away to hide.

Cody grimaced, she'd known it was going to be something like that, but it didn't make it any easier to hear.

"I'm sorry," Cody said quietly.

McKenna nodded, not looking at her, and Cody knew without a doubt that she was crying. Without stopping to think, Cody reached out and touched her shoulder, apparently that was the breaking point, because McKenna let out a soft sob. Cody moved to lean her head against McKenna's back. It was the only thing she could think of to do that wouldn't have the girl in her arms, which was really where she wanted her to be.

She could feel McKenna's body shaking and closed her eyes. It went against everything that she knew to let a woman cry and not do everything in her power to comfort her. Cody knew, however, that she'd be completely breaking her cover if she did, and if she was wrong about McKenna and she was actually working with the gang trafficking young girls, she'd have blown the case completely.

When McKenna finally calmed down, she turned around, which put her right in front of Cody, their faces only inches apart. There were still tears on McKenna's cheek and Cody did what years with Lyric had drummed into her; she reached up and wiped a tear away with her thumb. She heard McKenna suck in her breath and then she did the dumbest thing she'd done in recent history, she looked into McKenna's eyes.

Bam! She knew she was screwed before she even saw McKenna's lips part. Before she stopped to engage her brain, her libido took over and had her leaning in to kiss McKenna's lips gently. McKenna's lips were soft, and warm and, *Oh God help me...* was all Cody could think, before McKenna's lips were on hers. Cody's hands reached out of their own volition and slid up McKenna's arms, pulling her closer as she deepened the kiss. McKenna moaned softly against her lips and that was what broke the trance.

What the fuck am I doing! Cody's mind screamed. She broke the kiss and turned away. She knew it would look like she was confused, when in fact she was fighting to control her body that wanted desperately to turn right back around and ravish the woman on the love seat.

"Oh my God, Cody..." McKenna said, shock and shame evident in her voice.

It was more than Cody could take. She stood up and strode to the door, she didn't care if it was completely out of character for Cody Wyatt to stride anywhere. A few moments later she was out the front door and she broke into a dead run. She ran as far and as fast as her legs would carry her, finally collapsing on the grass in a park about four miles from the group home. She lay on the grass, looking up at the sky and thinking, *Fuck, fuck, fuck!* McKenna was going to be the death of her short career! *Stupid fucking idiot, what is fucking wrong with you?* her mind kept asking her over and over again.

Cody lay on the grass for at least two hours; it was getting dark by the time she got up. She started walking, it was fully dark by the time she made it to her motorcycle parked four miles from the house in the opposite direction. She unlocked the helmet from the bike and pulled out her iPod and headphones tucked safely inside. She plugged in her headphones and turned on the iPod. Then she pulled on the helmet and hit play. Linkin Park blared through her headphones, the song "What I've Done" played as she gunned the bike through the streets, hitting the freeway going over a hundred miles an hour, not caring which LAPD officers called Lyric. The words to the song blasted in her head, and she let the words push her farther and faster, gunning the bike and feeling the powerful engine leap forward.

She got to the house at eight that night and went into her suite of rooms through the side door, so she didn't run into her mothers. She took a shower and threw on jeans, her Harley Davidson rocker boots, and a black halter tank top that hugged her body and bared her back, showing off the six-inch long tattoo; a black treble clef surrounded by the colors of the rainbow. It was something most people never saw, but tonight she didn't care. Taking off the chain she wore and putting her platinum band in place on her left ring finger, and slid a black and gunmetal tribal pendant onto the chain and put it back around her neck. Grabbing her black leather biker jacket on the way out, she picked up the keys to her car.

As she opened the garage, she waited for the lights to come on. Lyric's black Ferrari sat next to a red one, Cody's Ferrari. Cody's wasn't as rare as Lyric's, there'd only been thirty-two of the 250 GTOs. Cody's model was a '66 275 GTB, a bit racier, especially in the red, but definitely Cody. She and Lyric had restored it together; she loved the car almost as much as she loved the woman who'd given it to her.

She climbed into the low-slung sports car, put the key in, and started it with a deeply satisfying rumble of power. Plugging her phone into the iPod jack, she cranked Def Leppard's "Slang" as she backed out of the garage. The words to the song were about how she felt that night, and she wasn't about to stop and think this one through.

A half an hour later, she pulled up to The Club. She walked over to the girl at the valet booth, stepping up just behind her so her lips were right next to the girl's ear.

"You see that car?" she whispered seductively, pointing to her car.

The girl nodded, her lips parted at the feel of this hot looking butch standing right behind her.

"I love that car more than any other possession I have…" She pressed the keys into the girl's hand, sliding her hand up her arm. "If it gets a scratch… You and I will have a problem… And we don't want that, do we?" she asked, her voice husky.

The girl shook her head, breathing heavily.

"There's a hundred in it for you, if you park it far from everyone else," Cody said, kissing the girl's ear. Then she turned and walked into The Club.

The girl stood holding the keys for a full minute before she could get her pulse under control.

Inside The Club, Cody headed straight for the bar and ordered a double shot of Herradura tequila, winking at the bartender. Taking the shot and throwing it back, she tossed a twenty and a ten on the bar and ordered a beer. The bartender handed her a Corona, knowing Cody and what she drank.

"Thanks babe," Cody said, smiling at the bartender.

She turned and headed out to the patio where she could smoke. Outside she found a chair and sat sprawled, her legs out in front of her comfortably. She pulled out her cigarettes and lit one, then tossed the pack on the table, and pocketed her lighter

"Cody?" Jet said from behind her.

Cody dropped her head back, looking at Jet and smiling, "Hey," she said.

"Haven't seen you here in a while…" Jet said, her look narrowed slightly.

"Last time I checked, I'm still legal," she said, grinning as she picked up her beer and took a long drink.

Jet chuckled, moving to sit in the chair across from her.

"Heard you got married," Cody said.

Jet grinned, nodding.

"Never thought you'd get married," Cody said, shaking her head.

"You and me both," Jet said, grinning.

"Damned shame," Cody said, shaking her head.

"Just leaves more women for you, Cody," Jet said, grinning at the younger girl.

"Uh-huh," Cody said, draining her beer and signaling the waitress.

"Get us a couple of shots, will ya honey?" Jet said to the girl, smiling, her light green eyes sparkling. "You know what I like," she said then and the waitress smiled slyly nodding.

"Dog…" Cody said, grinning.

"Yeah, yeah," Jet said, waving that aside. "So what's up?" she asked, sensing easily that Cody was on edge.

"Nothing," Cody replied.

"Bullshit, what's up?" Jet asked again, her look more direct this time.

Cody looked back at Jet; they'd hooked up a handful of times in the past. She liked Jet, she was genuine and not about the bullshit or the games. Cody liked that a lot.

Cody blew her breath out, shaking her head. "Shit case right now," she said, her tone low.

Jet nodded. "Anything to do with those informants I'm developing for your mom?"

"Well, we're on the same task force, so probably," Cody said, not surprised to hear that Lyric had made contact with the COID team.

Jet was probably the best source of informants in the department.

"So what's going on in your case that's got you so on edge?" Jet asked, raising a black eyebrow.

Cody looked back at Jet, wanting to say, *Take me to bed and let's talk about it while you fuck me…* But knowing that Jet was married, she instead looked around at the other women at the bar.

Jet noted that Cody didn't answer, and knew that pushing it wouldn't be productive. The waitress brought the shots back then as well as Cody's beer. Jet handed the girl a couple of twenties with a wink.

Taking a shot and holding it up, Jet grinned. Cody held hers up and they tossed them back.

"Damn that shit is smooth…" Cody said, shaking her head.

"That's why I stick to that instead of that other crap tequila," Jet said.

"Cody!" the DJ yelled from her booth on the patio.

Cody looked over at the woman. "What?" she yelled back.

"When are you just gonna give in?" the girl asked.

"To what?" Cody asked, grinning.

"Me, you idiot!" the girl yelled back.

Cody looked at Jet, who waggled her eyebrows and then turned herself around to take a look at the DJ who was putting her head-phones back on and looking at Cody. The girl was definitely the 'hot DJ' type, with curly black hair, a slim but shapely body and 'come fuck me' heels.

Jet swiveled back around and looked at Cody. "So when ya gonna give in?" she asked, her tone sly.

"Might be tonight," Cody said, her lips curled into a grin.

A few shots and beers later, Cody was feeling no pain, and she and the DJ were definitely flirting with disaster. After the third dance tune, Cody was shaking her head, her look disdainful.

"What, Cody?" the DJ asked over the speakers.

"Play something hard," Cody said, her tone insinuating, her tongue between her teeth.

The DJ started another song, but Cody shook her head. "Old school, babe!"

"Alright," the DJ said, again over the speakers. "This is for you Cody…"

The song "Bad Boys" by Whitesnake started and Cody put her hand up, pointing at the DJ and nodding. As the intro to the song began, Cody noticed a few of the usual group coming out of the bar to see what was going on. Cody was joined by Jet, Jericho, Quinn, Kashena, Sebastian, and Skyler in a rousing rendition of the song as they sang the lyrics and enjoyed themselves.

As the song ended, a lot of women clapped and whistled as Cody and the rest of the group laughed and did the shots someone had just sent over. The DJ played a slow song next, leaving her booth for a minute and walking over to the outside bar. A moment later she picked up a tray and walked over to where Cody sat. Everyone on the patio watched as the DJ sat on Cody's knee and set the tray on the table. It contained a shot, a lime, and a saltshaker. She leaned in and whispered in Cody's ear.

"Do a shot with me…" she said, her tone low and sexy.

She picked up the saltshaker, and pointed to her neck. Cody looked back at her for a moment, and then moved to lick the girl's neck. She handed Cody the saltshaker and Cody applied salt to the spot. The girl then handed Cody the shot and she threw it back, knowing she was way over doing it, but not caring in the slightest. Sliding her hand around the DJ's bare midriff, she pulled the girl to her, and slid her tongue over the girl's neck seductively, feeling her shudder against her. The DJ then picked up the lime and, leaning back, she slid the fruit over the curve of her breast, just above the slightly exposed darker skin of her areola. Cody leaned down, and licked the lime off her skin and felt the girl's hands in her hair, holding her head there as catcalls and yowls were issued by the crowd. Cody was grinning when she lifted her head again. She slid her hand around the back of the girl's neck and pulled her to her, and kissing her deeply to more cheering.

The DJ made her way back to the booth then, winking at Cody as she did.

"Holy shit, that was hot..." Jet said.

"Tell me about it," Quinn agreed.

"You still alive over there?" Sebastian queried.

Cody laughed, shaking her head. "I am way too fucked up for all this right now," she said.

She did her best to lay off the alcohol for the next hour. Jet helped by buying her something to eat and putting it in front of her, ordering her to eat it.

"You say the sweetest things," Cody said, grinning lasciviously at Jet.

Jet laughed, glancing at Fadiyah, her wife, who was finding the entire group highly entertaining. Jet had already told Fadiyah who Cody was; she kept no secrets from her new wife. She'd also told Fadiyah that Cody was having a rough time, and Fadiyah wanted her to help. Fadiyah completely understood the cop mentality and how cops helped other cops. She'd seen it enough when Jet had troubles, so she knew it needed to be returned and paid forward.

"Cody…" came the DJ's voice over the speaker again, her voice singing Cody's name.

Cody looked up, grinning at the girl, she did not give up…

"I get off at two," the DJ said, her tone sly.

"Get over here, and you'll get off sooner," Cody replied, widening her eyes at the girl.

There were a number of "Ohhhhs" from the group, and the DJ made a pretty good show of walking out of the booth with the song "Pass at Me" by Timbaland playing over the speakers. As the DJ got over to the table, Cody stood up; she knew literally everyone on the back patio was watching. The DJ grabbed her hand dragging her out to the small dance floor and began dancing seductively to the song, moving her body in gyrating movements, her look up at Cody unmistakable.

Cody sang the chorus of the song down to the girl, putting her hands on the girl's hips as she moved. The DJ put her arms up around Cody's neck, and moved in to press her body to Cody's as they moved to the song.

When it ended, the girl kissed Cody on the lips, then looked up at her. "I have a break in twenty minutes," she said. "Let's make it count," she said, winking.

Then she strolled back to the DJ booth. Cody watched her go, shaking her head. As she turned to walk back to her seat, she wondered if fate was really just fucking with her head at that point…

The DJ's break was spent upstairs in the office, and true to form, Cody had the girl screaming for almost the entire time. By the time they descended the stairs, the DJ's hand firmly in hers, every butch in the place was nodding to Cody and high fiving her. Cody shook her head and laughed at the inanity of the situation.

Cody spent the rest of the night getting propositioned right and left. Apparently, the DJ had no trouble telling anyone that would listen that she'd come no less than ten times in the twenty minutes.

"You're a legend…" Jet said, grinning as she sat down, pulling out her cigarettes.

"Fuck you," Cody said, starting to feel the weight of the night and the tension that wasn't easing.

Jet looked at her for a long moment, as she lit her cigarette.

"Don't tell me that didn't get you off," Jet said, shaking her head, as if it was impossible.

Cody looked back at her, taking a drag off her cigarette and narrowing her eyes in the smoke she blew out a minute later.

"Jesus…" Jet said, shaking her head, a grimace on her face. "That bad?" Cody's lips twitched as she lifted her beer to her lips draining the bottle.

"You always did with me," Jet said, her tone puzzled.

"Yeah, you were about the only one, Jet," Cody said, just drunk enough to admit that to the other woman. "Okay, time for me to go," she said, standing suddenly and reaching into her jacket pocket for her keys.

"Oh, I don't think so," Jet said, snatching the keys out of her hand and moving to stand as well. "It might be time for me to drive you home, but that's about it."

"I'm fine," Cody said, her tone even.

"Yeah and if you wrap that fuckin' Ferrari around a tree your mother'll fuckin' have my head. I don't think so Cody," Jet said.

Cody looked back at Jet, suddenly feeling all of the alcohol she'd indulged in and feeling the need to escape.

"Whoa…" Jet said, nodding to Sebastian as she saw Cody wavering.

Cody took one step and started to go down. Sebastian got there just in time, easily lifting the girl.

"I got ya…" Sebastian said gently.

Cody looked at him with bleary eyes and then dropped her head to his shoulder and was out.

She woke the next morning in her bed at the house, with the worst hangover she'd ever had and spent the morning throwing up everything she'd eaten since she was ten. She was sure she was going to die as she hauled herself up off the floor and back to her bed.

"Code?" Lyric queried from the doorway to her room.

"Cody is dead at this time," Cody muttered.

Lyric walked in and sat down on the bed, looking at her daughter and vaguely remembered getting that drunk over a woman once.

Savanna stood staring down at Lyric, who lay prone on her bed. She wore a tank top and underwear, and nothing else. It had been four days since they'd had their encounter, and Lyric had been avoiding Savanna ruthlessly. She said she'd been working, but Savanna wasn't sure what to believe. It had been a bit of a shock to wake up the next morning with Lyric gone from not only the bed and bedroom but the house as well.

She'd waited, hoping Lyric would realize something and come back, but she didn't.

Savanna had called Lyric a few times, and gotten voicemail every time, so she'd finally just left a message. Lyric hadn't called back. She knew she was getting the brush off and she wasn't willing to let Lyric off that easily. So she'd shown up at her apartment and sweet talked the superintendent into letting her in explaining that her friend was sick in bed and needed to be checked on.

Now, standing next to Lyric's bed, she could see that Lyric had been drinking; there was an empty bottle of tequila by the bedside. Savanna moved to sit down on the bed, expecting it to wake Lyric up but it didn't. So it was likely that Lyric had been drinking before she'd passed out or fallen asleep. Narrowing her eyes, Savanna decided to push things a bit. Reaching out, she ran her nail over the material covering a breast, Lyric stirred but didn't wake. 'Good and drunk then,' Savanna thought. She got up and kicked off her shoes, and got onto the bed, laying down on Lyric's right side, and putting her hand on Lyric's shoulder. She lay there watching the woman sleep, until she finally got tired and dozed off. She woke to the feeling of being watched.

Opening her eyes, she saw that Lyric was now awake and looking at her. Savanna stared back at Lyric, refusing to be the first one to speak.

It took a while, but Lyric finally sighed, shaking her head as she looked back up at the ceiling.

"What are you doing here, Savanna?" she asked.

"Well, I wanted to make sure you were still alive, first of all," Savanna said. "Since you don't bother to return phone calls suddenly."

Lyric glanced over at her. "Is Cody okay?"

"Really?" Savanna asked, her tone annoyed. "You have sex with me, and take off in the middle of the night and that's all you have to say?"

Lyric didn't answer, looking up at the ceiling, her look serious.

"I'm sorry," she said finally. "But I knew where that was going to end up with you and I didn't want to go through that." She shrugged. "I just figured it was better if I just got out of there."

"Yeah, I'll bet you did," Savanna said sharply.

Lyric looked over at Savanna, seeing not anger, but hurt in her eyes. That was what pulled her up short. Her eyes searched Savanna's and Savanna didn't turn away, wanting Lyric to see that she'd hurt her.

Lyric grimaced. "I'm sorry," she said shaking her head. "I didn't mean to hurt you, I just... You don't want to believe that—"

"No, Lyric, no, you're not going to say that again," Savanna said, her tone angry.

"It's true, Savanna," Lyric said, exasperated. "Even if you won't let me say it."

"Okay," Savanna said. "Tell me what happened the other night then?"

Lyric shrugged, shaking her head. "It's been months since I really got off... And then there was tequila..."

Savanna pursed her lips, nodding, her look saying she knew that it was what Lyric was going to say.

"So," Savanna said, "you're saying that now that you've gotten off and aren't drunk you wouldn't react the same?"

Lyric looked back at her for a long moment, not sure she wanted to answer that question.

"Savanna..." Lyric said, her tone placating.

"Answer the question, Lyric." "What difference does it make?" Lyric asked, her temper sparking then.

Savanna narrowed her eyes at Lyric. "You're afraid," she said.

"Of what?" Lyric asked, in a snide tone. "You?"

Savanna nodded. "Damned right."

Lyric laughed sarcastically. "Really?" she asked, her face a cynical mask. "And why would I be afraid of you?"

Savanna looked back at her. "Answer the question," she said again.

"No," Lyric said.

"Answer the question, Lyric," Savanna said, moving to sit up, looking down at Lyric.

"No," Lyric repeated, narrowing her eyes.

Savanna reached her hand out, once again sliding her nail over Lyric's nipple through the material of the tank top. Lyric jumped in reaction.

"Answer the question," Savanna said, heat in her eyes now.

"I don't want you," Lyric said, her tone cruel.

"Really?" Savanna asked, her eyes dropping to the nipple she'd brushed her nail across before; it was hard. She slid her thumb over it making Lyric gasp out loud.

"Stop," Lyric gritted out between clenched teeth.

"Make me," Savanna replied simply, as she continued to move her thumb.

Lyric was trembling by that time. "Savanna…" she groaned softly.

"Just tell me you want me, Lyric," Savanna said gently.

Lyric pressed her lips together, closing her eyes as she grimaced.

Savanna leaned down, putting her lips right next to Lyric's ear. "You want me, don't you?" she whispered, her hand moving to touch the other breast.

"Jesus…" Lyric groaned, unable to believe her body's reaction to Savanna's actions as well as her words.

"Just tell me you want me…" Savanna whispered, her hand sliding down Lyric's body, making Lyric gasp and groan when she stopped just at the top of Lyric's bare thigh. "Say it, Lyric…" she said, her lips touching Lyric's ear, her breathing heavy now too. "Just say it babe… We both know you want me… Just say it."

"Yes."

It was the simplest word that sounded like it was torn from Lyric's insides.

Savanna slid her hand past the leg of Lyric's underwear and touched her. Lyric immediately came, calling out Savanna's name over and over again as she did. Even as Lyric's orgasm subsided, Savanna moved her mouth to Lyric's lips, kissing her deeply, her body moving to lie against Lyric's. Suddenly Lyric was kissing her back, her hands in her hair, pulling her closer, moaning. They made love fervently, both of them orgasming together. Afterwards, Savanna lay over Lyric with her head against Lyric's chest. She felt exalted at the feeling of Lyric's hands still in her hair.

After a few minutes, Savanna moved to lie next to Lyric, levering herself up on her elbow so she could look down at her. Lyric looked up, her look searching.

"What are you looking for?" Savanna asked, her tone soft.

Lyric smiled softly. "I don't know," she said. "I guess I'm trying to figure out what's happening."

Savanna looked back at her for a long moment. "Do you want me to tell you?" she asked.

Lyric narrowed her eyes slightly, but nodded.

"Do you know why you can't ever find the right man, Lyric?" Savanna asked. "Why there's always something about them, that isn't right?"

"Why?" Lyric asked.

"Because," Savanna said as she leaned down to kiss Lyric's lips softly. Then she looked down at her again. "You're the man you want them to be."

Lyric looked completely shocked by that statement and started to shake her head immediately.

"Think about it," Savanna said. "You complain that a man doesn't open doors, or pick up the check. You always open doors for me and you always pay whenever we go anywhere... Why do you do that?"

Lyric blinked a couple of times, considering what she was hearing.

"You take care of the women in your life... Me... Cody..." Savanna said.

She leaned down, and kissed Lyric's lips again and was surprised when Lyric's hand moved to her cheek as she kissed her back.

"That, right there," Savanna said against Lyric's lips.

"What?" Lyric asked.

"Your hand, on my cheek... Is that how you wish men would kiss you?" Savanna asked.

Lyric's eyes searched hers again. "No, but it's the way I want to kiss you," she said, her tone strong, as she lay Savanna on her back and kissed her again.

"Oh, my God..." Savanna said then, her tone awed.

"What?" Lyric asked, grinning.

"The real Lyric Falco just showed up..." Savanna said, her eyes starting up at Lyric like she'd just met someone completely new, because she knew she just had.

Lyric smiled softly, knowing exactly what Savanna meant. Savanna's words had made something click in her head, and she knew she was right. It was why no man had ever been quite right.

"Hi..." Savanna said then, her smile seductive.

"Hi..." Lyric said, smiling back at her as she kissed her again.

Lyric pulled back then, her look unsure.

"What?" Savanna asked.

Lyric grimaced slightly. "I don't know exactly what to do," she said, her tone hesitant.

Savanna moved her hand to touch Lyric's cheek, her eyes looking directly into Lyric's.

"Yes you do," Savanna said. "Do to me what you wanted them to do to you..."

There was heat instantly in Lyric's eyes, as she nodded. In the end, Lyric took the time to slowly remove every article of Savanna's clothes, kissing her skin as she did and reveling in the beauty of Savanna's flawless body. Savanna pulled at the tank top Lyric wore and Lyric obliged by removing it, along with her underwear.

"Oh my God…" Savanna murmured admiringly as Lyric climbed back onto the bed.

Savanna sat up, sliding her hand over Lyric's incredibly toned stomach, shocked by the tattoo on her lower right abdomen. It was a black falcon; an artistic rendering that looked tribal in nature, with the name "Falco" in script letters under it in a rich blue. She looked up at Lyric then, her eyes wide and Lyric simply grinned, and moved to kiss her.

Savanna slid her hands over Lyric's shoulders and arms, feeling the corded muscles and feeling extremely turned on by the strength that Lyric held just under the surface.

Lyric made love to her then and only afterwards did they discuss the tattoo.

"Is that the only one you have?" Savanna asked, her fingers brushing over the tattoo again.

Lyric grinned, her look amused.

"What?" Savanna asked.

Lyric surprised her by sitting up and turning her back to her. Savanna was stunned to see a large tattoo, at least a foot long, of a black panther with blue eyes. It looked like it was climbing up Lyric's back, its long black tail curling down by Lyric's waist, its head turned and its mouth open in a roar. It was an amazingly detailed tattoo and Savanna had a hard time believing what she was seeing. She shook her head.

Lyric lay back down and grinned at her.

"I have to say I wasn't expecting that at all," Savanna said. "But it's very you."

"My father had a fit when he saw it the first time," Lyric said, grinning.

"I'll bet," Savanna replied.

Lyric reached over, pulling Savanna into her arms and making an "Mmm" sound as Savanna's skin slid over hers. "God this feels so good," she said, sounding slightly amazed.

Savanna smiled, moving to kiss Lyric's shoulder before she put her head against it. "Yes, yes it does."

Lyric lay marveling at how good she felt, it was insane to feel this good. Turning onto her side, she looked down at Savanna. Savanna caught an odd look on her face and canted her head.

"What?" she asked.

Lyric curled her lips in a grin, shaking her head. "Nothing, it's crazy."

"What is?" Savanna asked.

Lyric blew her breath out, shaking her head again. "It's going to sound nuts," she said, her look wondrous. "But I'm pretty damned sure I'm in love with you…"

Savanna widened her eyes, truly shocked by what Lyric had just said.

"Crazy, right?" Lyric said, rolling her eyes.

Savanna smiled. "No, not crazy," she said. "I know that I've wanted you desperately since the minute I met you."

"You have?" Lyric asked.

"Oh yes," Savanna said nodding. "From the second I laid eyes on you."

"And it took you this long to get around to jumping me?" Lyric asked, her eyes sparkling humorously.

"Well, you're not gay… remember?" Savanna said, her eyes sparkling as well.

Lyric grinned, nodding her head. "I remember."

They were both quiet for a bit, then Savanna heard Lyric sigh.

Glancing up at her, Savanna could see a worried look on Lyric's face.

"What are you worried about?" Savanna asked, pretty sure she already knew.

Lyric looked down at her. "I'm sure you can guess."

Savanna nodded, "Your family."

"Yeah," Lyric said, nodding and blowing her breath out.

"We don't have to tell them anything if you don't want to…" Savanna told her, knowing that Lyric's family was really important to her.

Lyric looked at Savanna for a long moment, obviously considering the suggestion. Then she shook her head.

"No," she said, "I don't want to lie to them, not about you."

Savanna couldn't help but feel warmed by Lyric's statement. Reaching up she touched Lyric's face, her eyes soft.

"You know," she said, "I think I just might love you too."

Chapter 4

Cody had gotten everything she needed to bust John Tucker. She'd found that he was a low down scum, and she was very happy to fill out the request for his arrest warrant. To her incredible relief, she had actually completely cleared McKenna of all guilt in the case. Even though John had done pretty much everything, he could to make sure that McKenna went down if he got into trouble. Cody had been smarter. Questioned Documents had determined that even though McKenna had signed the bank documents to start the account, every other signature on every other document was forged.

McKenna and John were asleep at five o'clock in the morning when they heard a pounding on their door and the words "Police!" yelled right before the door was broken open. To McKenna's shock, John jumped out of bed, and grabbed a gun he had in the nightstand.

"What are you doing?" McKenna asked him, shocked.

"Shut up!" he yelled at her, his eyes wild.

The police entered the room then and there was a tense moment where they yelled at him to drop the gun, their weapons trained on him. John finally dropped the gun, while McKenna looked on in horror. The officers moved to him, shoving him to his knees, and reading him his Miranda Rights.

A woman identifying herself an Officer Laslow took McKenna into the kitchen and talked with her at length about what John was being arrested for.

"Human trafficking?" McKenna asked, blinking in disbelief.

"Yes, ma'am," the officer said. "We have evidence that links your husband to at least four girls that have been forced into prostitution."

McKenna couldn't believe it and she still couldn't believe it two hours later when the last of the officers left her home. She was shocked when one of them handed her an envelope just as they left, with her name handwritten on the front.

Due to her undercover status, Cody had only been able to be at the execution of the arrest warrant because she wore black raid gear including gear that hid her face. She did, however, give one of the officers who was remaining on-scene for clean up a note to give McKenna when they were ready to clear out. She left the house, and walked to her car parked two blocks away and took off her gear. She climbed into the car and left the area. She never saw the car parked across the street with two men it, nor did she see one of the men's eyes narrow when she took off her cover, exposing her face. He looked over at the other man, the "SUR" tattoo on his neck clear.

"Ese es su, pequeno coño," the man said, *that's her*, and calling Cody a "little cunt."

McKenna opened the envelope and took out the folded piece of paper. The handwriting was neat, what McKenna would consider 'cop handwriting.' The note read simply, "I'm sorry, I couldn't tell you. If you want a full explanation, please meet me at the below address. It's up to you." It was signed, "*C*" in a kind of cursive letter. There was an address printed below in the same neat handwriting.

When McKenna walked outside she saw that there was a patrol car still there. The officer, who'd been leaning on his car, walked over to her.

"Taking her up on her offer?" the officer asked.

McKenna looked back at him surprised, but then nodded. He led her to his car and opened the front passenger door for her.

"She asked me to escort you if you decided to go."

She wasn't sure she knew who "C" was, but she had her suspicions. Cody had not been back to the house since the day they'd kissed. While part of her hoped that it wasn't Cody that had written the note, part of her did hope it was her, because it would mean she was okay.

They pulled up outside a house and McKenna walked up to the door. It was a nice, newer home in a pretty good neighborhood. She wasn't sure what to think at that point. Not knowing what else to do, McKenna rang the doorbell, feeling incredibly stupid at that moment. A woman answered the door, wearing jeans, black boots and a black tank top. Perhaps more importantly, a nasty-looking gun at her hip and a badge clipped to her belt. The woman's eyes were bright blue and they glanced over McKenna's shoulder, seeing the patrol car leaving. Her eyes went back to McKenna then, narrowing slightly, and then she gave McKenna an expectant look and that reminded McKenna why she was there.

"I'm here to see…" McKenna began to say, suddenly realizing that the note had said "C," so she didn't even know if Cody was the other woman's real name.

"You're here to see Cody," the woman said, looking at McKenna her look icy. "And you're McKenna," she said then, her tone acidic.

McKenna nodded, not sure what to say at that point.

"Cody's my daughter," the woman said. "I'm Lyric Falco."

McKenna blinked a couple of times. "Is that her real name? Cody Falco?"

"Yeah," Lyric said, her tone clipped. "And I'm telling you right now, if you're here to eviscerate my daughter, you're not getting through this door."

McKenna's eyes widened and that not too thinly veiled threat. Lyric Falco did not look like the kind of woman McKenna wanted to mess with Regardless, she drew her courage around her.

"Cody actually asked me to meet her here," McKenna said, holding up the note she'd received from the officer.

Lyric spared a second to glance at the note. "My kid likes to take her lumps all at once," she said, indicating that she thought her daughter was crazy. "That doesn't mean that she deserves them or that it's not incredibly stupid of her to do it."

Again, McKenna had no idea what to say, she knew she was facing a 'mama bear'. McKenna couldn't decide if it gave her comfort or made her mad to know that Cody had her so thoroughly convinced that she had no one in her life that cared about her. This woman very obviously loved her daughter dearly and was willing to do whatever it took to keep her from coming to any kind of emotional harm.

"You need to know this, though," Lyric said, her tone softening slightly. "Cody did everything in her power to protect you in this. If it hadn't been for her, you probably would have been the one being marched off in cuffs this morning." Lyric paused to make sure she was getting through to the girl. McKenna's eyes widened in reaction to what she was hearing. "You are married to a very bad man, Mrs. Tucker," Lyric said, purposely using McKenna's married name to drive home her point. "He pretty much had you set up to take the fall for this, and it was Cody that cleared you as a suspect. So, you think about that before you lay into her about whatever slights you feel she dealt you. She was doing her job, and you can rest assured that your husband is going down for a long time for his part in this and that's because my daughter did her job."

Lyric waited, wanting to make sure that this woman knew that Cody had practically turned herself inside out trying to make sure that none of the case touched McKenna.

When McKenna drew in a deep breath, her look appropriately affected, Lyric nodded to herself and stepped back, opening the door wider.

"Cody's in the back," she said, gesturing for McKenna to enter.

McKenna walked into the house. Cody definitely lived in a nice home, certainly better than McKenna had ever believed. She was still trying to reconcile everything her head when it came to this girl... woman she thought she'd known. Lyric led her through the house. In the kitchen, McKenna saw a woman with long red hair, standing looking out the window. When Lyric walked through, the woman looked over and her eyes connected with Lyric's who nodded in return.

"This is Savanna, my wife, and Cody's other mother," Lyric said, gesturing to the woman.

McKenna nodded to Savanna, seeing the concern in her eyes. Apparently, Cody had two women who loved her a great deal. Then McKenna saw Cody through the back sliding door. At least she thought she did, Cody's back was to the door. Gone was the green hair; it was now the same white blond as Lyric's, and instead of being loose and unruly as she'd always seen it, it was slicked back. She stopped, suddenly afraid to see what else was different about Cody. She could already hear music playing and it sounded like rock music, she wondered if this was the kind of music she was always listening to when she had her headphones in her ears at the house. Yet another thing she didn't know, McKenna thought.

Lyric and Savanna exchanged a look. Cody had told them what she had done with giving McKenna the address to the house. Lyric had thought she was completely insane and Savanna had been beside herself since then. The last thing she wanted was for Cody to have to face a possibly raving lunatic when she was still so sensitized to everything. Cody had explained that she had always planned on facing McKenna when the case was done, she just didn't know if McKenna would be willing to see her.

"Yeah, except she might be willing to see you long enough to rip you apart, Cody," Savanna had said, her voice fierce in her concern for her daughter's well-being.

"I can take whatever she needs to say," Cody had said, her voice complacent.

"You think you can," Savanna had responded.

Cody had looked at Lyric then who looked just as worried as Savanna, but she shook her head and shrugged. "You did what you felt like you needed to do. Just know that I'm going to do what I feel like I need to do too."

Cody had looked back at Lyric, wanting to ask what she meant, but not sure that Lyric would tell her anyway.

Savanna had heard everything Lyric had said to McKenna at the door, and she sincerely hoped that this girl, who was, according to their daughter, working to become a psychiatrist herself, would watch her words with Cody. Whether McKenna Tucker knew it or not, Cody was far from the hardened undercover cop she might believe. This case had drawn out every insecurity and fear Cody had ever had and right now, she was completely raw. The last thing she needed was for someone to rip into her for doing the right thing and her job.

Taking a step forward, McKenna opened the sliding door and stepped out. Cody's head turned and her eyes widened slightly at seeing McKenna. She'd just managed to convince herself that McKenna had opted not to come. Cody glanced behind McKenna and saw Lyric standing in the kitchen, her hands on her hips.

"I hope my mom didn't give you too hard a time," Cody told McKenna.

McKenna was looking at the cigarette in one of Cody's hands and the coffee cup in the other. It took her a minute to realize that Cody was looking up at her, waiting. McKenna blew her breath out, shaking her head.

"No, she was just letting me know what you did to keep me out of handcuffs this morning," she said, moving closer to get a better view of Cody.

Gone was the frumpy clothing and the heavy makeup. Instead she wore simple black capri work out style pants, a black tank top, and black tennis shoes with no makeup. Her eyes were no longer downcast and there was no sign of the clearly simulated shyness.

"Do you want to sit down?" Cody asked, her hazel eyes looking gold in the morning sun.

McKenna nodded, and sat in the chair that Cody had gestured toward.

Cody eyed McKenna warily. "I'm guessing you have questions," she said.

"Yeah, you could say that," McKenna said, doing her best to keep anger out of her tone.

"Ask," Cody said. "Whatever you want."

With that said, Cody sat back, her look open, far from the Cody that McKenna thought she knew. Even Cody's posture was completely different. She sat leaning to one side in the chair with one foot on the seat of chair. It was a very open, easy posture, not the closed up, pulled in posture of the person that McKenna had come to know as Cody Wyatt. The questions swirled in her head, and she did her best to put them in some semblance of order of importance to her.

"So you were in the home to figure out what John was doing?" McKenna asked.

"Yes," Cody said, "we were pretty sure he was getting the girls in the home to the Sureños so they could prostitute them."

"Were they being forced?" McKenna asked, looking worried.

"They were being threatened, yes," Cody said, sure that McKenna really wouldn't want to hear the details.

McKenna shook her head, looking disgusted. "How could he do that?" she asked, her tone reflecting her loathing.

Cody's lips curled in distaste. "Oh you'd be surprised what the nicest guys do."

"I just can't believe I thought I loved that man! Was he just fooling me the whole time too?

Cody grimaced, shaking her head. "I don't know," she said honestly.

"How did I not know? Am I really that stupid?" McKenna asked, looking absolutely morose at this point.

"You're not stupid, McKenna." Cody sighed. "He's just a bastard, and a sneaky one."

McKenna pursed her lips; it was obvious she was trying to decide if she should believe what Cody was saying. Then she looked at Cody.

"So obviously you're not seventeen," McKenna said. "How old are you really?"

"Twenty-two. I'll be twenty-three next month," Cody said.

McKenna drew in a slow breath then expelled it nodding, her look closed off.

"McKenna," Cody said, leaning forward, her eyes on McKenna's. "I'm really sorry, about having to lie to you. I had a job to do, and didn't know whether or not you were part of what your husband was doing…"

"I know, you were just acting," McKenna said flatly.

Cody looked back at her, surprised by the statement. "Not always," she said.

"When weren't you?" McKenna asked, leaning forward in her need to know that part.

Cody narrowed her eyes at McKenna knowing exactly what she was asking. "Ask what you really want to ask, McKenna," she said softly.

"What do I really want to ask?" McKenna replied, looking hurt. "Whether or not I was imagining things when I thought you wanted me?"

Cody nodded, her look pointed. "No, you weren't imagining that at all," she said sincerely, her eyes staring directly into McKenna's.

McKenna felt her pulse quicken; it was the one thing that had been driving her crazy since that morning. Had Cody completely played her? She nodded slowly.

"That last day you were there…" McKenna said, her tone cautious. "I have to know… Did you kiss me first?"

Cody's lips curled into the most engaging grin McKenna had ever seen, her hazel eyes sparkling with mischief.

"Yes," she said, biting her lower lip slightly.

McKenna blew her breath out in relief then.

Cody saw the relief and grimaced. "McKenna, I'm really sorry about that part, I know that you didn't know how old I really was. I also know that you were just responding to what you were seeing from me. I couldn't seem to keep out of trouble there…" she said, her voice trailing off as she shook her head ruefully.

"I really thought I was going crazy," McKenna said honestly. "First of all wanting another girl, and secondly wanting one that was underage!" She shook her head indicating her confusion.

"I know," Cody said. "And I really tried to stay away from you…"

"Except I kept looking for you and talking to you…" McKenna said, rolling her eyes.

Cody grinned. "Yeah, that was kind of nerve-wracking."

"Good," McKenna said, her tone matter-of-fact.

Cody laughed out loud, and McKenna found that she really liked the sound of Cody's laugh. She watched as Cody took a drink of her coffee, and lit another cigarette, taking a deep draw from it.

"I only ever saw you smoke once," McKenna said, having found it strange, most smokers usually smoked quite often.

Cody nodded, looking back at her. "Yeah, that really wasn't a Cody Wyatt kind of thing to do," she said, her look narrowed. "You actually made me break cover for the first time in my career."

McKenna looked back at her shocked, but then shook her head. "You had just met me…" she said, indicating that it wasn't possible that it had been her fault.

"I know," Cody said. "And I wanted you the minute I saw you."

McKenna's mouth dropped open at the admission. Then she gave Cody a querulous look.

"Is that normal?" she asked. "I mean do you usually want someone you're investigating?"

Cody chuckled, shaking her head. "No, never."

"Oh," McKenna said, nodding.

The back sliding door opened then, and two pit bulls darted out of the house. Lyric stood at the door.

"Sorry, Code, they were driving us nuts," Lyric said, smiling.

Cody laughed, and put her hand up to stop the dogs from running any further forward. They both stopped instantly and sat down.

"I got it, Mom, thanks," Cody said, smiling at Lyric.

McKenna watched as Cody stood and walked over to two tennis balls sitting on the ground. As she picked them up, she gave a short whistle and both dogs bounded over to her. She began tossing the balls for the dogs who ran after then, picked them up and brought them back to her. When they would reach her, she would use an upward flip of her hand to signal them to sit, which they did, then she would tell them "drop it" and they would drop the ball into her hand. Then she'd throw it for them again. They played for a few minutes, then finally Cody walked back over to her chair and sat down. The dogs walked over with their balls still in their mouths and lay down near Cody's chair, happily chewing on the tennis balls.

"They're yours I take it?" McKenna asked.

"Well, technically, yes," Cody said, grinning. "I basically get them out of the shelter, work with them to make them better, more well-mannered dogs, then I get them adopted."

McKenna nodded, looking both shocked and impressed at the same time. Then her look grew serious again. "So, Cody Wyatt is just a cover, an act?" she asked, wanting to know if she really didn't know Cody Falco at all.

Cody looked back at McKenna, knowing she should say "yes" and leave it at that, but for some reason she just couldn't.

"Cody Wyatt is who I used to be," Cody said, her expression somber.

McKenna looked back at her, her eyes searching Cody's. "Before..." she said, her tone leading.

"Before Lyric and Savanna saved me," Cody said.

"So... What you told me that night..." McKenna said. "About..." She hesitated saying the words, but Cody knew what she meant.

"Yeah, that was true. All of it."

McKenna's eyes widened. "Oh my God... Cody..." she breathed, feeling horrified at what she'd been through.

Cody took comfort in McKenna's reaction; it wasn't something she told people normally. In this case, she felt like she needed to be honest with McKenna, since she'd had to be so dishonest previously.

"How old were you?" McKenna asked gently.

"I'd just turned fourteen," Cody answered, her tone flat.

McKenna blinked a couple of times, feeling her heart break a little for the girl Cody had been.

"Will you tell me about it?" McKenna asked and saw Cody's chin come up slightly almost immediately. "Maybe not now," she added, "but someday?"

Cody looked back at her for a long moment, and McKenna realized that she was assuming she'd ever see Cody Falco again after this day. She realized it really bothered her to think she might not. After all, Cody was a police officer, and after this case she'd have no reason to see someone like McKenna again. Another thought occurred to her then.

"What happens now?" McKenna asked, realizing how little she'd thought about what was happening with her life at that point.

In her rush to see Cody, she hadn't had a chance to really ruminate on her situation or the situation at the group home at that point.

"Well, in terms of the group home," Cody said, "a judge has to put someone in charge of it… My mom is actually going to take it over for the time being, until everything is settled and the court goes to trial."

"Your mom?" McKenna asked. "Isn't she a police officer?"

"Lyric is on the same task force as me, Savanna is like you actually, only she's a board-certified psychiatrist, and she runs an LGBT group home not too far from yours."

"Oh," McKenna said, surprised by this information. Then she looked at Cody. "Are you the reason she's been appointed?"

"I asked her if she'd do it, yes," Cody said nodding.

McKenna drew in a deep breath, blowing it out slowly as she nodded. "I guess you've been protecting me all along, haven't you?" she said, her tone matter-of-fact.

Cody's lips curled in a grin. "Depends on how you look at it, but... really, I was protecting the kids at the home in this case."

McKenna nodded, still looking grateful.

"So what will happen to the house when everything is done?" she asked then.

"Well, that's a good question," Cody said, taking another cigarette out of the pack and lighting it. "Whose name is on it?" she asked.

McKenna looked back at her, a little bewildered. "Oddly enough, when we got married he put it in my name."

"Who paid for it?" Cody asked, her eyes narrowed.

"That's what's weird. We took out some money to do some improvements, but he made some excuse about his credit, so my parents did the refinance."

Cody looked speculative for a moment, then finally nodded. "Well, he may have inadvertently done you a solid there," she said. "The house is not likely subject to asset forfeiture. Of course, that's if you divorce him..."

"Oh, that's happening for sure," McKenna said sharply.. "Asset forfeiture?" she asked then, looking confused.

"Yeah, anything he bought with money he got from his illegal enterprise can be seized by the DOJ."

"Is that who you work for?" McKenna asked then.

"Yeah," Cody said, nodding.

"So you're not a police officer?"

"Technically I'm a special agent," Cody said, grinning.

McKenna nodded, looking like she was trying to assimilate everything.

They were both quiet for a few minutes. Putting both feet on the ground, Cody reached down to pet the dogs, and McKenna thought about her situation. The song on the phone changed then, and McKenna was surprised when she heard Cody singing along.

"Is this the stuff you were always listening to on your headphones?" McKenna asked.

Cody looked up and grinned as she nodded.

"Who is this?" McKenna asked.

"Linkin Park," Cody said.

"Do you listen to them a lot?" McKenna asked, noting that the music had a very hard edge to it.

"Lately again, yeah," Cody said, nodding.

"Lately?" McKenna asked.

"When things get a little bit sideways, they seem to help smooth the rough edges…" Cody said, unsure if she was making sense.

She knew Lyric would get it, but not everyone thought of music the way she and Lyric did.

"Sideways," McKenna repeated, her look thoughtful, then she nodded. "So what song do you listen to most right now?" she asked, the psychiatrist in her kicking in.

Cody thought about it for a moment, then reached over to her phone and found the song "Lying From You" and hit play, turning the volume up too. The song started out calmly enough, but then became hard and driving. Cody sang every word and looked like she definitely meant them. The song talked about pretending to be something she wasn't and how that meant she'd lied herself away from people she wanted to be near. It also talked about wanting people to push her away because it was just better to be alone.

When the song ended, McKenna looked back at Cody as she lit another cigarette. She could see that Cody's hands were shaking. She wondered if Cody meant what the song said, and if she meant it about her, that she was lying her "way" from her.

"Cody?" McKenna queried her look searching as she looked back at Cody.

"Hmm?" Cody murmured, as she lifted the cigarette to her lips again, her hands very definitely shaking.

"Who are you 'lying' yourself away from?" McKenna asked her tone soft.

Cody grinned sardonically, leaning forward to put her elbows on her knees and putting her hands together. Even then McKenna could see the tremor in them. She waited for Cody's answer.

Instead of answering, Cody simply looked back at her, her look telling McKenna she was right that she was thinking that she'd 'lied' her way from McKenna.

"What else do you do when things go sideways?" McKenna asked her voice still gentle.

Cody smiled softly, her eyes dropping from McKenna's. She was thinking that McKenna was starting to sound like Savanna. In answer, she looked over at the table, surveying the empty bottles of beer on it.

"You drink," McKenna said.

"In my defense, those aren't all mine," Cody said, grinning.

"Which ones are yours?" McKenna asked, looking back at the bottles.

"The Blue Moons," Cody said, her lips curled in a grin.

"Which is all but…" McKenna said, counting, "four of them."

Cody rolled her eyes. "Yeah."

"And how many weeks' worth is this?" McKenna asked, there were at least ten bottles.

"Weeks?" Cody asked her look puzzled.

"Months?" McKenna queried, seeing Cody press her lips together, her eyes dancing in amusement. "Days?"

"Day," Cody clarified.

McKenna's mouth dropped open as she took the time to count the bottles.

"Cody there's thirteen bottles here," she said, her tone sounding exactly like Savanna's at that moment.

Cody put her tongue between her teeth, her eyes widening in reaction.

McKenna just looked back at her, her eyes narrowed.

Cody chuckled. "Again, in my defense," she said, her eyes still sparkling, "that was last Saturday, which was the day after Friday…" Her voice trailed off to indicate that McKenna knew what Friday she was referring to.

"The day you kissed me," McKenna said, her tone taking on a humorous tint.

Cody nodded her eyes on McKenna's.

"You started on Friday with these?" McKenna asked, wanting to clarify.

"No…" Cody said, looking a bit abashed at that point. "I drank myself into trouble at The Club on Friday night."

"The Club?" McKenna asked.

"Gay club in West Hollywood."

"And how does one drink oneself into trouble?" McKenna asked, looking critically at her.

Cody caught the look and laughed, shaking her head. "Oh hell no, I'm just gonna plead the fifth on that one."

McKenna narrowed her eyes at Cody and the embarrassment of that night written on her face. It made her more determined to hear it.

"You said I could ask anything," she said.

"Oh…" Cody said, narrowing her own eyes this time. "That's low…"

McKenna gave her a *too bad* look, and smiled.

Cody blinked a couple of times, her look considering. "I never pegged you for a sadist…"

It was McKenna's turn to laugh, shaking her head. "I'm not, but your reaction is making me want to hear what happened."

Cody drew in a deep breath, and shook her head. "Let's just say that I was a bit… Over the top that night. And it's likely I'll never live it down."

"Over the top, how?" McKenna asked.

"Oh… You know, drinking, singing, dancing… carousing…"

McKenna narrowed her eyes on that last word. "Define carousing…" Cody's eyes widened at the tone in McKenna's voice, it was quite severe suddenly, and did she detect a hint of jealousy there?

"Uh," Cody stammered, her hazel eyes looking everywhere but at McKenna. "I'm definitely taking the fifth on that one, doc."

McKenna pursed her lips, the look on her face indicating that she wasn't finished with this topic. Cody couldn't help but grin at her. She leaned forward and clasped her hands together, one of her rings winking in the sunlight, which drew McKenna's eyes to them. McKenna reached out taking Cody's hands in hers and pulling them closer.

"Uh," Cody stammered, grinning.

"Relax, I'm letting you off the hook for now on the carousing thing," McKenna said, throwing her a *for now* look. "This is a class ring…" she said, touching the ring with the very distinct shape. She looked more closely at the lettering and numbers engraved on it.

She looked up at Cody sharply. "This is this year," she said, sounding surprised. "Cody this says PhD…"

Cody grinned. "I know, I suffered through the classes," she said, her tone indicating that she thought McKenna was crazy.

"You're a PhD?" McKenna asked, sounding dumbfounded. "How?"

"The usual way," Cody said cautiously.

"You're only twenty-two!" McKenna exclaimed.

Cody laughed, nodding. "Yeah, and I've had my GED since I was sixteen. I got my bachelor's when I was nineteen, my master's two years later and now this…"

McKenna frowned. "That's disgusting, Cody," she said simply.

"Why?" Cody asked.

"Because I'm twenty-five and I don't even have a doctorate."

"But you're getting a medical degree, right?" Cody said.

"Well, yes, because if I want to practice I need that, but…"

Cody nodded. "I know, Savanna has one. I don't need that though, I just wanted the degree."

"A degree is a bachelor's, Cody."

Cody smiled, shrugging. "I tend to be an overachiever."

"I guess," McKenna said, her tone still somewhat awed. "So what about this…" McKenna said, touching the platinum band on Cody's left ring finger.

"Lyric gave it to me the day she and Savanna got married. It was the day they found out my adoption was final," Cody said, smiling fondly.

McKenna nodded, seeing the love Cody had for her mothers in her eyes. It was really nice to know that Cody had these two women in her life.

Cody reached for another cigarette then, and once again McKenna noticed her hands were shaking. McKenna reached out, touching Cody's hand, her eyes searching Cody's face.

"Why are your hands shaking, Cody?" she asked, her voice soft again.

Cody looked back at her for a long moment, once again needing to decide what she did and didn't want to tell this woman. *You've told her everything else...* she thought to herself.

"I didn't take my meds this morning," she said, glancing at the house, wondering if her mothers were listening to this conversation.

"What are you taking?" McKenna asked gently.

Cody pressed her lips together, hesitating, but then finally answered. "Lithium."

McKenna's eyes widened slightly, and Cody's mouth flattened in consternation at seeing it.

"Can I ask what for?" McKenna asked then, her eyes searching Cody's face, like she was looking for the reason visually.

Again, Cody hesitated, wondering how many skeletons she needed to drag out of the closet today. Again, she figured she'd gone this far, why not at this point?

"Bipolar Depression."

"Which type?" McKenna asked.

"Two."

McKenna nodded, knowing that meant that the manic episodes Cody had weren't long or too severe. Regardless, she felt something new shift inside her. She'd wanted to protect and care for Cody Wyatt, now she wanted to protect and care for Cody Falco just as much, if not more.

"Why didn't you take them?" McKenna asked, thinking she already knew.

Cody looked back at her, her lips pursed.

McKenna nodded. "Because of me."

Cody nodded looking pensive and took another deep drag off the cigarette in her hand.

"Because meds would have smoothed things for you," McKenna said, her eyes searching Cody's as she spoke. "And you thought you deserved for things to be rough."

Cody inclined her head, her look grim.

"Cody…" McKenna began to say.

The sliding door opened again then, and Cody closed her eyes for a moment, now knowing that yes, her mothers were listening to every word.

"Cody," Lyric said, from the back door. "Come in here please."

"Mom…" Cody said her tone placating.

"Now, Cody," Lyric said, her tone all cop, all supervisor and worse, all mother.

Cody winced at Lyric's tone, and then she looked at McKenna smiling tightly. "I'll be right back."

McKenna glanced at Lyric and could see that she was looking at her. McKenna bit her lip and nodded to Lyric, hoping she was conveying her agreement with Lyric's ire. Lyric's blue eyes narrowed at McKenna, but then she watched her daughter as she stepped inside the house.

Lyric held her hand out with Cody's pill in it. "Take it, now," she said, her voice brooking no argument.

Cody picked the pill up, glancing over at Savanna who was giving her a *you know better* look. She put it in her mouth and swallowed it.

"Wanna check under my tongue?" Cody asked, her eyes flashing in anger.

"Want me to remind you about what happened last time you didn't take your meds?" Lyric asked, raising an eyebrow at her.

"It was one morning, Mom," Cody said.

"It's always just one morning, Cody," Lyric said, her look serious. "And then another, and another… I'm not going to lose you over a case, it's not going to happen."

Cody looked back at Lyric, and saw the pain her eyes. She reached out and touched Lyric's shoulder. Lyric pulled her into her arms and hugged her.

"Love you, Code," Lyric said, her tone affected.

"Love you too, Mom," Cody said, closing her eyes for a moment.

McKenna watched as Cody walked back outside. She'd heard the entire conversation with Lyric.

"Everything okay?" McKenna asked.

Cody nodded, sitting down again and reaching for the cigarette she'd set aside so she could re-light it. McKenna looked at her for a long moment, wanting to ask what had happened "last time," but knowing she didn't really have a right to ask for too many of Cody's secrets now.

"So..." McKenna queried.

Cody leaned back, taking a deep drag on her cigarette, her eyes narrowing as she blew out the smoke. "So, what?" she asked gently.

"What happens now?" McKenna asked, her eyes on Cody.

Cody canted her head. "I thought we talked about that already..." she said.

McKenna smiled softly at her. "I meant with us."

"Oh," Cody said, her eyes widening slightly, then she looked considering. "That's up to you, really."

"It is?" McKenna asked, looking surprised.

Cody nodded the look in her eyes sincere.

"If you want, you can leave here today and never really have to see me again, except for maybe court," Cody said, pulling her knee up to lean her elbow on it, in an unconscious defensive gesture. McKenna noticed it immediately.

"Or?" McKenna asked.

Cody looked back at her for a long moment, thinking about her answer. McKenna felt like Cody was trying to decide whether or not she wanted to give her another option. McKenna waited practically holding her breath for Cody to answer her.

"Or," Cody said, "you could stick around."

"Which one would you prefer?" McKenna asked, her eyes searching Cody's.

"Oh, no, doc," Cody said, shaking her head. "This is all your decision."

"But you can't tell me whether or not you want me to 'stick around'?" McKenna queried, repeating Cody's words.

"Nope," Cody said, shaking her head.

"Well, then I think I'll stick around and get to know Cody Falco," McKenna said her tone sure, her look defiant.

Cody's lips curled into a grin, as she nodded. "Okay…" she said.

"Was that the option you wanted me to choose?" McKenna couldn't help but ask.

Cody looked amused "That depends."

"On what?"

"On how well you want to get to know me," Cody said, grinning, her eyes sparkling mischievously.

"As well as you'll let me," McKenna said seriously.

Cody drew in her breath, tilting her head. "That could be a lot," she said, almost as a warning. .

"Then I'll take a lot," McKenna replied.

Cody looked quizzically back at her, then she inclined her head. "When did you want to start?"

"Is now too soon?" McKenna asked smiling.

Cody glanced at her phone, checking the time.

"Well, I'm headed to the gym here in a bit," she said. "And then the shelter… If you want to come you can."

"I want to come," McKenna responded immediately.

"Okay," Cody said, inclining her head.

"And I want you to take me to that club tonight too," McKenna added, surprising Cody.

"Uh," Cody stammered, "why?"

"'Cause that's part of getting to know Cody Falco," McKenna answered, crossing her arms in front of her chest stubbornly.

Cody licked her lips and pressed them together in consternation. "I'm not sure that's a really good idea…"

"Yeah, I'm sure you're not," McKenna said, grinning, "but I want you to take me anyway."

Cody drew in a deep breath and blew it out in a sigh. "Fine," she said. "But don't blame me if you don't like what you see or hear for that matter."

"If it's about you, it'll be interesting, I'm betting on that," McKenna said, her eyes sparkling humorously.

Chapter 5

Lyric had worked for three days almost constantly after she and Savanna had gotten together. She called Savanna regularly to let her know what was going on, not wanting her to think she was avoiding her again. By the time she got done with the paperwork from her latest case it was almost ten at night. She called Savanna, but figured she'd just have to see her the next day.

"Come over here," Savanna told her. "I need to see you…" she said, her voice soft.

"I'm gonna warn ya now," Lyric said, grinning, "I look like hell, and I'm dead on my feet."

"It's okay, I just want you here with me, babe…" Savanna said, smiling at her end of the line.

"I'll be there soon," Lyric said, smiling too.

"Drive carefully," Savanna said. "You know, like you usually don't."

Lyric chuckled. "Okay, okay…" she said.

A half an hour later, Lyric climbed the stairs up to Savanna's room. Savanna had heard her car pull up and was standing at the top of the stairs.

"Oh my God…" Savanna said, seeing the cuts and bruises on Lyric's cheek and neck. "What happened?"

"Nothing new," Lyric said, grinning.

"Come on," Savanna said, as she hugged her, and then led her over to the bed where the light was better.

She looked at the cut on Lyric's cheek, grimacing at the blood still there.

"This needs to be cleaned, babe…" Savanna said, touching just below the cut.

Lyric made a small groaning noise in the back of her throat. "Babe… I just want to sleep…"

"Okay, you lie down, and I'll clean your cut," Savanna said, grinning.

"Seriously?" Lyric said, raising an eyebrow.

"Yes, seriously, Lyric, if that cut gets infected it's going to scar," Savanna said. "And I don't want anything marring this beautiful face," she said, touching Lyric's other cheek.

"Sweet talk will get you anywhere…" Lyric said, grinning.

Savanna helped her take off her jacket and she sat down kicking off her boots and pulling her jeans off and laying them aside. She lay down on the bed and Savanna cleaned the cut and a couple of others she'd found on Lyric's arm and knee.

"You are definitely a mess," Savanna told her.

"Mmmhmm," Lyric murmured, already half asleep.

Savanna put aside the peroxide and cotton balls, and climbed into bed, sitting up against the headboard and touching Lyric's shoulder.

"Come here, babe…" Savanna said, her voice soft.

Lyric turned over onto her stomach and rested her head against Savanna's stomach, wrapping her arms around Savanna's waist. Savanna put her hands into Lyric's hair, running her nails over Lyric's scalp and stroking her back. Lyric was asleep moments later. Savanna picked up the book she'd been reading and continued to rub Lyric's back with her other hand.

She heard footsteps on the stairs and looked up.

"I saw Lyric's car…" Cody was saying and then she turned and saw Lyric lying half clothed with Savanna's hand on her back.

Savanna was sure she saw Cody's face turn to stone.

"You lied to me…" she breathed and then turned and ran down the stairs.

"Cody!" Savanna yelled, waking Lyric up.

"What? What happened?" Lyric asked as she moved to sit up.

Savanna heard the front door slam. "Damnit! It was Cody, Lyric, she came up here… She just ran off!"

"Son of a bitch…" Lyric muttered as she jumped up and threw her jeans on, jamming her feet into her boots and grabbing her jacket. "I'll get her."

Two days later, they still had no idea where Cody was. They were both worried sick. Lyric had spent hours driving up and down the streets looking for the girl, to no avail. She hadn't slept at all and Savanna found she was worrying about Lyric just as much as she was about Cody. She was watching Lyric talking on the phone, she was pacing back and forth.

"Okay, are you sure?" she was asking, reaching up to rub her face in frustration. "Okay, thanks." She hung up then, looking over at Savanna and shaking her head.

Giving a frustrated yell, Lyric threw her phone across the room. "Where the hell is she?"

"Lyric…" Savanna said cautiously. "Honey, you really need to get some sleep."

Lyric looked over at her, then shook her head. "I can't right now, Van… She's out there and I need to find her."

"I'm worried about her too, but there's only so much you can do… You haven't slept in days and I'm starting to worry about you too," Savanna said, her eyes pleading. "Will you please just come over here and lie down and close your eyes for a few minutes?" she asked then, touching the couch next to her. They were in the front room of the group home.

Lyric sighed, she didn't want to worry Savanna too. She walked over to the couch, picking up her phone on the way, and lay down, putting her head in Savanna's lap, looking up at her.

"What if she never comes back?" Lyric asked, voicing her fear.

"She loves you, Lyric, she'll come back," Savanna said, smiling down at her. She slid her hand over Lyric's hair, smoothing it back. "She was just shocked… It'll be okay."

"She said that you lied?" Lyric asked, her look perplexed.

"She thinks we lied to her about you not being gay, I hadn't told her about us yet. She's probably feeling a bit possessive of you."

"Of me?" Lyric asked.

"You've become incredibly important to her, Lyric," Savanna said. "And she's probably worried that I'm going to replace her in your life."

"Why would she think that?" Lyric asked, not understanding at all. "I thought she wanted us together."

"I think that she wants to be like you so much that being gay is really hard for her. So I think she wanted you to be gay like her. I'm not sure she wanted us together, I think she just asked you if you liked me in that way to determine if you were gay, and maybe to confirm to herself that you weren't..."

"So this is a betrayal to her?" Lyric asked, looking devastated.

"Right now, I think it is," Savanna said, seeing the distressed look in her eyes.

She knew that Cody was important to Lyric too, and she was suddenly worried that her relationship with Lyric may be in danger if Cody didn't approve. It was that realization that made her worry even more. She knew there was nothing she could do at this point in time to fix things. She just hoped that she was important enough to Lyric to try and work through things with Cody.

It was another full day before Cody walked back into the group home, a determined look on her face. Lyric was pacing on the back porch when one of the girls came running in to tell her. Striding into the house, Lyric walked into a confrontation between Savanna and Cody.

"Why did you lie to me?" Cody asked Savanna, her eyes flashing in anger.

"Cody..." Lyric said from behind her.

Cody spun around, her eyes falling on Lyric. "You lied to me too," she said, her look more hurt than angry now.

Lyric grimaced, shaking her head. "I'm sorry, Code… When I told you that I wasn't gay, I really thought I wasn't."

"But she changed your mind?" Cody said in a derisive tone.

"Yes…" Lyric said gently.

"You love her," Cody said then, seeing it in Lyric's face.

Lyric pressed her lips together, seeing the hurt in Cody's eyes and just wanting to take it away, but not knowing how to do that.

"Answer me," Cody grated out, her face a mask of anger.

Lyric nodded. "Yes," she whispered.

Cody looked like she'd been struck. "I hate you," she said, and turned to run out of the room.

"Cody!" Lyric yelled, her voice authoritative enough to make Cody stop.

Lyric strode to her and stood directly in front of her. Cody turned her head away, refusing to look at Lyric. Lyric glanced at Savanna who was watching the scene with a devastated look on her face. Shaking her head, Lyric knew she couldn't deal with that right now too. She needed to fix this with Cody first.

"Cody, look at me," Lyric said, her tone softer now.

Cody shook her head, her fists clenched at her sides.

Lyric stepped closer to the girl, reaching out and taking her chin to turn her head toward her. Cody tried to fight her, but Lyric wasn't having that at that point. When hazel eyes met blue, Lyric could see all the pain and fear in Cody's eyes. She pulled the girl into her arms then, hugging her. Cody's hands went out to her sides, refusing to let Lyric comfort her.

"I love you, Code… Please just talk to me…" Lyric said, her voice a gravelly whisper.

Cody squeezed her eyes shut, not wanting to hear what Lyric was saying, tears slid down her cheeks.

"Please talk to me…" Lyric said again, tears in her voice now.

Cody pulled back, looking at Lyric and suddenly she could see the devastation in Lyric's eyes, and how exhausted she looked. Letting out a sob, Cody put her arms around Lyric's waist, leaning her head against Lyric's shoulder and started to cry. Lyric held her, talking softly to her.

"It's okay, Code… It's okay… I'm here… I'm not going any-where… I'm always going to be here for you… always… I love you… I'm here, I'm here…"

Lyric's eyes connected with Savanna's as she did her best to calm Cody down. Tears were sliding down Savanna's face too. Lyric mouthed the words 'I love you' to Savanna who then cried harder. Lyric felt her heart break a little seeing Savanna so upset and hearing Cody crying as well. The two women in her life who'd suddenly come to mean everything to her were hurting and she was just trying to withstand the storm long enough to fix things.

Eventually, Cody calmed down enough for Lyric to move them onto the couch, though with Cody still leaning against her. She reached out her other hand to Savanna, who walked over to take it and let Lyric pull her down next to her on the other side of where Cody sat. Lyric slid her arm around Savanna's shoulders and held her close. She leaned over, kissing Savanna's lips softly, then turned to kiss Cody's forehead. The three of them sat there together for a while, letting everything calm down. The other kids in the group home saw the three and couldn't help but wish for a family too someday.

When Cody finally sat back, she looked over at Lyric and Savanna, actually seeing them now and seeing that they looked good together. Lyric looked at Cody, moving to kneel on one knee in front of the girl, and taking both of her hands in hers.

"Cody, you need to know that no matter what happens, I'm here for you, okay?" she said seriously. "But please don't run off like that again… You had me and Savanna worried sick about you."

Cody looked over at Savanna, who nodded. "Lyric hasn't slept for more than a half hour in the last three days…" she told the girl.

Cody looked back at Lyric, not fully taking in what she had said. She blinked a couple of times. "You were worried?" she asked, her tone questioning.

"Of course I was worried, Cody," Lyric said. "I know you were upset, but if we're going to be friends, you need to learn to stop and talk to me about stuff, okay?"

Cody looked back at her, her lips trembling. "Are we still friends?" she asked.

Lyric smiled softly. "Yes, we're still friends."

"I didn't mean it when I said I hated you," Cody said.

"I know," Lyric said. "Sometimes people say things they don't mean when they're mad."

"I didn't mean it," Cody said, shaking her head.

"Well, I did mean it when I said that I love you, Cody," Lyric said, squeezing her hands gently. "You are very important to me, and nothing and no one is ever going to change that."

Cody looked back at her, her eyes unsure.

"Tell me what you're thinking, Cody," Lyric said.

Cody chewed on the inside of her cheek, glanced at Savanna, then looked back at Lyric.

"You're afraid I'm going to replace you in Lyric's life," Savanna said gently.

Cody's eyes widened, as she looked over at Savanna then she looked back Lyric, clearly worried. She was worried that Lyric was going to be mad, because that was exactly what she thought. She had no idea how Savanna knew that though.

"Cody," Lyric said, moving to sit next to the girl again, "you loved your mom and your brother at the same time, right?"

Cody nodded slowly.

"So, I can love you and Savanna at the same time too," Lyric said. She saw Cody's doubtful look. "I know it's really hard and really scary, Cody, but you're going to need to trust me, okay?"

Cody looked back at her for a long moment, then nodded slowly. Lyric hugged her then, kissing her temple.

Later when Savanna had finally forced Lyric to go up to her bedroom and get some sleep, she made Cody something to eat and sat in the kitchen while she ate.

"Cody," Savanna said, her look gentle, "I know that people in your life have let you down before, but I can tell you that Lyric isn't like that. And if you'll let me, I'd really like to be someone else you can count on."

Cody looked like she was considering the idea, then she gave Savanna a slightly narrowed look.

"Do you love her?" Cody asked her, sounding very adult suddenly.

"Yes," Savanna answered without hesitation. "Yes I love her."

Cody nodded, looking satisfied with that answer.

Savanna couldn't help the grin that crossed her features. It was rather nerve-wracking having to get approval from a fourteen-year-old to date her friend!

"Where are you headed?" Savanna asked when Cody and McKenna walked into the house and she heard Cody's keys jangle.

"The gym," Cody said, grinning.

"Uh," Savanna stammered, looking at McKenna and then back at Cody.

"McKenna is going to hang around for a bit," Cody said, not wanting to get into a big discussion about it in front of McKenna.

"Okay…" Savanna said, her look questioning.

"See ya later," Cody said, as she reached into the refrigerator and grabbed a bottle of water.

She leaned over to kiss Savanna on the cheek, then pulled back to wink at her. Savanna shook her head at her daughter, thinking the kid really did like to keep her mysteries. As Cody and McKenna walked out to the garage, Lyric came into the room.

"Where's Cody going?" she asked.

"To the gym," Savanna said, her tone matter-of-fact like Cody's had been.

"Is the girl still with her?" Lyric asked, her lips quirked sardonically.

"Yes, apparently McKenna is going to hang around for a bit," Savanna said, using Cody's words.

Lyric chewed the gum in her mouth, her look a cross between amused and perplexed.

"She's your daughter…" Savanna said, shaking her head.

"Always is when you can't figure her out," Lyric said, grinning.

"Because she's just like you when I can't figure her out," Savanna said.

Lyric laughed, shaking her head and then kissed her wife.

"From the sounds of that conversation, I think that McKenna is pretty interested in our kid. I don't think we have anything to worry about."

"You say that now…" Savanna said.

"Babe, she's too old for us to choose her playmates," Lyric said.

"She was too old for that when she was fourteen, Lyric," Savanna said, grinning.

"Yeah, but she wasn't really hot for anyone then," Lyric said, widening her eyes playfully.

"And she's hot for this one?" Savanna said ruefully.

"Maybe that's a good thing, babe," Lyric said. "She needs something solid in her life, something to hold on to."

"Or something to drag down with her as she drowns," Savanna said, sounding worried.

"For a shrink you're sure pessimistic when it comes to your own kid," Lyric told her.

"Yeah, because I've seen her pattern, Lyric," Savanna said. "This could just be a segue to another break, if this girl hurts her."

Lyric looked back at Savanna for a long moment, knowing that Savanna was forever worried about Cody. She had every right to be, Cody was far from healthy emotionally and they both knew that. Lyric wanted to believe that Cody could be cured of her depression, but Savanna knew all too well that it wasn't likely to happen. It was the difference in being a clinical psychiatrist and a cop; Savanna knew the science of it, but Lyric felt like she knew Cody's heart, and she thought that McKenna could be just what Cody really needed to get her life on track.

Out in the garage, McKenna stood staring at the two extremely expensive-looking sports cars, her mouth hanging open.

Cody grinned at McKenna's reaction.

"That one's Lyric's," she said, pointing to the black Ferrari.

"And that one is…" McKenna said, nodding at the red one.

"Mine," Cody said, her eyes dancing in amusement.

"No way," McKenna said, shaking her head, thinking that Cody had to be teasing her.

"Trust me, it's mine," Cody said. "So is that," she said pointing to the black motorcycle sitting on the other side of the garage next to two others.

"The black one?" McKenna said.

"Yeah, the other two are Lyric's."

"What about Savanna?" McKenna asked.

"Savanna drives a Range Rover Autobiography, and in case you're worried she got gipped here, her Rover was about a hundred and sixty thousand, so…" Cody said, grinning. "Lyric just wants her safe."

McKenna nodded slowly, getting that Lyric pretty much protected Cody and Savanna fairly zealously.

"But you and Lyric get to be… not safe?" McKenna asked, as Cody walked over to the red Ferrari and opened the passenger door for her.

Cody chuckled, shaking her head. "Don't let Savanna hear you say that," she said, grinning.

In the car, Cody plugged her phone into the phone jack as McKenna looked around at the interior.

"This is gorgeous…" she said appreciatively.

Cody smiled. "Thanks," she said, sounding very pleased with the compliment.

Cody started the car with a loud rumble and grinned, McKenna could see that she enjoyed the sound. Cody backed out of the garage, and used the remote to close the door.

"So Ferraris are a thing for your family?" McKenna asked.

"Well, Lyric's family is Italian, so yeah, kind of their thing," she said, smiling. "My grandfather gave Lyric the black one, it's actually pretty rare. There were only thirty-two of them ever made… She restored it with him. When I turned sixteen she gave me this and she and I worked on it together."

McKenna nodded, seeing that Cody was very proud of her car, and also very connected to Lyric.

"You and Lyric are close," McKenna stated.

"Yeah," Cody said, nodding. "She's who I wanted to be when I grew up."

"And that seems to be going pretty well," McKenna said, grinning. "At least from what I've seen so far."

"Don't let Lyric fool you, she's pretty tough when she needs to be, and believe me, she's needed to be with me a few times. But I know she loves me and that she worries about me, and that's why she's tough."

"Times when she's needed to be…" McKenna repeated, glancing over at Cody.

"Yeah," Cody said, nodding as she accelerated onto the freeway.

The Ferrari engine hummed with power as Cody moved between cars, grinning as she shifted gears, with the car jumping forward in response. McKenna did her best not to be alarmed, because it looked like Cody was fairly confident in her driving, but it was still a bit unsettling. As she moved around yet another car, Cody glanced to her left.

"Fuck!" she exclaimed, as she continued to drive.

"What?" McKenna asked, completely mystified at the exclamation as she looked around them.

Cody curled her lips in derision shaking her head. "LAPD…"

A couple of minutes later her phone rang. Cody looked heavenward.

"Goddamnit," she muttered even as she answered the call on hands free. "Hi," she said, her tone even.

"Slow the fuck down, Cody!" Lyric gritted out angrily.

"I know, I know," Cody said, her tone agitated. "Jesus, do they have you on fuckin' speed dial?"

"You know better," Lyric said, her voice chiding, but calmer now.

"What's the point in having a sports car if you can't drive it?" Cody asked.

"It's not a jet, Cody," Lyric said.

Cody sighed. "Got it," she said, feeling defeated.

"Just be careful, please?" Lyric said then.

"Yes ma'am," Cody said, her tone respectful.

She hung up then, glancing over at McKenna to see she was watching her.

"What?" Cody asked self-consciously.

"Somebody called her about you speeding?" McKenna asked.

"They do that," Cody said.

"For everyone, or are you special?" McKenna asked.

"Lyric used to work with the LAPD, they know me from then, and they recognize my car… and my bike… and yeah, they almost always call her when I'm pushing it."

"Another reason she worries," McKenna said.

Cody didn't respond, she just sighed and nodded her head. McKenna sensed there was a lot she didn't know about Cody. She wondered if she'd ever know everything, but really wanted to get to know her more. She was an enigma, but an extremely appealing one. McKenna had never felt such a strong pull to a person as she did to Cody, even before she knew who she really was. Even Cody Wyatt had a way that had made her want to engage her, help her, do whatever she could to be near her. It was crazy, but knew she needed to see where this led. At that moment, she couldn't think of another place in the entire world she'd want to be, but in this car with this woman who she barely knew.

The intrigue about Cody only grew when they got to the gym. In the parking lot, Cody surveyed the cars parked there. Before even walking through the door, she knew that Jet, Jericho, Sebastian, and Quinn were there. Their cars were easy to pick out in a crowd. Jet drove a Maserati, Jericho a red Challenger Hellcat, Sebastian a black Hummer, and Quinn a midnight blue Mach 1 Mustang.

"Oh good..." Cody muttered as she got out of the car and walked around to open McKenna's door.

"What's wrong?" McKenna asked.

"Oh, this morning is just going all to hell," she said, grinning.

"Why?" McKenna asked as Cody closed the door.

Cody chuckled. "Just do me a favor, okay?"

"Okay..." McKenna said, smiling at Cody's odd behavior.

"Try to ignore at least half of what you hear in there, okay?" she asked.

"Oh my..." McKenna murmured.

Cody turned and led her into the gym. The girl at the front desk scanned Cody's card, and Cody signed McKenna in as a guest.

"How's it going, Cody?" the girl at the counter asked with a wide smile.

"Shut up, Denise..." Cody said, grinning, knowing that this was just the beginning.

Denise laughed. "You had to know…" she said, her tone chiding.

"Yeah, yeah…" Cody said, shaking her head, as she led McKenna into the gym.

Cody seemed to know a lot of people in the gym; they nodded to her, or called out a greeting. There were more than a couple of wide grins, and McKenna was really curious. It only grew when they rounded a corner and walked toward a group.

"Good morning…" Cody said formally to the group, foolishly hoping to influence their behavior.

No such luck.

"Cody…" Quinn said, her look sly, her Northern Irish accent very clear. "How ya doin'?"

Cody gave Quinn a quelling look, not that Quinn was paying any attention though, her attention was on McKenna.

"Quinn Kavanaugh, this is McKenna," Cody said. "McKenna, this is Quinn, that's Jericho," she said pointing to each of them as she said their names. "That's Sebastian, Cat and Jovina, and that's Jet. No Shenin or Sky this morning?" she asked.

"They're at the shelter," Jericho said.

"Then I'll see them there," Cody said, nodding.

"Kash is on call today and Sierra's on a big case, so you're safe there," Sebastian supplied, grinning.

"Safe?" McKenna asked, her look pointed.

"He's being facetious, and it's not appreciated," Cody said, narrowing her eyes at Sebastian. She then clapped him on the shoulder. "I do, however, appreciate the assist last week," she said, referring to him helping her home the week before.

"Any time, little one," he said, nodding.

Jet extended her hand to McKenna. Cody knew things were about to get out of her control, she also knew there was no way to stop Jet and her runaway mouth. She knew everyone in the group was watching the exchange, and simply shook her head.

"Hi, I'm Jet," she said. She cast a look at Cody. "Is this her?" she asked, her eyes returning to McKenna, searching McKenna's face.

Cody pressed her lips together, then nodded. "Yeah."

Jet gave McKenna another assessing look, then nodded her head. "I get it," she said, smirking.

McKenna looked at Cody. "I'm sorry?" she queried.

Cody looked back at her. "Jet was at The Club on Friday," she said by way of explanation.

"And she knows about me, how?" McKenna queried, sounding surprised.

Jet and Cody exchanged a look and then Jet smiled mischievously back at McKenna. "We should talk," she said and she wrapped her arm around McKenna's shoulders.

"Oh, hell no," Cody said, shaking her head. "Do not talk to her, she's trouble," she told McKenna.

"Sounds like she's trouble for you…" McKenna said, smiling brightly. "Which makes her my new best friend…"

Jet burst out laughing. "Oh, I like her…" she said, her smile wide.

"Son of a…" Cody muttered, shaking her head. She started to say something else, but Natalia was calling everyone into the class that was starting.

Cody gave Jet a final pointed look. "I'll kill ya, I swear…" Cody said, her look serious, but a grin already starting on her lips.

"Go on now…" Jet said, waving Cody on her way.

Cody gave Jet a narrowed look, but finally shook her head and walked away.

"Come with me," Jet said, hooking her arm around McKenna's.

Jet walked McKenna outside of the gym, where there were tables. Jet sat down at a table, pulling out her lighter and cigarettes.

"Do you mind?" Jet asked politely.

"No," McKenna said, shaking her head.

"So, what do you want to know about Cody," Jet asked, grinning.

McKenna smiled, looking down for a moment, then looked back at Jet. "How well do you know her?" she asked.

Jet shrugged. "Better than most, less than some," she said.

"What does that mean?" McKenna asked, narrowing her eyes slightly.

"It means, I've slept with her a few times, and we're friends," Jet said simply.

McKenna looked back at Jet, surprised by the statement. "You've slept with her?"

Jet grinned. "Trust me, honey, that does not make me unique in any way."

McKenna narrowed her eyes again. "Why?" she asked.

"Because Cody's slept with a lot of women," Jet said, her look serious.

"Define a lot," McKenna said.

134

"A lot," Jet repeated, her look pained.

McKenna nodded as she processed what Jet was saying. "So, what happened last Friday night at The Club?"

Jet looked back at her for a long moment. "What did Cody tell you?"

"She said she was a bit over the top and that she did a lot of drinking and carousing."

"Is that what she calls it?" Jet asked, grinning at the term.

"What do you call it?" McKenna asked.

"Scoring another notch for her bedpost," Jet said her look serious. "Exactly how do you know Cody?" she asked then.

McKenna looked back at Jet for a long moment confused. "In there, you asked Cody if I was her…"

Jet nodded. "'Cause I knew she was really wound tight on Friday, I took a shot that it had to do with you, and she confirmed it. Cody doesn't bring women around, unless they mean something to her."

"How many women have meant something to her?" McKenna asked.

"I think I was the last one," Jet said, no ego in her tone at all.

"And how long ago was that?" McKenna asked, feeling a bit jealous of Jet, and trying to tamp down on it.

"About a year and a half ago," Jet said. "And don't get me wrong, I didn't mean that much to her, we're a lot alike."

"Meaning?" McKenna asked.

"I didn't do commitment and I did a lot of women," Jet said, her tone serious. "Same as Cody."

"So she doesn't do commitment?" McKenna asked.

"Not that I've ever seen," Jet said, looking apologetically at McKenna.

McKenna nodded, her look contemplative.

"So she took someone home from the bar last week?" McKenna asked, wondering why Cody would be embarrassed about that. It sounded like regular behavior for her.

"Uh..." Jet stammered. "No, she didn't take her home..." McKenna looked back at Jet for a long moment. "The girl took her to her place?" she asked, her tone hopeful.

Jet laughed. "If she lived in the office at the bar, sure..."

McKenna's eyes widened. "She had sex with someone at the bar, in an office?"

Jet grinned. "While the girl was on a break," she added.

"How long of a break?" McKenna deadpanned.

Jet laughed out loud at that question. "Twenty minutes, but apparently long enough to have no less than ten orgasms, according to the girl."

"She had ten?" McKenna asked her look stunned.

"Cody's good," Jet said, smirking.

"That good?" McKenna asked, blinking a couple of times.

Jet nodded, her light green eyes sparkling mischievously.

McKenna closed her eyes for a long moment, trying desperately to ignore her body's reaction to this news. It made sense, even when Cody had just looked at her for a long moment, she'd had a reaction.

"You okay over there?" Jet asked. She knew that McKenna was supposed to be "straight," but she could easily see how affected the other woman was by what she'd just intimated.

McKenna looked back at Jet, narrowing her eyes. She sensed that Jet was definitely a smart ass. She also bet that Jet was just as good as Cody in the sex department; it was an inherent confidence that she could read on both women.

McKenna shook her head. "Every time I hear something else about her, I wonder if I know her at all…" she said, with a wistful smile.

Jet looked back at McKenna, her look considering. "Well, whatever you decide to do…" Jet said seriously. "Please just be careful with her."

"What do you mean by careful?" McKenna asked, sensing easily that Jet was very serious at that point.

"I think that Cody is a lot more fragile than people think," Jet said softly. "And I think it wouldn't take much to completely shatter her."

McKenna looked back at Jet, surprised by what she said, but realizing that she'd already felt that way about Cody all along. She assumed she thought that way because of what she'd believed about her as Cody Wyatt. It made sense; Cody definitely had a lot going on in her head. With bipolar depression, which McKenna seriously doubted many people knew about, Cody would be manic at times. She wondered if that was what had been going on that night at the bar.

McKenna finally nodded, indicating that she understood what Jet was saying. After a couple more minutes, they went back inside.

"Whoa…" Jet said when they walked back into the main gym. Lyric and Savanna were standing watching the class.

"What?" McKenna asked, glancing back at Jet.

"Lyric and Savanna have never shown up here before…" Jet said looking pointedly at McKenna. "They must really be worried…"

McKenna looked out to the floor where the class was going on. Cody going through the steps, but she kept glancing over at Lyric and Savanna with a sardonic look on her face. When the next song ended, Cody walked over to the wall where Lyric and Savanna stood, as McKenna and Jet joined them.

"What are you two doing here?" Cody asked her mothers.

"We've been meaning to check the place out…" Lyric said, not so convincingly.

"Bullshit," Cody said, her eyes narrowing slightly. Lyric's eyes narrowed as well.

"Honestly, Cody," Savanna said, making a point of getting between the two. "I've wanted to see what Natalia's class was about for weeks now."

Cody's eyes shifted to Savanna, her look wry. "And I'm supposed to buy that?"

"Watch your tone little girl…" Lyric said, her voice low.

Cody looked at Lyric then, and it was obvious that Cody was warring with the need to obey Lyric and the need to fight against their concern and obvious hovering.

"I know it's tempting," Lyric said, her tone even. "But do yourself a favor and let it go…"

Cody's jaw twitched with the clenching of her teeth, the tension clear in her eyes. Finally, she turned and walked away, grabbing her bag and heading out the back door of the room.

Lyric started to move to follow her daughter, but Savanna stopped her, looking at McKenna.

"Will you please go check on her?" Savanna asked McKenna.

McKenna nodded and headed in the same direction Cody had gone.

Jet, who'd watched the entire scene, looked over at Lyric. "Is she that bad right now?"

"We're worried, yeah," Lyric said, as Savanna nodded agreement beside her.

Jet nodded. "I think she's on edge too. But I also think that she…" She nodded toward McKenna who had just gone out the door. "Might be what Cody needs right now."

"Why?" Lyric asked.

Jet grinned. "She cares about her, and I can tell you that she's what Cody was keyed up about last week."

Lyric nodded. "Yeah, we know, she was a suspect in Cody's case."

Jet looked surprised; McKenna never did say how she knew Cody. "Not still a suspect I hope?"

"No," Lyric said, "but that's thanks to Cody busting her ass to clear her."

Jet nodded, narrowing her eyes. "Then Cody cares about her too," she said. "This might be a really good thing."

"We'll see," Savanna said, sighing.

"Cody?" McKenna queried. She was standing smoking her back to the door, leaning against the building with her head bowed.

139

"What did Jet tell you?" Cody asked without looking back at her.

"Just about Friday night," McKenna said.

Cody nodded, turning around to look at her.

"All of it?" she asked.

"About the girl…" McKenna said. "Was there more?"

"Just the part where I passed out and Baz and Jet had to get me home," Cody said, shrugging.

"Oh, just that…" McKenna said, rolling her eyes and grinning.

Cody started grinning too.

"They love you Cody, and they're worried," McKenna said. "And you've said more than once that you've given them plenty of reason to worry."

Cody nodded, taking a drag off her cigarette before stubbing it out. "I have," she said.

"Then let them off the hook a little bit," McKenna said.

Cody looked back at her. McKenna was playing peacekeeper and for some reason she didn't mind it at all.

A little while later they were getting on the freeway to head to the animal shelter. Cody was accelerating past a block of traffic.

"LAPD on the right ahead," McKenna said.

Cody looked over at her sharply, then started to grin.

"Are you cop spotting for me?" she asked.

"One less call from Lyric, right?" McKenna asked, her look pointed.

"Yeah…" Cody said, her eyes sparkling in mischief.

"Then yeah, I'm cop spotting for you," McKenna said, winking at Cody.

Cody shook her head, grinning.

Later at the animal shelter, McKenna watched transfixed as Cody worked with the dogs. She was lying on the ground on her belly, her chin on her folded arms talking softly to a terrified little Chihuahua. McKenna couldn't help but be fond of someone who would take that kind of time and energy to do such a thing for a shelter animal.

Cody had explained that the group she was working with at the shelter handled the most timid of the dogs. It was their goal to get the dogs used to people so they would be more likely to be adopted when they weren't cowering in their kennel. McKenna met Skyler, who looked fairly similar to Jet, with dark hair and light blue-green eyes, but with a completely different personality. She also met Shenin and Tyler Hancock.

McKenna sat in the play yard at the shelter and watched in awe at the patience and effort put forward by the group. She was amazed by Cody's ability, and the others in the group were telling her that Cody was always incredible with the dogs.

"They're easier than people," Cody told her later on the way back to the house.

"Why?" McKenna asked.

"Because they don't care what your problems are, they just want to love you," Cody said shrugging.

To McKenna that was quite telling.

McKenna hadn't wanted to go back to the house she shared with John so Cody had offered to let her stay with her. McKenna had agreed, wanting to spend more time getting to know "this" Cody. The truth was, McKenna was also avoiding having to think too much about what John had been doing behind her back. Staying with Cody gave her a safe haven for the moment. Since she had nothing with her but the clothes on her back, she and Cody had made a quick shopping trip so McKenna could buy a few things.

"You're going to have to go back there at some point, you know?" Cody told her, if nothing else to pack some stuff."

"I know," McKenna said. "I'm just not ready to deal with that yet."

"Okay," Cody said.

Chapter 6

That evening, the Cody and McKenna got ready to head out to The Club, as Cody had promised. McKenna looked sexy in a short jean skirt and a sapphire-blue blouse with knee high brown leather boots. Cody wore simple faded jeans that were tight on her slim shape, and a black top with her black Harley Davidson boots. Around her neck she wore a byzantine-style black chain and a thick black banded watch. She had a very sexy cool look about her, more so when she picked up her black leather biker style jacket.

At The Club, Cody got out and opened McKenna's door, already being called to by women in the parking lot. Cody handed the valet girl the keys to the Ferrari, winking at her.

"You remember what we talked about last week, right?" she said to the girl, who nodded. "Speaking of which," Cody said, pulling some bills out of her jeans pocket. She handed the girl a folded bill and leant close to her. "For last week, sorry I left before I got a chance," she whispered, then moved back to wink at the girl again.

McKenna looked at the girl as Cody turned away, and saw that longing in the girl's eyes. It wasn't the last time she saw that look that night. Cody was definitely an "A Game" player that was for sure. They were sitting out on the patio, Cody was smoking and drinking a beer, the rings on the hand holding the bottle sparkling under the lights. So many women greeted Cody and she smiled and nodded in return. She even kissed a few girls who came up to her. McKenna surveyed Cody, she was sitting with her legs slightly bent and wide apart, and hunched down in the chair very casually and relaxed looking. It was obvious to McKenna that this was how Cody always was at the bar. It was yet another side to the woman.

"So, you are here…" Jet said as she walked out onto the patio.

Cody shook her head. "You don't come here on Saturdays," she said to Jet.

"I'm making an exception," Jet said, grinning. She leant down to kiss Cody's cheek quickly, and then hugged McKenna.

"Hi," McKenna said, smiling up at Jet.

"Where's your wife?" Cody asked.

"She's got a test tomorrow," Jet said. "So, I'm solo."

"That sounds like trouble," Cody said, grinning.

"Uh-huh," Jet said. "By the way, Maggie's already heard you're here and she's looking for ya."

Cody looked back at Jet blankly. "Who?"

Jet looked back at Cody for a long minute, trying to discern if her friend was joking or not. "You never even got her name?" Jet asked.

Cody gave her a sidelong glance, closing one eye like she was trying to remember.

"The DJ, Cody, Jesus!" Jet said, laughing.

"Oh," Cody said, looking slightly embarrassed.

"You didn't even know her name?" McKenna asked looking shocked.

"Uh," Cody stammered, rolling her eyes.

Both McKenna and Jet shook their heads at her.

"Alright, I don't need you two teaming up against me here," Cody said, narrowing her eyes at them both.

Just then a black-haired woman walked out on the patio and spotted Cody.

"I'm gonna go get a drink," Jet announced wanting to get out of the way of what could be an uncomfortable conversation. "Cody, you drinking beer?"

Cody nodded.

"What are you drinking McKenna?"

"White wine?" McKenna replied.

"You got it," Jet said, winking McKenna then turned and walked into the bar.

McKenna looked at the girl as she approached and thought, *If I had even half the body...* The girl walked straight over to Cody and, grabbing a handful of Cody's hair, she pulled her head back and kissed her. Cody kept her hands on the arms of the chair for a full minute, but as the girl obviously deepened the kiss, Cody's hands reached up to hold her arms. When their lips parted, the girl stared down at Cody.

"Hi," she said, smiling.

"Hi back," Cody replied, grinning.

The girl then walked away and over to the DJ's booth.

"That's the DJ?" McKenna asked, looking at Cody.

Cody pressed her lips together, waggling her eyebrows. "You wanted to come here, remember?"

Jet came out of the bar then, and handed Jet a beer and McKenna a white wine.

"Holy shit," Jet said, grinning at Cody. "Do ya still have your tonsils?"

Cody laughed, shaking her head at Jet but she kept her mouth shut, unable to think of a clever reply.

The DJ started playing music then, and called out the first song.

"All you Cody!" she called over the microphone.

When the music started, Cody started shaking her head, and Jet started laughing, McKenna had no idea what was going on but could guess easily enough. The song was Ricky Martin's "Mr. Put it Down" and it did seem to fit Cody pretty well.

As the song ended, the waitress came over to the table, handing Cody a shot.

"What's this?" Cody asked, looking at the waitress.

"You're doing a shot with me," she said, winking at Cody.

"Uh…" Cody stammered. "I don't think…"

"Oh, so you'll do one with Maggie, but not me?" the waitress said, pouting prettily.

Cody shook her head. "Okay, okay," she said, holding up her hands in surrender.

The waitress, sat on the arm of the chair, holding a saltshaker and leaning down across Cody. Cody looked at McKenna over the girl's shoulder and saw that she was watching avidly. Cody narrowed hazel eyes at her, as she slid her tongue over the spot where the waitress's neck met her shoulder. She shook salt onto the spot and then licked it again, then turned her head she did the shot. The waitress moved back, holding out the lime wedge between her fingers. Cody sucked on the wedge, licking the girl's finger seductively when she finished, grinning up at the waitress. The waitress leaned down, taking Cody's face in her hands and kissed her lips.

McKenna found that she was feeling rather warm after that particular performance. As the waitress got up and walked away winking at Cody, Cody looked over at McKenna.

"You wanted to come here tonight, remember?" she asked again, grinning.

McKenna stuck her tongue out at Cody, smiling. "I remember, and I'm thinking I need to buy you a shot," she said, winking at Cody.

"Ohhh…" Cody said, smiling as she reached for her beer again.

A few minutes later, it was Jet who handed Cody another shot.

"I'm not doing one off you," Cody said, grinning.

"I bought your girl Casa Noble," Jet said, winking over at McKenna

"She's not getting anywhere near you," Cody said, her tone serious, even though her eyes were sparkling with humor.

"It's for her to do off of you," Jet said, winking.

Cody shook her head. "You are such a troublemaker," she told Jet. Then she looked over at McKenna. "You don't have to do this."

McKenna looked back at Cody, her eyes already a bit heated. "Oh, no, that's fine, I'll do it," she said, smiling as she stood up.

Cody looked up into her eyes, looking amused. She looked less amused when McKenna pushed the bottom of her skirt up so she could straddle Cody's lap. Cody's breathing increased, and her eyes grew heated, never leaving McKenna's.

"You're going to need to tell me how to do this…" McKenna said.

Cody licked her lips, as she slid her hands over McKenna's hips. She pulled her a little closer, causing both of them to breathe heavier.

"You lick," Cody said, her voice slightly husky, "wherever you want." Her eyes sparkled attractively. "Then you shake the salt, lick again… Ohhhh…" She moaned softly as McKenna leaned down and licked her neck at the base of her throat, making Cody shudder. McKenna's eyes connected with hers as she shook the salt, and then lowered her head once again to lick the salt.

"Take the shot," Cody said warmly, as she handed McKenna the shot.

McKenna drank the shot delicately, as Cody looked on biting her lip. Cody then held up the lime wedge that Jet handed her.

"Then you suck," Cody said, putting the lime to McKenna's lips.

McKenna did as she was told, her eyes looking down into Cody's the entire time.

"Now, that's how you do a shot…" Jet said, her voice low.

Cody and McKenna laughed. McKenna put her hands to Cody's shoulders as she moved off her lap, sliding her skirt back down a moment later and sitting back in her chair again.

"I need another drink…" Cody said standing up and winking at McKenna as she walked inside the bar.

Jet grinned, watching Cody go, then looked back at McKenna.

"You're gonna kill her at that rate," she said, smiling widely and giving McKenna a wink.

"Or me," McKenna said, blowing her breath out. "Jesus… is it hot in here or is it me?"

"Oh, it's definitely you, sweetheart," Jet said, smiling.

McKenna looked back at Jet and knew that she was definitely every bit as sexually dangerous as Cody. She thought that Jet's wife as probably crazy to let Jet be at the bar alone. Then again, McKenna hadn't seen Jet look at one woman yet, so it was pretty obvious that Jet was in love with her wife.

Cody came back a few minutes later, with a fresh beer, one for Jet and another wine for McKenna. It was another hour before McKenna decided she needed to buy Cody a shot. Cody looked over at her when the shot arrived, narrowing her eyes. She took the shot from the waitress, picked up the lime and the saltshaker, and then stood.

McKenna looked at her confused. "Come with me," Cody said, sliding the saltshaker in her pocket and holding out her hand to McKenna.

McKenna glanced at Jet, who raised a black eyebrow, a grin on her lips.

Taking Cody's hand McKenna stood up. Cody led her into the bar and upstairs to a particularly quiet corner. There she turned to McKenna, moved her to the corner of the wall, and set the shot and the lime on the windowsill nearby.

"Let's do this properly," Cody said her lips at McKenna's ear. "Without the crowd."

McKenna felt her breath catch in her throat simply at Cody's closeness. She was surprised when Cody slid her hands around her waist, and lifted her so they were eye to eye. Cody pressed against her, pinning her to the wall to keep her there. McKenna put her hands to Cody's shoulders as she looked into Cody's eyes feeling her heart beating wildly.

Cody lowered her head, and slid her tongue sensually from the base of McKenna's throat to her ear. McKenna moaned softly, her body already pulsing from the excitement coursing through her. Reaching into her back pocket, Cody pulled out the saltshaker and sprinkled some on the spot, and then slowly and extremely sensually licked it off. She picked up the shot, drank it, and then picked up the lime. She slid her hand up McKenna's chest and pulled aside part of her blouse, exposing a section of breast above the nipple. She slid the lime over it, then lowered her head and licked it off. McKenna grabbed Cody's head, holding here there, breathing heavily, and feeling her body shaking with need.

She felt Cody's lips on her skin, and then she felt Cody's tongue slide past the material to touch an extremely hard nipple. McKenna was gasping in her orgasm instantly, her hands grasping at Cody's hair. Cody's lips then found McKenna's, and she kissed her deeply as McKenna came again, wrapping her legs around Cody's waist as Cody pressed closer, causing yet another orgasm. McKenna grasped at Cody's shoulders, feeling like she was going to explode as wave after wave rolled through her body. Cody's hands slid under the blouse caressing her skin and causing more unbelievable sensations. McKenna lost all sense of reason wanting Cody's skin against hers, but Cody stopped her when she tried to pull at her clothes.

"Not here, honey," Cody said in a husky voice.

McKenna wanted to protest when Cody moved back, gently setting McKenna on unsteady feet.

"I got you…" Cody whispered, as McKenna grasped at her to keep from falling to the ground. Her body suddenly felt like it was made out of rubber.

Cody moved to lean against the wall, holding McKenna against her. McKenna laid her head against Cody's chest and could feel Cody's heart beating fast. She couldn't believe how incredibly good she felt, even though they were standing in a bar, and she'd just come God knew how many times, in public, although there was no one around where they were. Regardless, they were still in the bar, but McKenna hadn't cared about that, all she'd cared about was the feeling of Cody's mouth on hers, and her hands and what it was doing to her body.

"I think I get the ten times in twenty minutes thing now..." McKenna said softly.

She heard a rumble of laughter from Cody's chest and looked up. Cody was grinning down at her. "You do, huh?"

"Mmmhmm," McKenna purred. "I think I need another shot," she said, smiling.

"Oh lord," Cody said, smiling back at her.

After about twenty minutes, Cody took McKenna's hand again, and led her back downstairs and up to the bar, where she bought her another shot. McKenna didn't really need instructions this time, but Cody gave them all the same.

"Lick," Cody said, sitting on a barstool, which put her eye to eye with McKenna.

McKenna lowered her head, licking along the low neckline of the shirt Cody wore, her hands at Cody's waist.

"Salt," Cody said, grinning.

McKenna shook the salt on the spot, sliding her hands up Cody's torso. Before Cody could tell her, she licked it again. She flicked her thumbs upward, brushing over Cody's nipples, her body hiding the action from onlookers. She felt Cody's body jump slightly and her quick intake of breath.

"Suck," Cody said, her voice a husky whisper in her ear.

McKenna lowered her head to Cody's neck, just above her collarbone and sucked at Cody's skin. She could feel Cody's low moan vibrate against her lips and her hands in her hair seconds later, holding her there. When she finally moved back, she was satisfied to see a dark bruise where her mouth had been and the slightest trickle of blood, which she quickly ducked to lick off Cody's neck. When she pulled back, she saw that Cody was watching, her eyes holding both heat and amusement.

"Marking your territory?" Cody asked, as she grinned.

"Exactly," McKenna said, her look challenging.

Cody inclined her head. "Nicely done," she said.

McKenna pressed her lips together, for some reason insanely pleased that Cody liked what she'd done. A few minutes later they rejoined Jet out on the patio, and she whistled lowly when she saw the hickie.

"Letting a girl mark you now?" Jet asked, raising an eyebrow at Cody.

Cody licked her lips, her eyes widening at Jet. Jet shook her head, giving her a rueful smile. She was thinking that Cody was well and truly caught at that point. She was happy to see it. McKenna noticed the exchange, but didn't say anything. She'd already been pretty sure that Cody normally wouldn't have gone for something like a hickie on her neck. It had been why she'd been thrilled that Cody hadn't been mad. She knew it was ridiculous, but she wanted Cody all to herself, at least for that night.

An hour later they walked into Cody's side of the house. McKenna looked around noting the framed Linkin Park album cover posters as well as some others. She walked over to one of them, and glanced back at Cody, who was leaning against her door watching her.

"Who's this?" she asked, pointing to the poster.

"Queensrÿche," Cody said, smiling. "Operation Mind Crime, first album Lyric ever gave me."

McKenna smiled, nodding. Not surprised by that at all. There were others as well, a British flag with "Def Leppard" in the center, and another from the album Pyromania.

"All about the music, huh?" McKenna asked, glancing back at Cody again.

"Always," Cody said, smiling.

Her room was spacious and the furniture was black Mission style, simple, but substantial. It was very 'Cody' McKenna thought. The bed was covered with a deep purple comforter with black accents.

"Purple?" McKenna asked.

"Favorite color," Cody said, her look indulgent.

"Hmm," McKenna murmured, as she moved to look at the few pictures on the dresser.

There were pictures of a younger Cody with Lyric and Savanna. There was a separate picture of Savanna and Lyric, a wedding picture, obviously. Savanna wore a white wedding gown, and Lyric wore a black tuxedo; they were facing each other, their heads together. Lyric's hand was on Savanna's cheek looking tenderly at her new wife. Savanna's smile was brilliant, her eyes looking straight into Lyric's.

"Wow," McKenna said, looking at the picture.

She felt Cody move to stand behind her and look over her shoulder.

"Yeah," Cody said, smiling. "That's my favorite one."

"It's awesome," McKenna said. "You can see how much they love each other in that one shot."

Cody nodded, smiling fondly. She slid her hands around McKenna's waist then, lowering her head to kiss McKenna's neck softly. McKenna slid her hands over Cody's arms, leaning back against her, dropping her head to Cody's shoulder, leaving her neck open to Cody's lips, which Cody took full advantage of. Within minutes, McKenna was grasping at Cody's arms and pressing back against her.

Taking one of McKenna's hands, Cody led her over to the bed. She stood in front of her and lifted the edges of McKenna's blouse, sliding it up and over her head. Smoothing her hands over McKenna's skin, she reveled in finally touching the person she'd had far too many fantasies about. She looked down into McKenna's eyes and saw she looked a little nervous.

"Is this okay?" Cody asked softly.

McKenna nodded, her lips trembling slightly. "Yes, I just don't know what to do…"

"Just follow me," Cody replied cavalierly.

With that she slid her hands up McKenna's back, unclipped her bra and removed it. She moved her hands over her breasts, then slid her hands down McKenna's body as she knelt on one knee to slide McKenna's the skirt off. All the while her hands continuing their exploration of McKenna's body.

McKenna looked down at Cody, unable to believe this was the 'girl' she'd thought she was only twenty-four hours before. This was no child, this was an incredibly sensual woman who made her want her more than anything in the world at that very moment. While she knew she was still avoiding thinking about anything too deeply, McKenna also knew that her reactions to Cody were very strong. She was surprised by the intensity. Refusing to worry or overthink things, McKenna reached out her hand and touched Cody's cheek, shuddering as Cody continued to touch her, their eyes locked on each other's.

In one fluid motion, Cody stood up and her lips captured McKenna's. She then slowly pushed her back onto the bed positioning herself over her, with her arms braced on either side of McKenna's body. There was something incredibly sensual about the fact that Cody still had all of her clothes on. The chain she wore was cold against McKenna's skin, but it just turned McKenna on even more.

Cody made love to her, moving her body over hers making her moan and grasp at clothing. After the third or fourth orgasm, McKenna started pulling at Cody's clothes, desperate to get them off. Cody grinned down at her, then got up to stand at the side of the bed. She kicked off her boots, and stripped off her shirt and bra, then finally unbuttoned her jeans.

McKenna moved to sit up and put her hands to the waist of Cody's jeans instead, looking up at Cody as she removed the offending garment and the boy shorts under them. When she was finally able to see Cody's body she sat back and let her eyes move from the lean muscle of her arms and shoulders and down to her lightly defined flat stomach. Her body was incredible. She moved her hand over Cody's abdomen, looking up her the entire time. Cody grinned and climbed onto the bed, sliding her arm under McKenna to lift her and move her higher onto the bed, then sliding her body over McKenna's.

"Cody…" McKenna breathed as her entire body lit up with renewed excitement instantly.

There wasn't a doubt in McKenna's mind that Cody had done this millions of time. Cody knew exactly how much pressure to exert, and where to exert it, she knew when to lower her head to kiss skin, and slide her tongue over a nipple. McKenna found herself screaming as she held Cody's body to hers, bucking against her. It excited her even more when Cody's breathing became uneven and she groaned, moving her body faster against McKenna's.

"God, God…" Cody chanted. Her head moved from side to side, her body tensed, and then she gave a shout of pure ecstasy, which sent McKenna right over the edge again as well.

Cody lay against her afterwards, her knee bent next to McKenna, where McKenna suspected she was concentrating her weight since she was still light against her. McKenna pulled at her, wanting Cody's full weight against her. Cody groaned as she slid her leg down, her body pressing against McKenna.

"God… Kenna…" Cody breathed against her neck, her voice husky.

McKenna wrapped her arms around Cody, thoroughly enjoying the feel of Cody's skin against hers, feeling Cody's muscles move and shift as she reached up to stroke McKenna's cheek, her face still pressed against McKenna's neck. McKenna fell asleep with Cody's hand still in her hair.

Dawn was just breaking the next morning and Cody sat in the backyard smoking, music playing on her phone next to her. She'd pulled on her jeans and a tank top; it was windy and cold but she didn't seem to notice.

"Code?" Lyric queried, stepping out of the house.

"Hey," Cody said, smiling.

"What are you doing out here?" Lyric asked, pulling her jacket around her.

Cody held up a cigarette, grinning.

"Ah," Lyric said, then reached into Cody's pack and took one out for herself.

"You're smoking again?" Cody asked.

"Only occasionally," Lyric said, her tone unrepentant.

Cody nodded. "Uh-huh," she murmured.

Lyric looked at her daughter, she could see how relaxed she was, there wasn't even the tiniest hint of tension in her face or in her posture. It allayed a little of Lyric's fear, seeing her that way. Then she noticed something else. Leaning forward she flicked the hickie on Cody's neck.

"You let her do that to ya?" Lyric said, looking surprised.

Cody grinned again. "And so much more…" she said, her tone extremely self-satisfied.

"Oh ho…" Lyric said, her mouth open in a surprised smile. "That good, huh?"

Cody bit her lip, closing her eyes for a moment, then nodded, looking at Lyric her eyes dancing in excitement.

"Well, alright then," Lyric said, nodding her head, her eyes sparkling. "How long's it been?" Cody looked considering. "'Bout a year and a half."

"Holy shit…" Lyric said, looking stunned.

"I know, right?" Cody said with a wry grin.

"So, what do you think that means?" Lyric asked, her eyes narrowed slightly.

"That I got there with her?" Cody asked.

"Yeah," Lyric said. "I know this girl means something to you, Code, it's obvious. Jesus just the way you look right now says it."

Cody looked pensive, then finally blew her breath out shaking her head. "I don't know for sure."

"What do you think you know?" Lyric asked. "How do you feel?" she asked, reaching out to touch Cody's chest, her hand over Cody's heart. "Here."

Cody sighed, closing her eyes for a moment again. "I feel absolutely amazing right now, Mom, better than I've felt in a long time."

Lyric nodded. "Is that because of her, or because you finally got properly laid for the first time in a year and a half?" she asked, with a sly grin.

Cody laughed out loud, appreciating Lyric's way of asking harder questions.

"That's the part I don't know for sure," Cody said. "I feel so much right now, I can't tell what's just a complete lack of sexual tension for a few minutes, or… more."

Lyric nodded. "Well, when the lack of sexual tension takes hold," she said, winking. "Your heart will tell you how you really feel."

"Is that how it worked for you and Mom?" Cody asked, having heard the general story of how Savanna had essentially had to force Lyric to admit she had feelings for her, by way of sex.

Lyric smiled, her eyes soft. "Code, once I finally accepted the idea that I was gay, I knew I was in love with your mother. It was instant."

"Really?" Cody asked, her eyes widening. Then they dropped to the side.

"What?" Lyric asked, sensing that Cody had just had a thought she was surprised by.

Cody looked back at her, chewing on the inside of her cheek.

Lyric canted her head. "What, Code?" she asked again, knowing she needed to get it out of the girl.

"Would it be crazy…?" Cody began, but then shook her head. "No, never mind, its nuts."

Lyric gave a knowing smile; she'd been where Cody was now. "What is?"

Cody drew in a deep breath, looking back at her mother. "If I'm in love with her," she said simply.

Lyric gave a short laugh. "I asked your mother the exact same thing the night I told her I was in love with her."

Cody's eyes widened, her look considering. "So it's not too crazy?"

"Wasn't for me," Lyric said. "I've loved your mother every minute since that night."

Cody nodded, knowing that what Lyric was saying was true; she could see Lyric's love for Savanna and Savanna's for her every day.

"So maybe it's time you get your ass back in there with your girl…" Lyric said, grinning.

"Maybe," Cody said, smiling, stubbing out her cigarette.

"Cody," Lyric said, her tone serious suddenly, her eyes searching Cody's face. "Are you okay? I mean, really okay?"

Cody looked back at Lyric, seeing the worry in her eyes.

"I really am, Mom," Cody said, nodding. "The last twenty-four hours have been completely insane, but… I feel good, really good."

Lyric nodded, looking pleased. "Love you, Code."

"Love you too, Mom," Cody said, standing up and leaning down to hug Lyric. "You better get back to Mom, she's probably getting cold without you."

"Uh-huh." Lyric grinned and stood up.

Back in her bedroom, Cody dropped her clothes on the floor and climbed into bed next to McKenna who lay sleeping on her side. Cody positioned herself behind McKenna, and gently slid her arm under her so she could pull her closer. She wrapped her arms around her, enjoying the feeling of them being so close. McKenna stirred.

"Cody?' she murmured tiredly. "Where did you go?"

"Just out to smoke," Cody said, kissing McKenna's bare shoulder.

McKenna sighed and snuggled back against her, turning her head to kiss Cody's shoulder. They fell asleep that way.

Lyric slid into bed next to her wife and lay on her side, with her arm over Savanna's stomach. Savanna stirred immediately and turned her head to look at Lyric.

"Everything okay?" she asked softly.

"Oh yeah," Lyric said, moving to nuzzle her wife's neck. "I think Cody's in love with McKenna," she said offhandedly.

"What!" Savanna asked, fully awake suddenly.

Lyric chuckled. "I said, I think that Cody is in love with McKenna."

Savanna turned over on her side, looking back at Lyric.

"Why do you think that?" she asked.

"Well, one, because I saw the kid's face and she's completely gone when she talks about the girl. You saw it today too, you know it," Lyric said, narrowing her eyes slightly at her wife. "And just now she basically said she thinks she is."

Savanna thought about the possibility. Cody certainly hadn't been acting like she normally did when it came to this woman. Their daughter had always been fast and loose with women, never sticking with one for long, and rarely letting them as far into her life as she'd let McKenna in the last twenty four hours. The gym and the animal shelter were huge things for Cody, she didn't share them with just anybody. McKenna being around Cody's friends, and seeing her at the shelter where Cody was completely open was a big step for their daughter. It made sense.

Savanna nodded finally. "But do we think that McKenna feels the same?"

Lyric shrugged. "Well, she's still here, even after everything with the case…"

"True," Savanna said. "But she's married to a man," she reminded her.

"Sometimes we don't know who we are until we meet the right person, babe, you taught me that," Lyric said.

Savanna looked back at Lyric. "You weren't married to a man, Lyric."

"I know, but I was also in pretty heavy duty denial about my sexuality. This girl doesn't seem to have that particular impediment."

"So they did sleep together," Savanna said, thinking they probably had, but not sure.

Lyric grinned, her eyes sparkling.

"What?" Savanna asked, knowing her wife well enough to know that she was dying to tell her something.

"She got Cody… uh… home," Lyric said, trying to be humorous.

They'd discussed Cody's admission to Lyric about not 'finishing' and Savanna had said that it was perfectly normal for someone who'd suffered the sexual traumas that Cody had to have that kind of problem.

Savanna stared back at her wife. "She did?" she asked, surprised.

Lyric nodded.

"Well, then that's why Cody thinks she's in love with the girl," Savanna said.

Lyric rolled her eyes. "Well, Code did say it's been over a year and a half since the last one…"

Savanna stared back at her, blinking a couple of times. "A year and a half?" she repeated, in disbelief.

Lyric chuckled, nodding her head.

"Christ, I get two days out and we have a problem…" Savanna said, smiling at Lyric with her tongue between her teeth, her eyes dancing in amusement.

"Uh-huh, I know, trust me," Lyric said sounding put upon. "That's why I get things thrown at my head when I work too much."

"Yes you do," Savanna said, grinning unapologetically.

"Well, she did say that it might be the sudden complete lack of sexual tension," Lyric said. "So I think she's got her head on straight about this."

Savanna nodded considering Lyric's words. Then she suddenly slid her hand over Lyric's bare shoulder.

"How many days has it been?" she asked seductively.

"Who cares?" Lyric replied, moving to kiss Savanna's lips sensually.

Savanna's arms wound around Lyric's neck, pulling her close and pressing her body closer. Lyric's hands pulled at her, as she moaned against her lips. Minutes later, they were both crying out.

"That never gets old…" Lyric said, breathing heavily, as they lay together afterwards.

Savanna reached down smacking her ass. "It better not!" she exclaimed.

Lyric chuckled, moving to kiss Savanna's lips again.

The next morning McKenna slid out of Cody's bed and went into the bathroom. Cody stirred and rolled to her stomach, clasping a pillow under her head with both arms. When McKenna came back into the room, she was shocked to see the tattoo on Cody's back. She walked over to the bed and sat down, reaching her finger out to trace the black treble clef design. Cody stirred again, turning her head and opening one eye.

"What are you doing?" she murmured tiredly.

"Checking out your art work," McKenna said, smoothing her hand over the tattoo, noting the rainbow outline of the musical symbol.

"Mmmm…" Cody murmured, closing her eye again, and smiling warmly.

McKenna lay down on her side facing Cody with her elbow propping her head up, taking in Cody's profile. Cody sensed she was being watched, and opened one eye again.

"It's all about the music, isn't it?" McKenna asked, her tone amused.

"Always," Cody said, repeating what she'd said the night before. "But that's about Lyric too."

McKenna nodded, having suspected that as well.

"Are you awake now?" Cody asked tiredly.

"Probably," McKenna said, glancing at the clock on Cody's nightstand. "It's six a.m., when I normally get up."

"We didn't go to sleep till like one," Cody said.

McKenna smiled. "I know, but my internal alarm clock is pretty set. That doesn't mean you can't go back to sleep."

Cody rubbed her face on the pillow under her head, then turned over onto her back, groaning as she did.

"I can't lie here in this deafening silence, though," Cody said, reaching over to pick up the remote to her iHome and hitting a button.

Music filled the room suddenly, and Cody grimaced comically turning the volume down with her eyes squeezed shut. McKenna watched with an amused grin on her face. So this was Cody in the morning.

"Deafening silence," McKenna repeated. "Is that what it sounds like to you?"

"It sounds really loud," Cody said, nodding.

McKenna nodded her look contemplative. "So do you have any other tattoos that I don't know about?" she asked, grinning.

Cody went still for a moment, and McKenna instantly recognized uncertainty in Cody's eyes. McKenna reached out her hand touching Cody's cheek, her eyes searching.

"What is it?" she asked softly.

Cody looked back at her for a long moment, then bent the knee of her left leg, moving aside the sheets to reveal the "SUR" tattooed on her thigh.

McKenna looked at the tattoo, then she looked up at Cody. "What does SUR stand for?"

"Sureños, they're a Mexican street gang," Cody said, her voice breaking slightly on the word.

"Why do you have it?" McKenna asked, her voice as gentle as she could possibly make it, sensing that this was a big deal to her. This was not like the other tattoo.

"It's not like I had a choice…" Cody said, her voice trailing off as she swallowed convulsively. "You know how ranchers brand their cows?" she said. She kept her tone even, but her eyes told a completely different story.

"Oh Cody…" McKenna said, her eyes shining with tears.

McKenna's look was so completely devastated for her that Cody had to close her eyes to shut it out for a minute. Her lips trembled slightly as she fought to control her emotions.

"That's why I do what I do, Kenna," Cody said, when she had control of her emotions again.

McKenna looked back at her but Cody still had her eyes closed. When she opened them, McKenna could see all the pain and desolation in them and her heart ached for Cody. She reached out her hand and laid it on Cody's shoulder, her eyes looking into Cody's.

"I'm so sorry, Cody," she said, her voice tremulous. "I can't even begin to imagine what you've been through in your life. "But you are so amazing to have come through it the way you have."

Cody gave a short sarcastic laugh. "Well, coming through it is true enough, but I'm not sure there's anything amazing about it."

McKenna sat up in her surprise at what Cody had just said. "How can you not see how amazing you are?" she asked, her tone serious. "Cody, you do a job that saves people's lives," she said. "You deal with the most horrible people, and take monsters off the street… How do you not see that as amazing?"

Cody looked back at McKenna, sensing McKenna's tension and her obvious surprise that Cody didn't know this about herself. Cody narrowed her eyes looking doubtful.

"I do it while taking Lithium and screwing every woman in town," Cody said, her tone self-castigating.

"That's coping, Cody," McKenna said. "And I hate to hear you talk that way about yourself."

Cody looked back at her, surprised by what she'd just said, unable to think of a response. Blowing her breath out, she shrugged, shaking her head.

McKenna put her hand over Cody's heart, then looked directly into her eyes.

"You have an incredible heart, Cody," she said softly. "You just have to let people see it."

Cody blew her breath out, grimacing. "Yeah, that's always the problem."

"What is?" McKenna asked.

"Letting people see," Cody said, her eyes downcast.

"Why?" McKenna asked.

"Because if they see your weakness they can take advantage of it," Cody said, sounding very much like the street kid she'd been years before at that moment.

McKenna heard it in her voice and saw it on her face.

"Not everyone wants to take advantage of your weakness, Cody," McKenna said.

Cody's eyes looked into hers, her look doubtful.

"Is that what you think I'm trying to do?" McKenna asked her then.

"No," Cody answered immediately, making McKenna's heart skip a beat.

"I don't want to hurt you," McKenna said gently, shaking her head slowly, her eyes on Cody's.

Cody's lips trembled and her eyes softened. "I know," she said.

"Is that why you're letting me see you?" McKenna asked her voice still very soft.

Cody nodded, her look affected. "No one else has ever seen this much," she said, her voice a whisper.

"That scares you, doesn't it?" McKenna asked.

"More than you'll ever know."

McKenna drew in a deep breath, blowing it out in a sigh. "I just want to…" she began, her voice trailing off as she shook her head.

"Want to what?" Cody asked, her eyes searching McKenna's.

McKenna hesitated, because the words that came to mind just sounded inadequate for the way she felt.

Cody sat up so her face was only inches away from McKenna and reached out to gently touch her.

"What do you want, McKenna?" Cody asked, her voice intense, but gentle at the same time.

McKenna lifted her eyes to Cody's. "I want to love you."

Cody's lips parted in reaction and she leant in and kissed McKenna's lips gently. "Then love me," she said as she pulled back, her voice a quiet plea.

Tears sprang to McKenna's eyes instantly, and she reached for Cody, who pulled her into her arms, holding her tightly against her. Cody held her in her arms, her hands stroking her hair, her lips against McKenna's temple. McKenna pressed her face against Cody's neck, breathing in the scent of her and feeling completely at peace. It was the most incredible, wonderful feeling and McKenna couldn't believe how simple it had been. Cody wanted to be loved and McKenna wanted to love her, how could it have been any different? McKenna didn't know, but she knew that she'd been meant for this woman. She felt it to her very core.

Later that morning, McKenna's phone rang and she pulled it out of her purse, seeing that it was her parents.

She grimaced. "I need to take this, it's my parents," she said, and she got out of bed and walked into the bathroom.

Cody lay on the bed, staring up at the ceiling, music still played on the iHome. She could hear McKenna talking and didn't want to eavesdrop so she turned the volume up on the speakers, not overly loud, but enough to mask whatever McKenna was telling her parents.

A new song came on just as McKenna hung up the phone and she stood in the bathroom listening to the words. They talked about how she had no idea if love was real because she was damaged too much to know that. It spoke to abuse and having things taken away. McKenna guessed that Cody was talking about her innocence.

McKenna walked out to the bedroom to see exactly what she expected; Cody was singing the words and staring up at the ceiling. The song was Plumb's Damaged, and the words of the song went straight to McKenna's heart. She walked over to the bed, staring down at Cody as she sang.

As the song faded out, Cody moved her hand and pressed McKenna's to her heart, her look meaningful. It told McKenna that Cody was trusting her with her heart at this point. McKenna nodded, accepting the unspoken entreaty that she not break it.

"So how'd that go?" Cody asked when McKenna sat down on the bed next to her.

"Well, they're shocked, and they want me to go visit them."

"Okay. And how are you feeling about all of this?" Cody asked then.

McKenna breathed out a sigh and shook her head. "I feel like I had to be the world's biggest fool not to see what he was doing," she said, trying to express her feelings genuinely. "I wonder if part of me always knew he wasn't the man I thought, he was too perfect. But now that I know what he really is, I just feel sick. How could he be that horrible and me not know about it? Am I really that naïve?"

Cody sat up and touched McKenna's face. She felt a strong need to protect this woman.

"I can't imagine what you're going through with this," Cody said, her voice soft. "But you gotta know that he planned it this way, and he did a lot to hide from you who he really was."

"I just want to hit him," McKenna said. "I want to punch him over and over until he hurts the way he hurt those girls."

Cody chuckled. "Well, rather than violence that'll only get you arrested too, let's let the court handle him, okay?"

McKenna nodded, knowing Cody was right.

"And you're still okay with us… this?" Cody asked, gesturing to them as a couple.

McKenna didn't answer right away, wanting to try to make sense of everything that was in her heart and head. "I can't explain it," she said, shaking her head, "but this feels right somehow. You know?"

Cody curled her lips in a derisive grin. "Don't I know it," she said, with a humorous tone to her voice.

McKenna laughed softly, shaking her head.

Chapter 7

Later that day McKenna got to see yet another side of Cody Falco. They were at the LGBT group home run by Savanna. Cody held her hand as they walked up the stairs leading up to the front door of the house. Cody opened the door and stepped inside, glancing around as she did.

"Cody, Cody, Cody!" a young girl chanted excitedly as she ran up to Cody.

Cody had to let go of McKenna's hand quickly as the girl launched herself into Cody's arms. Cody hugged the girl, smiling, turning with the girl in her arms and winking at McKenna.

When the girl finally let Cody go, she looked at McKenna.

"Who're you?' she asked suspiciously.

"Easy now…" Cody said, her tone amused. "This is McKenna. McKenna, this is Christie."

Christie looked like she was about twelve. She had blond hair that was pulled back in a few different braids with colorful rubber bands. She had a very young-looking face, but her brown eyes were wary, far too wary for someone so young as far as McKenna was concerned.

"Hi Christie," McKenna said, smiling.

Christie narrowed her eyes, her look skipping from McKenna to Cody and then back.

"Why are you here with Cody?" she asked then, her tone supporting the suspicious look she was giving her.

"Chris," Cody said sternly. "She's with me and you need to be respectful of that."

Christie looked at Cody again, as she chewed on the gum in her mouth. "With you, like *with* you?" she asked, her tone leaving no room for misunderstanding what she was asking.

"Yes," Cody said, her tone more gentle now.

Christie looked at McKenna again, her look assessing, then she looked back at Cody again. "You're never with anyone, Cody."

Cody's lips curled into a grin. "Yeah, well, I guess I am now, huh?" she said, a slow smile spreading on her lips.

Christie looked like she didn't like that answer, but then she put her hands on her hips, in a sudden show of sassiness. "But just till I'm eighteen, right?"

Cody laughed, nodding. "Of course," she said.

Christie gave McKenna a *so there* look and walked off, turning her head to wink at Cody.

"That was… interesting," McKenna said, giving Cody a sidelong glance.

Cody grinned. "Yeah, she kinda has a crush," she said. "It seems to help her talk to me a bit, which is what Savanna says she needs."

"So you don't just work with dogs…" McKenna said, grinning.

"Dogs are just easier," Cody said, her look serious.

McKenna nodded, understanding that completely.

"McKenna?" queried a girl that walked down the stairs.

McKenna recognized Julie from the group home that had been shut down due to John's crimes.

"Cody?" Julie said then, recognizing McKenna much easier than she had Cody.

"Yeah," Cody said, nodding.

Julie looked shocked. "Is that really you? 'Cause you look totally different."

Cody nodded, blowing her breath out. "Yeah, we need to talk, okay?" she said. "I need to talk to all of you," she said, looking around for the other girls from the home.

"Cody," Savanna said from the doorway to the back patio. "I've got everyone out here," she said. "Julie was just joining us."

Cody nodded, turning to McKenna. "I need to talk to them, do you want to stay in here, or…?"

"No, I want to be there," McKenna said.

Cody had already told her that she intended to talk to the girls from the home, explain who she was, and what she had been doing there. She needed to know if anyone else had been victimized, and this was the best and easiest way to get that information.

They walked out to the sunroom at the back of the house. Savanna closed the doors and looked over at Lyric who was lounging near the far windows. Both of her mothers being there meant they were still keeping tabs on her somewhat. Savanna and Lyric noted that she was holding McKenna's hand. Lyric raised an eyebrow at her wife, by way of saying *See?* Savanna made a face at Lyric, as she moved to sit in one of the chairs on the patio. She looked at the five girls sitting on the couches and chairs. Then she looked at Cody, gesturing for her to proceed.

Cody nodded and stood in front of the girls, leaning against a nearby table. She pulled out a cigarette and held it up. "Anyone mind? she asked.

All the girls grinned, shaking their heads. Cody lit the cigarette as her eyes scanned over the girls. They were all pre-teen or teenagers, their ages ranging twelve to seventeen but they all looked a lot older and more hardened by their lives out on the street. Lyric, Savanna, and McKenna had all noted that Cody's hands were shaking slightly. Lyric looked over at McKenna who mouthed, "She took it," indicating that Cody had indeed taken her meds that morning. There was just some stress even Lithium couldn't keep at bay.

"So, I don't know what you've heard," Cody said, her tone matter-of-fact, "but I'm not Cody Wyatt." Her look was pointed. "I'm actually Cody Falco, and I'm a special agent for the California Department of Justice. I work for a human trafficking task force. It's my job to stop people who are using young people to make money by selling them into sexual slavery." Her look was serious and somber. "I have personal experience with this shit, and it destroys lives." She looked at the girls, noting that they all looked shocked. "The reason the house is closed at this point is because we arrested John Tucker for multiple counts of human trafficking and money laundering. I know a couple of you knew that already," she said, looking at two of the girls, Julie being one of them. "So, if you have any questions, this is your chance to ask."

McKenna watched Cody, seeing the 'cop' part of her come out. She was completely self-assured and her confidence was high. She suspected that the shaking hands were simply because she didn't like now knowing how the girls were going to react to her information.

"How old are you really, Cody?" one of the girls asked.

"Twenty-two," Cody answered.

"Whoa," the girl replied, widening her eyes.

Cody grinned engagingly. "Yeah, I'm old," she said, taking another draw off her cigarette.

"You smoke, Cody?" another girl asked.

"Like a train at this point," Cody said, grinning.

"How long are we gonna be here?" another girl asked. Her name was Rosa, and she didn't look like she was happy about the situation at all.

"Well, we have to see what happens with the case," Cody said, glancing at McKenna. "But if it goes right, McKenna might be able to reopen it."

"What's she doing here? She's married to him, right?" Rosa asked, her tone snide.

Cody narrowed her eyes slightly. "McKenna's not involved in that," she said, her tone strong.

"How do you know?" Rosa asked, her look full of attitude.

"'Cause I'm good at my job," Cody said, her tone more pointed.

"Were you fucking her then too?" Rosa snapped.

Cody took a deep breath, forcing herself to remain calm, when she really wanted to smack the girl for being a bitch. She also wanted to say, *Are you still pissed because I wouldn't fuck you?* Not that the girl hadn't tried every way to Sunday to get her into bed.

"We were not involved then," Cody said, her tone even.

Rosa leaned back in her chair then, her arms crossed, her dark eyes flashing still, but she stopped asking questions. She'd had her sights on Cody from day one, but the girl wouldn't give in. Now she knew why, it irritated her.

"One last thing," Cody said. "I need to know if John tried to get to any of you, other than you two," she said, glancing at Julie and another girl called Tammy.

"He asked me once if I wanted to make some money," one of the girls said. Cody remembered her name was Barbara.

"What did you say?" Cody asked her eyes narrowing slightly.

"I said *cool,* but…"

"But what, Barb?" Cody asked.

Barbara shrugged. "It didn't sound right," she said. "He wanted me to take pictures or something…"

Cody closed her eyes for a second, then blew her breath out, looking over at McKenna who looked somewhat ill suddenly.

"Did he bug you about it?" she asked.

"He asked a few times, but I just blew him off," Barbara said.

Cody nodded. "You've got good instincts, always listen to them," Cody told her. "If you'd be willing to give me a statement that would be great."

"Sure," Barbara said, nodding.

Cody pulled out her badge wallet containing her business cards and handed them to all the girls. "If any of you need anything, I want you to call me," she said, her tone sincere. "And if any M-13 members try to contact you, or harass you in any way, I want you to call me any time, day or night. Do you all understand?"

"Do you carry a gun, Cody?" Julie asked, her eyes wide as she looked at the badge clipped to the black leather wallet.

Cody turned, lifting the back of her shirt, showing them the holster at her back with the fairly nasty looking gun in it.

"Holy shit, girlfriend is strapped!" Rosa said, grinning.

Cody grinned. "That's all," she said, signaling an end to the meeting. "If any of you want to talk to me privately, I'll be here for a bit."

All of the girls nodded, standing up and talking to each other. Cody walked over to McKenna, looking down at her, her eyes searching McKenna's.

"You okay?" she asked McKenna.

"Yeah," McKenna said, blowing her breath out. "It's just really hard to hear. It's one thing to have learned what he was doing, but it's another to actually hear it from these poor girls… Part of me really wanted to believe it was just a bad dream or something… I feel so stupid…"

"You weren't stupid, Kenna, he knew what he was doing," Cody said, her tone soft.

McKenna blew her breath out, nodding her head. She put her hands on each of the ends of the denim vest Cody was wearing, her head bowed, leaning it against Cody's chest. Cody leaned down, kissing the top of her head affectionately.

Lyric and Savanna noted the two talking and saw the sweet gesture.

"Told ya," Lyric said to Savanna.

Savanna glanced back at Lyric. "You are all-knowing babe, all-knowing," she said, her tone far from sincere.

Lyric laughed, smacking her wife on the butt, Savanna laughed then too.

"Cody?" Julie queried softly, walking up to where Cody and McKenna were standing.

Cody turned to look at Julie. "Hey," she said, her voice gentle, "you okay?"

Julie nodded. "Thanks to you," she said, her tone sincere.

"I'm glad I could help," Cody said.

"How did you know I was hurt?" Julie asked.

"That day in the study," Cody said. "When I dropped the pencil."

Julie looked surprised. "I thought that was weird," she said, shaking her head.

"Well, sometimes you do what you gotta do to figure out what's going on," Cody said, smiling softly.

"You said you have personal experience with this…" Julie said, her tone cautious.

Cody nodded. "Yeah," she said, her tone somber.

"Like what?" Julie asked.

Cody felt McKenna's hand slide into hers, she squeezed McKenna's hand gently.

"Like exactly what you went through," Cody told the girl.

Julie looked shocked. "No lie?" she asked.

"No lie," Cody said, shaking her head. "I was fourteen."

"How did you get out?" Julie asked.

Cody raised her head, nodding toward Lyric and Savanna talking on the other side of the room. "They saved me." Julie looked over at the couple and then back at Cody, nodding.

"Well, you saved me," Julie told Cody. "And I won't ever forget that."

Cody smiled, her eyes misting with tears. She reached out and took Julie into her arms.

"Thank you for that," Cody said her voice gravelly with emotion.

"What would you think about me adopting Cody?" Lyric asked Savanna one morning.

They were lying in Lyric's bed and had just made love. Savanna's head rested on Lyric's stomach, she lay cross ways on the bed. She looked up at Lyric.

"How long have you been thinking about this?" Savanna asked, her tone mild.

Lyric grinned. "A week or so," she said.

"Or since she came back that last time," Savanna said.

"Or since then," Lyric added, her grin wide.

Savanna moved to sit up. "I think that you'd be fantastic as a mother," she said, her tone sincere.

Lyric looked back at her. "Would you be willing to do it with me?"

Savanna's brows furrowed. "Huh?" she asked. "Oh, you mean help you with the paperwork? Sure."

Lyric grinned and reached up to pull Savanna down to her. She kissed her, then pulled back to look at her.

"No, I meant being her mother with me."

Savanna looked back at her for a long moment. "Are you asking what I think you're asking?"

"If you think I'm asking you to marry me, then yes, I'm asking what you think," Lyric said, her tone so matter-of-fact it was maddening.

"So you just drop a question like that into the middle of a sentence and think that's okay?" Savanna asked her tone incensed as she sat up again.

Lyric laughed her blue eyes sparkling. "I thought it would be easier that way."

"Easier than what, Lyric?" Savanna asked sounding flabbergasted.

"Than the whole one knee thing... You know how complicated that can get, there's the where to do it and how to do it and did I do it right... And did they really put a man on the moon, and is Elvis really dead..."

By the time Lyric's voice trailed off Savanna was laughing and shaking her head.

"Only you," Savanna said, her tone amused.

Lyric sat up, taking Savanna's face in her hands. "I love you, Savanna, and I want you, me, and Cody to be a family. So will you do me the honor of becoming my wife?"

"Oh, see that's much, much better..." Savanna said. Whatever she was going to say next was lost when Lyric kissed her deeply.

"So, what do you say?" Lyric asked, her blue eyes searching Savanna's.

"I say that I'd love to be your wife, Lyric," Savanna replied.

"Good," Lyric said, sounding very pleased with herself. "Now help me with the adoption paperwork."

Savanna laughed, shaking her head.

Two days later Savanna and Lyric took Cody to dinner, ostensibly to celebrate their engagement. Lyric had presented Savanna with a ring consisting of chocolate and topaz diamonds and it winked and shined in the lights of the restaurant.

After they'd ordered, Lyric looked over at Cody.

"So we have a question for you," Lyric said.

"Okay," Cody said, looking at them both suspiciously.

Savanna looked at Cody, reached across the table and held out her hand to her. Cody took Savanna's hand, looking worried suddenly. When Lyric did the same thing, Cody took Lyric's hand with her hand shaking.

"What's going on?" Cody asked, her tone fearful.

"Cody, we want to know if you want to be our daughter?" Lyric asked.

Cody went completely still, and Lyric and Savanna exchanged a look, both wondering if the girl was really ready for this.

"You mean it?" Cody asked, her look indicating that she wasn't even daring to hope that they did.

"Of course we mean it, Cody," Savanna said with a wide smile.

Cody looked to Lyric.

"My idea, so of course I mean it," Lyric told her.

Cody jumped up from the table and threw herself into Lyric's arms.

"Woah…" Lyric said, trying not to fall out of the chair, even as she held Cody to her. "I'm thinking this is a yes…" she said, smiling fondly.

"Yes, yes, yes…" Cody chanted quietly against Lyric's shirt.

Lyric and Savanna exchanged a look, smiling. They had a nice dinner talking about their plans, where they'd live, whether or not Cody could paint her room any color she wanted…

Three days later, things went straight to hell. Cody disappeared again, and Lyric was frantic. She questioned every person in the group home. On the third day, she finally caught a break, finding something out from one of the kids who was rarely at the house. All she had to hear was one name. "Sureños," and her blood ran cold.

"Who are the Sureños?" Savanna asked, watching as Lyric put on her vest and loaded her gun, before putting it in her shoulder holster.

"They're a Mexican gang… And they run a human trafficking ring…"

"You don't think Cody…" Savanna started but her voice trailed off as she grew pale.

"Stay with me babe," Lyric said, reaching out to steady Savanna.

"What are you going to do?" Savanna asked, her tone worried.

"I'm going to go get our daughter," Lyric said, her tone serious.

"You can't just walk in there," Savanna said, knowing enough about any kind of criminal operation to know that.

"Watch me," Lyric said, her eyes blazing.

"Lyric wait, you can't…" Savanna said, suddenly frantic. "You'll get yourself killed!"

"I'm not leaving our daughter there a minute longer, Savanna, I don't have time to do things by the book!" She leaned in to kiss Savanna. "Give me twenty minutes, then call 911 and report it here's the address I'm headed to." She gave Savanna a serious look. "You have to wait the twenty minutes, Van, if they hear sirens before I get to her, they'll kill her, do you understand me?"

Savanna nodded, looking terrified.

"I'm sorry, I gotta do this, Van, you know that," Lyric said.

"I know," Savanna said, nodding. "But I'm scared."

Lyric nodded. "I know." Then she leaned in, kissing Savanna one last time. "I will get her out of there, if it's the last thing I do on this Earth. Just remember that I love you," she said, her look somber.

Savanna hugged Lyric then, doing her best not to try to hold her back. She knew that Lyric needed to go after Cody, she was just afraid this would the last time she'd see her.

"I love you, Lyric… So much…" Savanna said.

Lyric nodded, moving to the door. Then she was gone.

Lyric climbed into her car and started it with a roar. She glanced at the group home one last time, hoping it wouldn't be the last time she saw it. She shook her head, not the time to think like that. Putting the car into gear, she sped off. Queensrÿche's "Screaming in Digital" poured out of the speakers. Lyric used the screaming guitars to center herself, and focus her on what she needed to do. She had to push away the visions of what could be happening to Cody, if she was even still alive.

She got to her destination in record time. Glancing at her watch, she noted she still had seventeen minutes until Savanna would call the police. She looked around as she got out of the car. She was half a block from the hotel she was headed for. She prayed that she had the right intel and that was where they had Cody. As she approached, she saw Sureños hanging around. She didn't make eye contact, but kept walking, acting like she was headed to her own room. She got up to the second floor without incident. Glancing at the room numbers, she knew she only had a few more to go. Looking down the corridor she could see two Sureños standing by a door chatting.

Lyric slowed, shifting her neck, doing her best to focus. As she walked toward the two men, she glanced around her like she was lost. She moved her hand to her waist, scratching her belly. Both men looked at her, but didn't see her as a threat, she was just a woman after all. Lighting fast, she pulled her gun out, and pointed it at both of them.

"Now, nice and slow…" she said, smiling sweetly. "Open that door, and you better pray that my daughter is in there and okay, or I'll make you sorry you were ever born," she practically growled.

The two guys looked at each other, and then back at her.

"We don't know what you're talking about lady," one of them said.

Lyric reached up under the back of her jacket, pulled out the Kaybar knife she was carrying and stuck it to the guy's crotch. "You know what I'm talking about now?" she asked, her lips twitching with anger.

"Yeah, yeah!" the guy said, putting his hands up.

"Move…" Lyric growled.

They moved toward the room door and opened it. Lyric shoved them inside. Glancing around, she saw Cody huddled on the bed and had to look away, knowing she couldn't take seeing her that way and focus on getting them out of there alive.

"Get in there, now," Lyric said, pointing to the bathroom.

The men did as she said. She'd just locked them in the bathroom and turned to Cody when she felt the burning pain of a knife sliding into her side. She jumped to the side, spinning as she did, and faced a man twice her size. She had the time to think, "Where the hell did he come from?" before he lashed out and hit her in the face. She dropped her gun, but held on to the Kaybar knife she'd used on the men now locked in the bathroom.

She heard Cody scream her name.

Pure adrenaline was the only thing that kept her on her feet. She lashed out with the knife in her hand, catching him in the arm, because he'd expected her to go down. He charged at her, and she had to dive out of his path to keep him from taking her down. She knew if he got her on the ground she was dead and so was Cody. She spun around to face him, as he staggered up obviously shocked that she'd avoided him.

"What's a matter?" Lyric asked sarcastically. "Only used to attacking little girls?"

"I'm gonna fucking kill you, bitch!" the man growled.

"You're gonna try," Lyric said, her tone confident.

The man gave a yell of anger as he charged her again. Lyric stepped aside and punched him in the face as he passed her, but he surprised her by whirling around and grabbing her. She brought her knee up, catching him in the face and his hands dropped. She saw her gun, lying on the ground a foot away and dove for it, grabbing it as she hit the floor. She rolled, and saw that he was coming at her. She fired without a second's hesitation. He fell to the floor dead.

Lyric climbed to her feet, panting, and holstered her gun. Cody ran to her and threw her arms around her. Lyric grabbed her up in a hug, as she heard sirens.

"Okay baby girl, okay… I got you… You're okay…"

"Lyric you're bleeding!" Cody cried as she saw the red spreading over the white tank top Lyric was wearing.

"It's okay," Lyric told her. "I'm okay."

Officers came running into the room then, and Lyric held the side of her jacket up so they could see her badge.

An hour later, a bandaged and bruised Lyric climbed out of her car, with Cody running around the car to help her. Savanna came running out of the house, hugged Cody then looked at Lyric.

"Oh, honey…" she said, seeing the bloody shirt and the nasty bruise on her face.

"Oh, I've looked worse after a fight," Lyric said, grinning.

"Don't tell me that," Savanna said, shaking her head.

The three of them went inside, the family reunited. Later after settling the rest of the house, Savanna went up to her room. She found Cody and Lyric asleep on her bed. She stood looking at her girls and thinking she had no idea what she'd do without these two blessed creatures in her life.

As she climbed into bed that night, Lyric kissed Savanna, thinking that things with their daughter were finally stabilizing. McKenna seemed to have a good effect on Cody.

"What do you think about taking a vacation?" Lyric asked Savanna.

Savanna looked back at her surprised. "A vacation?" she said. "I've heard of those…" she said, her voice trailing off.

"Yeah, they're those mythical things that people take occasionally to decompress…" Lyric said, grinning, and moving to lie on her back.

Savanna moved to lie next to her, putting her head on Lyric's shoulder.

"You think we need to decompress?" Savanna asked.

"I think we need to blow ourselves up and start over," Lyric said, shaking her head.

"That bad, huh?" Savanna asked.

"I don't know about you babe, but I'm holding on by the skin of my teeth these days," Lyric said.

Savanna moved to sit up to look down at her wife, as she searched Lyric's eyes she suddenly started to see how tired Lyric looked.

"How have I missed this?" Savanna asked sounding suddenly devastated.

"We've both been holding on tight, babe…" Lyric said.

"We can go wherever you want," Savanna said, her voice determined.

"Good," Lyric said, nodding. "I'll make arrangements."

Cody had to go into the office the day after the meeting at the home. McKenna went with her since she really didn't have much to do with no house to look after. She was hoping to get on as an intern with Savanna's house, but hadn't heard whether or not it was approved. Savanna had been more than willing to have McKenna at the home, knowing that the girl needed to keep up her internship or she'd be in danger of delaying her degree.

In the kitchen Cody poured coffee into a travel mug, and reached for cream in the refrigerator.

"Still wussing it up, huh?" Lyric asked, grinning as she walked into the kitchen. "Good morning," she said to McKenna who stood on the other side of the counter watching Cody.

"Good morning," McKenna said, smiling.

"Just because I can't drink that mud you, grandpa and uncles drink doesn't mean I'm a wuss," Cody said, grinning.

"Tell yourself what ya need to," Lyric said, chuckling as she moved to sit on a bar stool next to where McKenna was standing.

"Stop picking on her," Savanna said, as she walked into the kitchen. "Good morning McKenna," she said then, smiling at the girl.

"Hi," McKenna replied.

Savanna poured coffee into a mug for Lyric and handed it to with a kiss.

"See, this is coffee…" Lyric said, tipping the cup toward Cody.

"You say coffee, I say mud…" Cody said in a singsong voice, as she winked at McKenna.

"Wuss," Lyric said still grinning.

"Crazy person," Cody replied.

"Girls!" Savanna exclaimed rolling her eyes.

Lyric and Cody grinned at each other.

It was obvious to McKenna that this was a fairly routine morning for this family.

"Gotta go," Cody said then as she picked up her gear bag and her coffee.

"Do more than drink coffee today, Cody!" Savanna called after her.

"Got it," Cody said, leading McKenna out to the garage.

In the car, McKenna looked over at Cody. "What did she mean by that?"

Cody chewed at the inside of her cheek. "She meant I need to eat."

"That's a problem?" McKenna asked as Cody started the car and backed out of the garage.

Cody shrugged. "Sometimes."

"And the thing about the coffee?" McKenna asked.

Cody grinned. "Taste it," she said, gesturing to her coffee in the cup holder.

McKenna picked up Cody's cup and took a sip coughing a moment later.

"Wow, that's strong," she said, blinking a couple of times.

"Yeah, and that's with cream, Lyric takes it black."

"Okay, I see what you mean there," McKenna said, grimacing.

"She grew up on the stuff," Cody said. "My grandad and uncles all drink it like that. They keep telling me that Lyric had it in her baby bottle."

McKenna laughed, shaking her head. "CPS would have had a field day."

"Oh that's nothing," Cody said. "Lyric was a bit of a hell-raiser from what I've been told."

"So, you said your grandfather and uncles… They're Lyric's family?" McKenna asked.

"Yeah, Savanna just has her dad too."

"You have all the moms," McKenna said, winking.

Cody chuckled. "Yeah, I guess so," she said smiling fondly.

"What about your other parents?" McKenna asked her tone gentler now.

Cody glanced over at her. "I don't see them," she said simply.

McKenna nodded. "So they are living then?"

Cody shrugged. "I assume so. I mean, I know my dad is dead, he died before I left. He was a drunk and got himself killed in a car accident."

"Oh," McKenna said, sensing that it was a turning point in Cody's life, no matter how casually she mentioned it. "So then it's just your mom?"

"My birth mother," Cody corrected tightly. "And a little brother, till my mom remarried."

McKenna noted the tension in Cody's posture, and knew she was touching on a very sensitive topic. She did her best to proceed with caution.

"Was he the reason you left?" McKenna asked gently.

Cody didn't answer at first, her lips curled in a sneer, then she nodded.

McKenna nodded too, knowing there was more there, but not wanting to push too hard.

They were both silent for a few minutes.

"He's a Baptist preacher," Cody said, her tone even. "And a child molester."

McKenna winced. "Cody…" she said, her eyes reflecting the pain she was feeling for Cody.

Cody's lips curled into a derisive grin. "Yeah, I know," she said simply.

Cody's driving became much more erratic; she switched lanes quickly and passed within inches of other cars. McKenna knew that Cody was reacting to the conversation. She could easily see why Lyric got constant updates on her daughter's driving from other officers.

Another thought occurred to her then, but she decided she'd better wait until they weren't hurtling down the freeway to talk about that particular thought.

They got to the office a little while later, and Cody signed her in and led her to her office.

"You have your own office?" McKenna asked, looking surprised.

Cody chuckled. "Yeah, don't be too impressed, it's because I'm kind of noisy when I'm here. And it's not really much of an office, more like an afterthought," she said as she opened the door.

She was right; the room was small, like it had been converted from a closet. It was very neat, however. Cody gestured for her to precede her as she pulled folders and things out of the box that hung next to her door.

Inside the office there was two chairs and modular counters instead of a desk. There were more Linkin Park and other rock band posters on the walls. Law enforcement paraphernalia littered the room. There were things like a silhouette target with holes in the very center, there was a gray t-shirt that said "FUCK THE POLICE" in large blue letters, and then below it in smaller letters it said, "NO, REALLY I HEAR THEY'RE GREAT IN BED," as well as cuffs and a baton on the wall. Then there was the windbreaker hanging on the back of Cody's chair that had a large black patch with yellow letters that read "CALIFORNIA DOJ" and the word "POLICE" in larger letters below them. When Cody turned the chair, McKenna saw that there was a TRaCE badge on the other side. It was an interesting window into Cody's other world and McKenna found herself fascinated.

The first thing Cody did was to connect her phone to her computer and turn her music on as the computer warmed up. McKenna watched as Cody read through items in the folder, signing off on some things, making notes on others, and tossing things into a box marked as "Out" as she finished with them. Her phone rang a few minutes later and McKenna got to hear what she considered Cody's cop side once again.

"Falco," she answered, then listened for a minute. "Wait, when did that come in? No, I thought that wasn't going to be in till next week? Okay… right… Well, hell, BFS is getting faster on me…" She laughed out loud then. "No, I'm not fucking anyone in BFS currently, but thanks for asking," she joked. "No, I can pick it up, I don't want it getting lost… No, there was trace on it, but they couldn't get a print, but there was a second option there… I got it, okay, yeah, he said that would work. Okay, good, thanks!" she said, then hung up a moment later.

"BFS?" McKenna queried.

"The Bureau of Forensic Services," Cody explained. "They're the nice people that helped me clear you," she said, grinning.

"Oh," McKenna said, nodding. "Maybe you should sleep with one of them to thank them for me," she said, grinning as she winked at Cody.

Cody gave a short laugh, shaking her head at McKenna. "You've been hanging around me for too long already."

"Oh, I don't think so," McKenna said softly.

Cody looked back at her, seeing the sweet smile on her face. She quirked a grin, her eyes sparkling.

A while later there was a knock on Cody's door.

"Come," Cody said loudly to be heard over her music.

A young woman, with brown hair up in a messy ponytail, and a much-harried expression walked in, smiling at McKenna and glancing at Cody's outbox.

"Hey Brenda," Cody said, reaching over to pick up the items in her outbox and handing them to the woman.

"Look what the cat dragged in…" Brenda said, grinning at Cody.

"It happens," Cody said, smiling. "Hey Brenda, this is McKenna. McKenna this is Brenda, she's the poor soul here that has to try to keep people like me organized."

"It's not easy, let me tell ya!" Brenda said, rolling her eyes and smiling at McKenna.

McKenna smiled at the other woman, nodding her head. "I can imagine."

"Oh, Cody, I was told to remind you to eat," Brenda said.

"Let me guess…" Cody said sarcastically.

"You know I always do what Lyric tells me, honey," Brenda said, winking. "Love that woman!"

"Well, love me more and her less, will ya?" Cody asked, rolling her eyes. "You work for our group, not hers…"

"And I'm loving you more by telling you to take care of yourself, Cody," Brenda said, her tone mothering, although she didn't seem old enough to be a mother.

"Blah, blah, blah…" Cody muttered, which got her a smack on the arm.

"Behave yourself!" Brenda said, winking at McKenna, then she turned and left with a final, "Eat Cody!" as the door closed.

McKenna looked back at Cody. "I guess this eating thing is a well-known problem with you?"

Cody looked at her for a long moment, then shrugged. "I never really ate much to begin with, but the Lithium kills my appetite completely."

"Well, that's not good," McKenna said, her tone worried.

"Don't you start…" Cody said her look narrowed.

"With as physical as you are, Cody, eating is kind of major…" McKenna said, her tone earnest.

"I do alright," Cody said, her tone even as she turned back to her computer tapping at the keys quickly.

McKenna looked at Cody's back, shaking her head. "Do you let anyone take care of you?"

Cody stopped typing and turned her head to the side in an indirect backward glance. "Is that what you're trying to do?"

"It's what I'd like to do," McKenna said wistfully.

Cody turned around giving McKenna a suspicious look.

"Why?" she asked sharply. She didn't trust people saying they wanted to take care of her.

"It's part of loving you, Cody," McKenna said, her look indicating that she thought Cody would know that. "It's making sure you're happy and healthy and okay."

Cody looked like she was trying to assimilate what McKenna was saying and not really grasping it fully.

"You've had people take care of you, Cody," McKenna said. "At the very least Lyric and Savanna."

"You mean the *only* ones who have," Cody said, her tone mild, her eyes looking down at a spot on the rug.

"What about your friends?" McKenna asked.

Cody shrugged looking complacent.

McKenna narrowed her eyes. "You don't let people take care of you," she said, answering her own question from before.

"Only people who signed up to do that," Cody said, her tone matter-of-fact.

"Meaning Lyric and Savanna," McKenna said.

Cody nodded.

"And you don't think anyone else should have to?"

"I don't want anyone else to," Cody said.

"Why?" McKenna asked.

Cody looked back at her for a long moment, trying to decide what to say.

"Just say it, Cody…" McKenna said. "Don't scrub it for me, just say it."

An amused smile played at Cody's lips at McKenna's phrase, then she shrugged again. "I don't want anyone to take care of me, because I don't want to count on it."

"Because if you count on it…" McKenna began, her voice trailing off as she looked back at Cody pointedly.

"Just another down," Cody said, her tone cynical.

"Down?" McKenna asked, recognizing the term that people with depression tended to use to describe the lows in their moods.

Cody looked back at McKenna thinking, *Really?* McKenna knew exactly what she meant.

"So you won't let anyone take care of you, because you think that they'll stop at some point."

"Doesn't everybody?" Cody asked. "I mean, eventually, right?" she added her look serious.

"Not necessarily," McKenna said. "I mean, sure it happens that people drift out of your life, but you can't spend your life in a vacuum Cody."

"I do alright," Cody said again.

Cody turned back to her computer again, and McKenna sensed that the conversation was over. It bothered her that Cody was so closed off when it came to people in her life. Whereas she'd been open with her, she now started to feel what others probably felt with Cody a lot. It spoke to the deep-seated issues that Cody had. She had major trust issues, though from the sounds of what Cody had told her so far, she had good reason for them.

McKenna knew that Cody needed consistency in her life, and someone who would stick around. Other than Lyric and Savanna, who Cody felt had 'signed up' to stick around, no one else had. It seemed to McKenna, however that Cody did the pushing away before a person could walk away. That would make it tough for anyone to stay around if Cody refused to have you around. McKenna just hoped that Cody would let her stay long enough to make a difference.

A few nights later, after another day spent at the office, Cody got a text message. At a red light she read the message, her brows furrowing as she set the phone down.

"What?" McKenna asked, seeing the look on Cody's face. "Who was it?"

"It's Rosa…" Cody said, looking pensive.

"From the group home?" McKenna asked.

"Yeah," Cody said, nodding. "She said she wants to meet me to talk about something."

"Which is what you told them to do, right?" McKenna asked, not understanding Cody's hesitation.

"Yeah…" Cody said. She clearly had reservations about it that McKenna didn't understand.

"You don't want to meet with her," McKenna said, her look perplexed. "Why?"

"Remember how she lampooned me for 'fucking' you?" Cody asked.

"Yeah," McKenna nodded.

"Well, I'm thinking she was pissed because I wouldn't fuck her," Cody said, her tone matter-of-fact.

"She wanted you to…" McKenna said, her voice trailing off instead of using the word Cody was using.

"Oh yeah," Cody said, her mouth set in a hard line. "On a number of occasions and in various states of undress."

"Wow," McKenna said, shocked that this had been going on, but then again not so surprised. Cody was Cody after all. "I guess she'd have been shocked all to hell if she'd met Cody Falco, huh?" she asked, her grin wide.

Cody gave a short laugh. "Yeah, I doubt she'd have known what to do with that," she said, her tone wry.

"So are you going to meet her?" McKenna asked.

Cody lips twitched in irritation; on the one hand she'd told these girls if they needed anything or wanted to talk, they should reach out to her, but on the other hand, Rosa could just be making a new play thinking the rules had somehow changed.

Making an irritated noise in the back of her throat, she picked up her phone and texted Rosa back saying she'd be there and to send her the address.

She looked over at McKenna who was watching her.

Cody rolled her eyes. "I guess I'll take my chances."

That night Cody knocked on a door in a bad part of town. She reached up under her jacket she touched her gun at her back reassuringly. She would have preferred to meet in a public place, but Rosa had insisted that she couldn't let anyone see her talking to a cop.

Rosa opened the door to the house and gestured for Cody to come in. Cody walked inside, listening for sounds of anyone else in the house. She didn't hear any.

"Whose house is this?" Cody asked.

"A friend," Rosa said simply.

Cody looked back at the girl. She would have been pretty if she hadn't let the streets make her hard. Her insistence in using dark eye makeup and red lipstick made her look more garish than attractive.

"So what's up?" Cody asked, when Rosa didn't say anything else.

"Well, I wanted to talk to you about the case…" Rosa said, her eyes looking everywhere but at Cody, which was the first indication to Cody that she was lying.

"Okay," Cody said, her tone even. "What about it?"

"Jesus, you just wanna get right to it, don't you?" Rosa said seductively, her eyes screaming come on.

"Rosa…" Cody sighed. "I'm a cop, I'm not sleeping with an underage girl, period."

"But who's gonna know, Cody?" Rosa asked. "'Cause I won't tell anyone…" she said, sliding her hand up Cody's chest as she moved closer.

Cody lifted her chin, stepping back and putting her hands up in a halting gesture.

"Just give me a chance, Cody… You could see how good I am…" Rosa said, moving closer still.

Cody backed up a couple of steps and into the kitchen table. Rosa took that opportunity to move in and locked her lips to Cody's, her hands sliding up Cody's chest, caressing and touching. Cody yanked her head back, breaking the lip lock.

"Rosa!" she snapped. "I told you no, get it through your head."

Rosa apparently didn't get things very easily, because she pressed closer to Cody, looking up at her in an attempt to be seductive.

"What could that juera do for you that I can't?" she asked, her hands sliding down to Cody's waist.

Rosa's lips were on hers again, and Cody felt Rosa's hands sliding to her back.

"Don't even fucking think about it," Cody growled against her lips, as she reached up to grab Rosa's shoulders to shove her away.

Rosa's face contorted in a sudden rage and she launched herself at Cody, all flying fingernails and fists. She caught Cody's throat with her nails, raking four bloody welts down her neck before she could grab her hand. Rosa wasn't done; she grabbed a knife that had been lying on the kitchen table and slashed at Cody with it. Cody raised her arm, blocking the blade but felt it slice her forearm. Fortunately, the force of her block knocked it out of Rosa's hand. Cody grabbed her extended arm, and with speed born of experience spun Rosa around, twisting her arm up behind her back and taking the girl down to her knees in one move.

"What the fuck is wrong with you!" Cody yelled.

Rosa struggled against Cody's hold, screaming.

"Rosa, stop!" Cody yelled, trying to hold on to the struggling girl without hurting her.

"You'll be sorry, you fucking cunt, you'll be sorry!" Rosa screamed. "They'll fucking kill you, they'll fucking cut you up into food for their pit bulls!"

"What are you talking about?" Cody asked, going cold suddenly.

"M-13 are gonna fuck you up…" Rosa practically sang.

Cody lifted Rosa's arm up higher, making her gasp.

"Who in M-13?" Cody asked sharply.

Rosa cackled. "You like wanna name or something? Are you fucking stupid? They're gonna kill you, bitch… You should never fuck with them, you stupid cunt."

Cody fought the urge to beat the shit out of the girl out of the pure rage she was feeling at that moment. Instead, she pulled out her cuffs, hooking one to Rosa's wrist and the other to the leg of the table. With that she walked out of the house, pulling out her cell phone and dialed dispatch.

"Dispatch," the operator answered.

"Yeah, dispatch, this is SA Cody Falco, Badge number three eight seven six seven."

There was a slight pause, then the dispatcher said, "Go Agent Falco."

"Can you send a black and white to 879 MLK Boulevard, I have a female suspect hooked up. Tell them to charge her with assault on a peace officer, and I'll come in to make a statement later."

"10-4 Agent Falco, do you need medical?" the dispatcher asked.

Cody lifted her arm and saw it was covered in blood. She flexed it and , winced at the burning pain. "Nah, I'm good."

As she drove home she considered what Rosa had said. She wasn't sure if the girl was lying or not, she could have been. The fact that she'd specifically called out M-13 wasn't significant since Cody had mentioned them that day at the LGBT house. Still, it was something she knew she needed to look into. Lyric had told her earlier that day that she and Savanna were going out of town in two weeks. The last thing Cody wanted was for this to get back to Lyric and mess up their vacation plans.

With that in mind, Cody entered the house through her own entrance, rather than through the garage. She figured at that time of night Lyric and Savanna would be having dinner, and she didn't want them to see the blood on the sleeve of her jean jacket.

Lyric, Savanna, and McKenna were having dinner, talking about McKenna's background and where she'd gone to school. She'd told them that when she was sixteen her family had moved to the Manchester area of New Hampshire and that she'd gotten her bachelor's in psychology from Dartmouth. Lyric and Savanna had exchanged a look, it sounded like McKenna was from money. They weren't sure if

Cody was aware of that or not. Having been a street kid, Cody tended to have an attitude about "rich people."

They were all three surprised when they heard music coming from Cody's side of the house. Lyric and Savanna looked at McKenna as if for an answer but she just shrugged.

"I guess the meeting was short? I'll go see," she said. She got up from the table and walked toward Cody's rooms.

When McKenna walked into the bedroom, she heard the shower running. As she walked into the bathroom she saw Cody standing in the shower, one arm up over her head braced on the wall,. Her head bowed allowing the water to run over her head and down her back. The other arm was down at her side. Then McKenna saw the blood dripping from her hand.

"Oh my God, Cody!" McKenna exclaimed.

Cody's head snapped up. "Quiet!"

"What happened?" McKenna asked, opening the shower door and reaching for Cody's hand.

Cody turned and then McKenna saw the bloody welts on her neck.

"Cody, my God, what happened?" McKenna asked, touching the skin where the nail marks ended, heedless of the water splashing on her clothes.

"Did Rosa do this?" she asked, reaching for Cody's hand to carefully lift her arm.

"Yeah," Cody said simply, reaching up to redirect the showerhead so McKenna wouldn't get completely soaked. "Came with a warning too," Cody said, her tone conversational.

"What warning?" McKenna asked, taking a washcloth to dab at the blood on Cody's arm trying to see the cut.

"That M-13 are gonna kill me," Cody said, her tone still so casual that McKenna looked up at sharply.

"Are you serious?" McKenna asked.

Cody shrugged. "I am, I just don't know if she was."

"This seems awfully serious," McKenna said, gesturing to the nail marks and the arm she was still trying to clean.

"Oh, that was because I wouldn't let her get to me," Cody said, her look wry. "The threat came after that."

McKenna looked up at Cody, her eyes searching Cody's face. "Why are you so calm right now?"

"Think this is the first time I've been threatened?" she asked, a grin at her lips.

"Well, no, maybe not," McKenna said, her tone faltering.

"No," Cody confirmed. "I just have to decide how serious the threat is," she said. "But we do not breathe a word of this to Lyric and Savanna."

"Cody, why?" McKenna asked, looking worried.

"They're going on the first vacation they've taken in years. I don't want this to fuck up their plans."

"If you're in danger though…" McKenna said.

"I'm always in danger, Kenna," Cody said, sounding tired suddenly.

McKenna looked up at Cody, seeing the weariness in her face.

"Okay, well, this doesn't look too bad," she said, her hand on Cody's arm. "Those need to be cleaned," she said, gesturing at the nail marks. "God knows what that girl had under her talons!" she said, her tone snide.

Cody grinned at McKenna's tone.

"Feeling a little possessive, honey?" Cody asked.

"No," McKenna said, her look narrowed. "I'm feeling a lot possessive and a lot like I want to go rip her hair out!" she said, smiling sweetly.

Cody chuckled. "Well let me finish my shower so I can clean this up," she said, making a shooing gesture to McKenna.

McKenna left the shower, and went to change her clothes. She was sitting on the bed reading when Cody emerged from the bathroom wearing a tank top and sweats. Cody lay down on the bed next to her.

"Let me see your arm again," she said, setting her book aside.

Cody dutifully lifted her arm. The blood had clotted and the cut luckily wasn't very deep.

"I hope she's going to pay for this," McKenna said, leaning down to kiss the cut gently.

"She's probably being booked for assault on a peace officer as we speak," Cody said.

"Good," McKenna said.

Cody grinned, she enjoyed McKenna's possessive streak. She moved to sit up, facing McKenna and reached out to touch her cheek.

"You're so cute when you're possessive," Cody said, smiling.

McKenna narrowed her eyes at Cody. "It's not cute," she said.

"What is it then?" Cody queried, still grinning.

McKenna gave her a baleful look. "I don't like that you're taking this so lightly, Cody."

Cody looked back at her for a long moment. "It's part of the job, Kenna, I get threats, I get hurt sometimes… It's not a big deal."

"Well, it is to me, okay?" McKenna said tearfully.

"Oh honey…" Cody said, moving to gather McKenna in her arms, holding her close. "I'm sorry, I know this isn't your world," she said softly. "But I'm okay, really."

McKenna shook her head against Cody's shoulder. "She could have killed you Cody," she said, her tone affected.

"No, honey," Cody said. "I'm much more careful than that. She caught me off guard a little bit, but I wasn't in danger of dying, okay?" she said, bending her neck to look down at McKenna, her lips near McKenna's ear.

McKenna nodded and just then her phone rang. Cody glanced over at the phone on the nightstand.

"Babe, it's your parents again," she said.

"Oh," McKenna said, reaching for the phone and moving to sit on the side of the bed. "Hello?" she answered. "Hi Mom, yeah sorry I meant to call you back tonight, but something came up… I know, I'm sorry… Things are a little bit hectic right now… I know, and I do need to… What?" she asked, her tone surprised. "Mom, I can't come home right now…" she said anxiously. "I'm sorry you're worried, but… Yes, it has to do with him… Yes, it's a big thing… I just… No, I don't want to just… Okay, okay, I'll come, I know, Mom, okay," she said then, glancing at Cody who had moved to lean against the headboard.

When McKenna hung up a few minutes later, she sat back on the bed facing Cody, setting her phone back down on the nightstand.

"Going home?" Cody asked, her tone mild.

"Yeah," McKenna sighed. "They know something's going on and they're worried."

Cody looked back at her surprised. "You haven't told them what's going on?"

McKenna looked hesitant. "No, I haven't."

Cody canted her head to the side, her look assessing. "Do they like John?"

"No," McKenna said, shaking her head. "They were completely against me marrying him."

"How'd you meet him anyway?" Cody asked. She realized then that she knew very little about McKenna's life with John.

"He was a guest speaker at Dartmouth once, he asked me out after," McKenna said, shrugging.

Cody looked back at her, her eyes reflecting surprise.

"Dartmouth?" Cody repeated, a little shocked.

McKenna nodded. "Yeah, after my sister… My parents moved us to New Hampshire, so I ended up at Dartmouth when I decided to go into psychology. They're back in San Diego again now though, my father's firm has an office there."

"So, your parents didn't like John, huh?"

"No," McKenna said, "they were worried that I was just bowled over by his 'big heart'… And they were right…" Her voice trailed off as she thought once again about how stupid she'd been.

Cody gave McKenna a pained look. "I'm sorry babe," she said. "He's a real son of a bitch."

"Yes, he did," McKenna said, her tone grim. "And now I have to go back and tell them all of this and…" Her voice trailed off as she shook her head.

Cody reached out touching her cheek, not sure what to say at that point. She pulled McKenna into her arms and held her tight.

"So how's that going to go over?" Cody asked after a few minutes.

"Oh, it's going to go over like a lead zeppelin," McKenna said. "My mother is really big on making people feel stupid for their mistakes."

"Ouch," Cody said, her tone sympathetic.

"Yeah…" McKenna said

"I guess I'm lucky Lyric and Savanna don't do that, otherwise I'd never hear the end of it…" Cody said, grinning self-effacingly.

"Hmmm…" McKenna murmured. "I still have questions about that, but I'll ask them when I'm not freaked out about facing my parents."

A look of surprise flickered across Cody's face. "I'm guessing bringing the bi-polar, butch lesbian you're seeing now wouldn't be any help, huh?" she asked, grinning.

McKenna looked up at Cody. "I know you mean bringing the incredibly sexy special agent with a doctorate in psychology with me," she said, her eyes narrowed at Cody for her alternate description of

herself. "And I don't know that anything would help at this point...
But having you with me would make me feel better if that counts."

Cody smiled softly, her eyes showing that she appreciated
McKenna's description of her "It counts."

"Then you'll come with me?" McKenna asked.

'I'll drive," Cody said, winking at her.

Chapter 8

Cody and McKenna left the house early the next morning, making the short drive down to San Diego.

McKenna looked every bit the dutiful daughter, looking fresh and clean in her flowered dress with black heels, her hair pulled back attractively from her face with combs and her makeup perfect. They'd gone back to McKenna and John's house a couple of days before so McKenna could pick up as much of her personal property as she could, since it was likely that the house would be forfeit when the case was done. Cody had gotten special permission for McKenna to pick up her personal property that had been hers prior to the marriage.

When they'd been walked around McKenna and John's house, Cody could see that McKenna was looking around, as if she was looking for signs of John's betrayal in everything. In their bedroom McKenna had skirted the bed, refusing to look at the place where she'd slept next to a man who'd turned out to be a monster. As she'd shoved clothes from her dresser into a bag, McKenna found herself looking at the picture she and John had taken on their honeymoon. They were smiling and so happy. Without a word, she picked up the framed picture and threw it across the room hearing it shatter into pieces. Cody stood by, waiting.

John hadn't bought her much, except for the wedding band she'd worn. McKenna had left that behind on his dresser.

For the trip Cody dressed smartly, wanting to make a good impression on McKenna's parents. She wore her black slacks, the ones she usually wore for court, and a crisp white-collared shirt. She matched it perfectly with a tailored black jacket with white pinstripes that fell to her mid-thigh and her heeled Harley Davidson leather boots.

McKenna also wore a delicate gold chain with a heart-shaped pendant and small gold hoop earrings. Cody wore a necklace of black cord with sliver accents and a black and silver triskele pendant hanging from it. She'd explained to McKenna that the triskele was a representation of the Trinacria which was the Sicilian symbol.

"Because the island of Sicily is essentially a triangle," Cody had said, showing McKenna what a Trinacria looked like. It is the head of Medusa encircled by three bent legs. "The three bent legs represent the three capes of Sicily and the wheat stalks on Medusa's head represents the fertility of the island. Medusa represents the goddess Athena's protection of the island; Medusa's head is mounted on her shield."

It was yet another side of Cody that McKenna hadn't seen; her pride in Lyric's heritage. She'd told McKenna that she had no idea what nationality her own family was, so she'd adopted Lyric's.

Cody also wore her usual platinum band on her left ring finger, her silver and black class ring, and two other silver rings. She looked very different from McKenna, but definitely with a style of her own. McKenna found Cody's look very attractive, and every time she saw her in a different outfit, she was consistently awed by her.

Cody liked McKenna's style as well. It was sexy, but with an air of sophistication that she hadn't really gotten to see when McKenna was at the group home. It had been like McKenna had dressed down around the kids. Now that she was out of that environment, Cody felt like she was seeing the real McKenna, and she liked it a lot.

The drive was uneventful; at one point Cody reached over to hold McKenna's hand, sensing McKenna's tension. Cody's tension increased as they got off the freeway and drove the winding Soledad Mountain Road. The houses seemed to get bigger and more expensive the farther they went and the closer they got to the ocean. When they turned onto Via Estrada Way, there was one house that was entire block long.

"Jesus cazzo Chirst," Cody muttered. *Jesus fucking Christ.* It was something Lyric was given to doing often and a habit she'd picked up when under stress.

"What was that?" McKenna asked.

"That was mortal terror," Cody said, grinning.

McKenna chuckled. "Oh, sounded like Italian."

"Funny…" Cody said, even as she turned into the drive of McKenna's parents' house.

"Holy shit..." she uttered then, beholding the huge Italian renaissance-style home with its terracotta tiled roof and its expansive driveway.

"You okay?" McKenna asked, amused to see Cody's trepidation. She hadn't figured Cody would fear anything, least of all a house.

Cody looked over at her as she put the car in park. "Did you forget to tell me how rich your family is?"

"It's their money, not mine," McKenna said, shrugging. She looked over at Cody then, her look searching. "Is this going to be too hard?"

"For what?" Cody asked, her tone mild.

"You," McKenna asked, sensing Cody's tension and seeing the way her thumb was worrying at the platinum band on her finger.

"I'll be fine," Cody said. "I can fake anything," she said, winking at McKenna roguishly.

Cody got out of the car then, and strode around it to open McKenna's door, putting her hand out to help her out of the low-slung car. McKenna moved close to Cody as Cody closed the car door, putting her hand to Cody's cheek.

"Thank you for coming with me," she said softly, looking up into Cody's eyes. "I'm going to apologize in advance for any stupid thing my mother says."

Cody grinned. "I'm going to accept that apology in advance then," she said and then leant down to kiss McKenna's lips softly.

When their lips parted, McKenna heard someone clearing their throat quietly and glanced over to see her mother standing at the gate to the courtyard.

Cody looked at McKenna's mother, she could see where McKenna got her beauty from. McKenna's mother was every bit as beautiful as McKenna, with a few added years, wrinkles, and much more jewelry and expensive-looking clothes. Her mother also had an aristocratic air to her, it was called out in her posture, and in the way she held her head. Also in the way she was looking at the two of them, her gaze steady and icy.

"Hello mother," McKenna said, turning to face her mother. Her hand dropped behind her and she extended her fingers towards Cody, who took her hand and squeezed it gently.

McKenna held onto Cody's hand and walked toward her mother, only letting go long enough to hug her mother formally.

"Mother," McKenna said, stepping back, even as she reached her hand out to Cody again. "This is Cody Falco," she said, still very formal. "Cody, this is my mother, Rebecca Hayden."

Cody's eyes met Rebecca's and she inclined her head, a polite close-lipped smile on her face. She saw the immediate flaring of Rebecca Hayden's nostrils. Cody figured that McKenna's mother had been expecting her to look ashamed that they'd been caught kissing moments before. Cody Falco didn't apologize for being who she was, not to anyone. It was something the Haydens would come to find out over the course of their first meeting with her.

"We're around the back on the veranda," Rebecca said. Cody could hear the condescension it her tone as clear as day.

She turned and led them to the front door and opened it. McKenna held Cody's hand and felt the hesitation as they crossed the threshold. Glancing back, she saw Cody mouthing the words "holy shit" as she gazed around at the house.

Cody was quite stunned by the opulence of the house. The entryway was tiled with porcelain tile, and the staircase they faced was made of intricately carved mahogany. The living room was open with vaulted ceilings and the stone and marble fireplace had a mantle that went from floor to ceiling. There were rod iron terraced walkways on the second floor that promised even more opulence upstairs. The walls wore a warm rich brown, with mahogany crown molding and baseboards. Even the furniture screamed money. To say Cody was intimidated was an understatement but to her credit, other than the silent exclamation, none of it showed on her face. McKenna squeezed her hand gently, as her mother continued to lead them out through a pair of double doors onto the terrace.

The terrace had a view of the ocean, with a huge built-in fireplace and entertainment area that included an infinity pool. Cody did her best to appear unimpressed. The last thing she wanted McKenna's parents to think was that she was with McKenna for her family's money. They'd have no way of knowing that Cody wasn't even aware that they had money until five minutes before.

A man was waiting for them. He stood from the chair he'd been sitting in, and moved to hug McKenna. It was obvious that he'd been worried about his daughter. It didn't however keep him from looking Cody over as he hugged his daughter.

"Dad," McKenna said, smiling at her father. "This is Cody Falco," she said, gesturing to Cody, her eyes on Cody. "She's a special agent for the Department of Justice. Cody this is my dad, Thomas Hayden."

"A police officer?" Thomas asked, looking surprised.

"Yes," Cody said, taking a step forward and extending her hand to him, her eyes looking directly into his.

Thomas's eyes narrowed slightly, even as he took Cody's hand, shaking it firmly.

There was a moment where everyone stood uncomfortably. Cody looked out at the view, then looked back over at McKenna. McKenna smiled softly at Cody, so glad that she was there with her, and praying that her parents didn't make Cody uncomfortable.

"Why don't we sit down?" McKenna suggested.

McKenna moved to sit on a small couch with its back to the fireplace and put her hand on the seat next to her, looking at Cody. Cody got the message and casually sat down next to her. Cody's body language spoke volumes, these people did not intimidate her. McKenna on the other hand, sat with her hands folded in her lap, was clearly nervousness.

Thomas moved to sit in the chair closest to McKenna, and Rebecca sat in the chair across from them, her eyes on Cody the whole time. Cody looked at Rebecca, her face composed in a serene, confident look.

McKenna took a deep breath and expelled it slowly.

"So I'm sure you're wondering what's going on," she said, her tone matter-of-fact. "The truth is that John has been arrested."

"What!" Thomas exclaimed, his look shocked.

He looked at Cody, then back at his daughter. "What was he arrested for?"

McKenna looked over at Cody, knowing she wouldn't use the right terms. Cody caught McKenna's look and knew she wanted her to tell them.

"He was arrested for three counts of human trafficking, and two counts of money laundering."

Thomas Hayden looked pale, as he swallowed convulsively, realizing what that meant for his daughter.

"We told you that man was no good, McKenna," Rebecca said, her voice scornful. "You never listen to us, you always have to do things your own way. See what a mess this is now? And don't think your father is going to clean it up for you, either!" she said sharply.

"I don't need daddy to clean anything up for me," McKenna said, her tone soft.

"You aren't foolish enough to think this won't come around to you, are you?" Rebecca practically snapped, her eyes flashing. "That man was a con artist and don't think he didn't figure out a way to protect himself."

"Good thing I figured out what he was doing to protect himself before it hit McKenna then," Cody said, her tone even.

"What?" Rebecca queried, looking at Cody like she'd just appeared out of thin air.

"I was the investigating officer on the case," Cody said, her tone matter-of-fact. "And you're right, he was setting McKenna up to take the fall, but I was able to prove that he was forging her signature, and cleared her completely before charges were filed."

"You investigated the case?" Thomas asked, looking at her, thinking she looked awfully young.

"Yes sir," Cody said.

"No offense, young lady, but you don't look old enough to be a very seasoned investigator," Rebecca said, in a steely tone.

"Seasoned enough to take John down and protect your daughter while I was at it," Cody replied, her tone pointed, her hazel eyes sparkling with ire.

"Thank you for that," Thomas said, throwing his wife a quelling look. "What can we do honey?" he asked then, looking at McKenna. "Where are you staying?"

"I'm staying with Cody right now," McKenna said, glancing over at Cody. "And I'm really okay."

"How is this going to affect that house we financed for you two?" Rebecca asked, her tone still strident as she referred to the group home John and McKenna had run.

Again, McKenna glanced at Cody, who grinned at her.

"Technically," Cody said, "since you and Mr. Hayden paid for the house when they got married, and McKenna is divorcing John, it isn't considered a marital asset, therefore not subject to asset forfeiture."

Thomas nodded. "She's right," he said. "They will, however seize anything you and John bought during the marriage, so that house you were living in..." His voice trailed off as she realized that his daughter would lose her home because of John's misdeed.

"I know," McKenna said, nodding as she saw her father's pained look. "It's okay, I wouldn't want that house now anyway, knowing what John was doing."

"What exactly was he doing?" Thomas asked, looking at Cody this time.

Cody uncrossed her legs and leaned forward, her hands on her knees, to look over at Thomas.

"He was using the group home as a cover to launder money and lure girls into prostitution through a local street gang."

"Oh my God..." Rebecca railed.

"How were you able to figure out what he was doing?" Thomas asked, curious about Cody Falco.

"I work for a task force that deals with these types of cases all the time. We know that street gangs are getting into human trafficking in a big way because it's a high profit industry with not a lot of risk. One of my friends developed an informant that told her about John's group home and that girls were being culled from it. I went in undercover and got the information I needed to make the arrest."

"And clear me," McKenna added.

"And clear you," Cody said, smiling at her.

Thomas noted the exchange between his daughter and Cody and sensed that there was more there than a police officer and cleared suspect.

"So you're an undercover police officer? I imagine because you look so young," Thomas said.

Cody nodded, a grin curling her lips. "Well, I'm only twenty-two, but yeah, that's why I'm able to infiltrate these places so easily."

"And that's how you met McKenna?" he asked her then.

"Yes," Cody said, her look direct.

"And you're involved with our daughter," Rebecca said, her tone disapproving.

Cody looked over at Rebecca, narrowing her eyes slightly. "Yes, I am," she answered, her voice clear and strong.

"Is that why you worked so hard to clear her?" Rebecca asked, making it sound like Cody's motivations were suspect.

Cody didn't answer for a moment, letting the question hang in the air. She raised her eyebrow slightly at Rebecca and then said, "I did it because it's my job to avoid arresting innocent people, it's usually known as justice."

Rebecca pursed her lips angrily, her eyes narrowing. "And you just happened to fall into bed with her?"

"Mother!" McKenna exclaimed, ready to say more, but Cody's hand on her arm stilled her. When she looked over at Cody, she saw Cody was looking at her mother.

"Your daughter is an amazing person, Mrs. Hayden," Cody said, her voice completely calm, her look direct. "And I found myself drawn to her in a way that I never have with anyone else. If to you that means that I fell into bed with her then yes, that's what happened. I like to think there's a bit more to it than that though, but I wouldn't expect you to understand."

Rebecca stared back at Cody, her mouth hanging slightly open from the reproach she'd just heard in this young woman's voice. She snapped her mouth shut to sneer at Cody.

"I'm sure the fact that she comes from wealth, means nothing to you whatsoever," she said, her tone accusatory.

"Sweetheart," Cody said, her tone acidic. "I don't give a shit about your money. If I've learned one thing doing this job, it's that money doesn't equal class, it never has, and it never will."

With that, Cody stood up and strode over to the other side of the terrace, a good five hundred feet away. There she pulled out a cigarette and lit it with shaking hands, keeping her back to them. McKenna threw her mother a reproachful look and shook her head as she stood up and walked over to Cody.

Thomas watched as McKenna stepped up to Cody. He saw the way her hand slid up Cody's back, standing next to and leaning into the other woman. There was very definite affection there. At one point he saw Cody turn her head to smile warmly down at McKenna and it tugged at his heart.

"Can you believe the nerve of that woman?" Rebecca whispered harshly.

"What I can't believe is the way you're acting," Thomas said, his tone mildly chastising.

"What does that mean?" Rebecca asked, looking shocked by his reproach.

"It means that that woman kept our daughter out of jail, and if you open your eyes, you'd see that our daughter cares about her just as much as that woman just admitted to caring about her. Shouldn't that be enough to keep a civil tongue in your head?"

Rebecca looked back at Thomas for a long moment, he'd always been easier on McKenna than she felt he should be. She knew it was because of the way that they'd lost their other daughter, Dana, and he was afraid to drive McKenna away too.

"Look at them, Rebecca," Thomas said, gesturing to the two women standing at the other end of the terrace.

Rebecca looked over at Cody and McKenna. She saw McKenna's hand moving back and forth on Cody's back, her smiling face up-turned to Cody's As she watched, McKenna reached up and touched Cody's cheek. Cody turned her head saying something and grinning at her. There was definitely a connection between the two, but Rebecca still didn't trust it.

"Are you okay?" McKenna asked as she reached Cody. She slid her hand up her back, feeling the tension there.

"I'm fine," Cody said, her lips twitching in self-irritation. "I'm sorry I lost it back there, but she pissed me off."

"She pissed me off too," McKenna said, her tone reflecting that irritation.

"And this is why I don't date rich girls," Cody said, grinning.

"You date anyone?" McKenna asked, grinning too.

"Well, no, but this is why I wouldn't date a rich girl if I dated," Cody replied.

"Uh-huh," McKenna said, smiling up at Cody. Then she said, "We can go, Cody. It's okay if you want to go."

"No, it's okay, I'm okay," Cody said, shaking her head, lifting the cigarette to her lips again. McKenna saw the tremor in her hand.

"Cody your hands are shaking," McKenna said reaching her hand up to touch Cody's cheek, concern evident in her voice.

Cody blew her breath out. "There's only so much Lithium can do, babe," she said, grinning.

"I'm sorry," McKenna said again.

"It's okay," Cody said, finishing her cigarette. She picked up a foot to put it out on the bottom of her boot, then pocketed the butt. "Let's go back."

As the two turned, Cody took McKenna's hand firmly in hers, her look at Rebecca pointed. She was done playing nice. They walked back over to the couch, Cody waited for McKenna to sit first, then she sat down, looking at Rebecca. Cody sat forward, her body language showing that she was now in the conversation fully, no longer a simple spectator.

"So where were we?" Cody asked, her tone sarcastic. "Oh yeah, the part where you think I'm a gold digger," she said, putting her finger up in a kind of tabulating gesture, then she twirled her finger in a semi-circle. "Carry on."

Rebecca looked shocked by Cody's change in demeanor but Cody didn't look like she cared.

"You have to understand the way it looks to us," Rebecca said, her tone placating.

"No, I actually don't," Cody said strongly, shaking her head. "Because you don't know a thing about me. You think because I'm a cop I can't be worth anything, right?" she said, her look direct. "But what you don't know is that my mother's family goes back many generations in Sicily, and they have plenty of money. I don't consider any of that money mine, just as I don't consider any of the money you and Thomas here have is McKenna's." Her eyes narrowed. "I'm dating your daughter because I love her, and if that's not a good enough reason for you, then I'm sorry, your priorities suck."

"You what?" McKenna said, her look shocked.

Cody turned her head to look at McKenna and seeing the shocked look on her face, she started to grin. Thomas and Rebecca watched the exchange avidly.

"You what?" McKenna asked again, her tone stronger, her look searching Cody's face.

Cody turned her body to face McKenna as best she could on the couch. "I love you," she said softly.

The look of joy that swept over McKenna's face was almost painful to see, but then she narrowed her eyes.

"And you didn't think to mention that sooner?" she asked her tone teasing.

"Well... Meetin' the 'rents and all..." Cody said, her tone humorously offhanded as she rolled her eyes.

McKenna pursed her lips and blew her breath out through her nose. "I supposed I can let you off the hook for that," she said, nodding. "Considering..." She nodded toward her mother who was watching them closely. Then she gave Cody a direct look. "Say it again," she said, her tone soft.

Cody put her hand to McKenna's cheek, her eyes staring into McKenna's. "I love you," she said, her voice soft but sure.

McKenna took Cody's face in both of her hands, leaning forward to kiss her lips softly. Pulling back she smiled and said, "Thank you for letting me love you back."

"We'll see how long ya wanna do that," Cody said winking at her.

"Yes we will," McKenna replied, the look in her eyes challenging. "My guess is forever, but maybe longer."

"Uh-huh," Cody said, grinning.

McKenna narrowed her eyes at Cody, but then looked over at her parents and saw that they were watching them.

"Sorry," she said, her tone breezy. "First time she's admitting to being in love with me, so I kinda had to clarify."

Thomas grinned at his daughter, then glanced at his wife, who seemed absolutely stunned.

"So, tell us more about your family, Cody," Thomas said after a few long moments of silence, his smile open.

Cody leaned back in the chair again, once again crossing her leg at the ankle, her arm on the back of the couch.

"What do you want to know?" Cody asked, her look straight forward.

"What does your father do?" Thomas asked.

"Don't have one," Cody said simply.

"She has two mothers," McKenna said, moving to sit back and lean against Cody, who immediately put her arm around McKenna's shoulders.

Thomas looked taken back for a moment, but then recovered nicely.

"And what do they do?" he asked.

"Lyric is a cop like me, only she's a supervisor, because she's been doing this a lot longer, and Savanna is a psychiatrist who has a private practice and runs an LGBT group home, like McKenna did."

"Impressive," Thomas said, nodding, then looking at McKenna. "That's what you're planning to do isn't it honey?"

"Yes," McKenna said, "but Savanna's already board-certified and everything, I still have a ways to go. I'm hoping I can finish my internship at Savanna's group home."

Thomas nodded, looking pleased, then looked at Cody. "And you're in the family business," he said, grinning.

"Oh, you have no idea how true that is," Cody said, grinning. "My grandfather retired from the police department as an assistant chief. One of my uncles is a captain, the other is a Special Agent Supervisor, like Lyric, and the youngest one is a sergeant for the LAPD."

"So it really is a family business," Thomas said, smiling.

"Yes sir," she said, nodding. "What exactly do you do?"

"I'm the enemy," Thomas said, chuckling. "I'm a lawyer."

"Oh, not all lawyers are the enemy," Cody replied. "Don't suppose you know one that could help Kenna with her divorce though."

"In fact I do," Thomas said, winking at his daughter.

"I don't want anything from that marriage," McKenna said, "except out."

"And the group home, babe," Cody said. "The kids'll need you."

McKenna nodded. "Yes, that too."

They talked for a while about the ins and outs of the divorce and what would happen with the group home. Cody really liked Thomas. Rebecca sat silent through most of the conversation, but had stopped being adversarial.

By the time they drove back to LA that night, McKenna was very happy they'd gone.

"My dad likes you," McKenna said, glancing over at Cody as she drove.

Cody smiled. "I like him too," she said. "Your mom..." she said, letting her voice trail off.

"She'll grow on you," McKenna said, grinning.

"So does fungus," Cody replied sourly.

"Stop it!" McKenna said, laughing as she swatted at Cody's arm.

Cody laughed, grabbing McKenna's hand and bringing it up to her lips to kiss it softly and then holding it with her elbow resting on the center console.

"So, family money in Sicily?" McKenna asked.

Cody grinned. "Yeah," she said, "not that we care that much over here."

"Still," McKenna said. "Not something I knew either."

Cody shrugged. "Isn't mine, so I don't mention it, unless some battle-axe is backing me into a corner with hers."

McKenna laughed at the term Cody used. "I see," she said, nodding.

Later they lay in bed, having just made love. McKenna looked up at Cody, a question in her eyes.

"What?" Cody asked, feeling very comfortable and sated since having orgasms with McKenna didn't seem to be an aberration after all.

"That first day I was here," McKenna said cautiously. "Lyric mentioned the last time you stopped taking your meds..." she said, letting her voice trail off as she looked at Cody to judge her reaction.

Cody remained relaxed, nodding and waiting for McKenna to finish.

"What happened?" McKenna asked, her look apprehensive.

"Which time?" Cody asked, her tone derisive. "I've done it more than once," she said, her tone self-effacing. "And it's almost always bad when I do. I've laid down a few bikes, I wrecked the Ferrari twice," she said, her tone bitter. "The last time was the worst though. Which is probably why they're so hyper-vigilant about me taking my meds."

"What happened last time?" McKenna asked, her look pained, because she knew just from the descriptions she'd heard already that if this was worse it wasn't going to be good.

Cody settled more comfortably on the bed, lying on her back and sliding her arm around McKenna's body to pull her closer.

"I decided to go take care of the Sureños myself," she said, her tone condescending.

"Oh God…" McKenna said, her look worried.

"Yeah," Cody said, her tone sardonic. "Probably not my best idea ever."

"What happened?" McKenna found herself asking again.

"Oh, I got the crap beat out of me before Lyric saved the day again," Cody said.

"Again?" McKenna asked.

"Yeah, it was the second time she had to go get me back from them, so yeah, again," Cody said, her voice so casual, McKenna was partially lulled by it.

"Wait," she said, putting her hand on Cody's arm. "When was the first time?"

"When I was fourteen and they had me locked up in a hotel room servicing men for three days," Cody said quickly. It didn't lessen the impact of the words though.

McKenna felt sick at the picture Cody had just painted. "Oh my God, Cody…" she breathed.

"You say that a lot, you know," Cody said, her look wry.

McKenna gave a flabbergasted laugh. "I guess I do," she said. "But you just keep telling me things that would have broken any normal person, and yet here you are alive, and pretty damned healthy considering."

"Yeah," Cody said, not sounding convinced of her "emotional health."

Little did either of them know that that emotional health was about to be sorely tested.

A week after the meeting with McKenna's parents, Cody walked into the house of the leader of M-13, her hands out to her sides, her badge prominently hanging on a chain around her neck.

"What do you want, pig?" Julio, one of the lieutenants of the gang, spat.

"I want to know which one of you wants to try to kill me," Cody asked, her tone even.

"Is that an offer?" one of Julio's hangers-on asked.

Cody's eyes fell on the man, her look pointed. "One at a time, honey," she said, winking at him sarcastically.

"What the fuck are you talking about?" Julio asked. He didn't like this cop coming in interfering with his business.

"Your girl, Rosa," Cody said. "She said that M-13 are gonna kill me, so I'm here to find out which one of you wants to give it a shot."

"Juera es loco!" called out one of the other members of the gang.

Cody looked at him calmly. "Sometimes," she said.

"I don't know what the fuck you're talking about, cop, I didn't order no hit on you," Julio said, the vein in his neck standing out in his tension. "So I don't know what that stupid puta was sayin'."

Cody looked back at Julio for a long minute, trying to discern whether or not he was telling her the truth. She'd had it with looking over her shoulder, so she'd done some digging and traced Rosa to Julio; she'd been his girl at one point in her young life. She'd decided to take the bull by the horns so she could breathe again. Now she wasn't sure if she was getting the truth or not.

"None of your boys would do it for fun?" Cody asked.

"If any of 'em fuckin' smokes a cop without my say so, I'll cap 'em myself," Julio said, his look at his people pointed. "That's trouble we don't need."

Cody nodded. "Then I guess we're good," she said, grinning.

With that she turned and walked out of the house. The gang members all looked at each other like the cop must be crazy.

Cody wondered the same thing as she pulled into the lot at the jail. She wanted to talk to Rosa again, to see if she could get anything out of the girl. The last thing she wanted was to dismiss a threat that was real. She figured one last visit with the girl would tell the tale. Twenty minutes later she walked out of the visitation room having gotten nothing but more bullshit from Rosa. Shaking her head, she blew her breath out, figuring it was now time to just dismiss the threat and move on. As she turned to head back out to check-in, she literally ran into John Tucker being led out from another visitation.

"Little Cody…" John said, his tone leering.

Cody stood looking up at him. "How's jail, John? Comfy?" she asked sarcastically.

"I hear you're fucking my wife," John said, smirking.

"Better than you did," Cody replied.

John's nostrils flared in anger at that, but then his eyes fell on Rosa who was being led out of the visitation room. A smile crossed his face as he looked back down at Cody.

"Still barking up that tree?" he asked.

"I never barked up that tree," Cody said. "Underage girls were your thing, John, not mine."

"Still think it's M-13 that's gonna kill ya, you little cunt?" John snapped.

"What?" Cody asked, going very still.

John gave a sarcastic laugh. "Not as fuckin' smart as ya think you are, little Cody. They're gonna take out your cunt of a mother and then you."

Just then, a man left the visitation area John had been led from; Cody's eyes connected with him as he walked past. He was Mexican, about nineteen years of age. She recognized him, he'd been a kid back then, but she knew it was him. His name was Martin, and he'd been around the gang all the time… Then it hit Cody, he was Churro's brother… Churro was the man Lyric had killed the night she'd rescued her when she was fourteen. Then Cody saw the SUR tattooed to his neck.

"Son of a bitch…" she breathed. John started laughing as they led him away.

"So long little Cody!" John yelled.

But Cody didn't hear him, because she was running to catch up to Martin. When she did, he turned to look at her, his eyes as cold as ice, then he started to smile and Cody felt her blood run cold. Blindly she reached for the doors, and ran outside to get a signal on her cell phone and dialed Lyric's number.

Lyric answered on the second ring, she was putting her gear bag in her car.

"Hey Code, what's up?" she said, moving to lean against her car.

"Mom! You gotta be careful, they've put out a hit on you!" Cody yelled, running toward her car.

"What? Cody, calm down…" Lyric said

It was too late. Cody heard the report of the rifle over the receiver. There were multiple shots, and Cody heard the phone hit the ground and the screeching tires.

"Mom!" Cody screamed, standing where she was. "Mom!" she screamed again, but somehow she knew it was no use.

Dropping her phone she staggered, and went down to her knees as a wave of nausea swept through her. The idea that Lyric had just been shot ricocheted around in her head making her wince painfully.

She gave a yell of pure frustration and pain, scaring people around her. She forced herself to her feet, scooped up her phone and began to run toward her car. She started it with a roar, throwing it into gear even as she dialed her phone. She called dispatch to ask about the incident, they reported to her that Lyric had indeed been hit and that an ambulance was on its way. Cody headed for the office, driving at breakneck speeds, and not caring how many lights she blew to get there.

They were loading Lyric into the ambulance when she got there, and she climbed inside just as they closed the door. Cody had to grit her teeth to keep from passing out. Lyric was unconscious; according to the EMT she'd been hit three times with AK-47 rounds. Cody moved to sit next to Lyric, she heard the heart monitor beeping erratically. Reaching out she grabbed Lyric's hand, holding it tight, putting her head down to Lyric's ear.

"Come on Mom, you gotta fight, okay?" Cody said, tears streaming down her face.

They lost Lyric's pulse three times in the ambulance before they reached the hospital. As soon as the ambulance stopped, Cody got out of the way, knowing that if Lyric had a chance to survive this they needed to do their jobs and she needed to stay out of the way. As she climbed out of the ambulance, she made the phone call she never wanted to make in her lifetime.

Savanna answered the call on the fourth ring, sounding harried.

"Mom…" Cody said, her voice breaking as she started to cry again.

"Cody, what is it?" Savanna asked, instantly worried.

"Mom, it's Lyric…" Cody said, her voice a barely audible whisper. "She's been shot… You need to get here… You need to get here now…"

"Oh my God…" Savanna said, falling to her knees as she closed her eyes. "No…" she said, with tears in her voice. "No… no… no…"

One of the assistants took the phone from her then.

"Hello?""This is Cody," Cody said. "You need to get Savanna to Cedars now, Lyric's been shot."

"Oh my god!" the woman exclaimed. "Okay, okay, we'll get her there, Cody, you wait for her!"

Cody hung up the phone, and slid it into her pocket as she walked into the emergency room.

A half an hour later, Cody was stood like a stone statue waiting to hear word of Lyric's condition. Jet arrived after hearing the news, and made straight for Cody and hugged her. Cody squeezed her eyes shut, forcing herself not to break. She was holding on to her control with the iron will that had gotten her through life when she was young and things were hopeless.

"Have you heard anything yet?" Jet asked.

Cody shook her head, her look haunted.

Lyric's unit all showed up, hugging Cody in turn and asking if she'd heard anything. Cody continued to shake her head, her knee starting to bounce in agitation. When Savanna arrived, she ran straight to Cody. Cody held her mother, while she cried almost hysterically.

"I can't lose her, Cody…" Savanna said at one point. "I can't lose her…" she repeated.

"I know, Mom, I know," Cody said, her voice soft. "She'll be okay, you know Lyric is as tough as they come…"

Lyric's father and brothers arrived. They again hugged both women, asking if they'd heard anything. A short while after, Cody handed a still distraught Savanna off to Lyric's oldest brother and went outside to smoke. Standing against the side of the quad she was in, she could see Lyric's brothers talking.

"I can't do this…" Lyric said, her tone tremulous.

"Okay…" Savanna said, her tone gentle. "We can just play it like always…" Savanna said. "Like any other dinner with them."

Lyric looked back at her, her eyes searching Savanna's, then she shook her head. "No, I need to tell them the truth about us," she said, her tone strong again.

They were sitting outside of the Falco family home, the house Lyric had grown up in and they were supposed to tell Lyric's family about them and the fact that they were not only a couple, but were getting married and adopting Cody. They hadn't brought Cody to meet the family yet because they wanted to make sure her family was okay with them first before they exposed Cody to any negativity.

Lyric's family had met Savanna previously at dinner, though back then she'd just been Lyric's friend and they'd happily accepted her into their group. But things had changed, and Lyric didn't like lying to her family so she wanted to tell them everything. Wanting to do something and doing it, however were two different things.

Blowing her breath out, Lyric nodded to herself, then reached over to open the car door. She got out and walked around to the passenger side, opening Savanna's door and holding out her hand to help her out of the car. Savanna squeezed Lyric's hand gently, smiling up at her.

They walked up to the front door, Lyric blew her breath out again, and then reached for the door. Inside she called to her dad.

"There she is!" Jacomo Falco called, smiling broadly at his daughter and grabbing her up in a bear hug. "And miss Savanna," he said, moving to hug Savanna too.

"Easy pop, don't break her!" Lyric said, laughing.

"She is too skinny!" Jacomo exclaimed, holding Savanna's arms out to her sides, looking at her. "I bet the boys don't like that!" Jacomo said, chuckling.

Savanna and Lyric exchanged a look, Lyric rolled her eyes, shaking her head from behind her father. Lyric's three brothers arrived shortly thereafter. Mario who was the youngest of the boys at thirty-three, classic tall dark and handsome described Mario perfectly, he was a patrol officer for the LAPD. Then there was Saldino, or Sal, the middle brother with sandy-brown hair like their mother's had been and dark eyes. He was thirty-six, and already married with two kids. His wife was called Sara and their kids were both boys, who looked exactly like their father. Lastly, there was JJ, Jacomo Jr, the oldest at thirty-seven, he was well on his way to being a Lieutenant for the LAPD and a complete hound dog according to Lyric. His handsome looks and easy smile made him a real hit with the ladies. Jacomo was hoping that Savanna would be interested in either Mario or JJ, so he was always pleased when Lyric brought her to dinner.

After dinner and a lot of good-natured ribbing, they all sat around the table having red wine that came from Falco vineyards in Sicily. It was a tradition that had been in place for many years. Lyric drank two glasses of the potent wine to gather her courage. Finally, she felt brave enough.

"I have an announcement," Lyric said, her eyes on Savanna.

There was silence around the table, and every eye in the place was on her.

"What is it Lirica?" Jacomo asked, using the Italian word for her name, which he often did.

Lyric looked around at her family, her stomach in a huge knot, terrified that the smiling faces would soon turn to frowns or worse grimaces of disgust.

"I'm in love," she said then, her voice trembling.

"What?" Jacomo asked. "You are in love with a boy that no one in the family has met?" he asked, his tone shocked.

Lyric pressed her lips together, tears glazing her eyes. "You have met the person I'm in love with, Daddy," she said, her tone soft.

"What? When?" Jacomo asked, looking around at Lyric's brothers to see if they knew who Lyric was talking about. They were all shaking their heads, looking as confused as he was.

Lyric stood on unsteady legs, and stepped over to the chair Savanna sat in, putting her hand on Savanna's shoulder, her look at her father pleading.

Jacomo looked confused. He looked at Savanna and then back at Lyric.

"What are you saying?" Jacomo asked his tone heavy.

"I'm saying that I'm in love with Savanna," Lyric said.

"What!" Sal exploded. "Basta! This is not funny Lyric," he said a frown on his lips.

"Well, it's a good thing I'm not joking then," Lyric said, her look defiant.

Sal's mouth fell open then he stood and pulled his hand back, like he intended to hit Lyric. Savanna jumped to her feet, not about to watch that happen, but Lyric was faster, blocking her from interfering with an outstretched arm. She stared back at her brother, a challenge on her face.

"Do it," she growled. "But don't think for a fucking second I won't hit you back."

Sal gave a short sarcastic laugh.

Lyric stared back at him, her look still openly defiant. "Try me," she said, motioning to him with her fingertips.

"Basta! Enough!" Jacomo said, taking control of the situation before his children came to blows. "Saladino, sit down!" he ordered, an order Sal complied with immediately. "Lyric, explain to me how this is possible."

Lyric looked over at Savanna, then moved to hold her chair for her until she was seated, then she sat back down. Jacomo took in the gallant gesture and glanced at his other sons, who were both watching their sister as well.

"I don't know how it's possible, Dad," Lyric said, her tone plaintive. "I just know that I love her," she said, looking at Savanna, her eyes softening. "She's my best friend and the very best thing in my life."

Jacomo looked at his daughter, his thoughts warring, but he could not deny how happy his daughter looked when he looked at Savanna.

"And you?" he asked Savanna. "How do you feel about my Lirica?"

"I love her more than I've ever loved anyone in my life," Savanna said without hesitation, her eyes shining.

Jacomo picked up his wine, draining the glass and pouring another.

"We're getting married, pop," Lyric said then, causing him to pour more into his glass. Lyric looked on, amused. "And we're adopting Cody too."

Jacomo looked surprised. "Then we will need to meet this child," he said, nodding.

"We can do that," Lyric said, her eyes going to her brothers. "But I'm not bringing her here if there's even the slightest chance of any kind of negative reaction."

JJ and Mario both held their hands up, shaking their heads.

"Got no problem with that, baby sis," Mario said.

"Me either, Lyr,"JJ said.

Lyric's eyes fell on Sal then. "What about you?" she asked, her tone sharp.

Sal looked back at her, his lips twitching in consideration. "I would never treat a child badly."

"Well, she's going to be my child, and I'll kill anyone that tries to hurt her. She's had enough pain her life," Lyric said, her tone strong.

"Lirica, no threats," Jacomo said, his tone chiding.

The following week, Savanna and Lyric brought Cody to the house. She was expectedly nervous even though Savanna and Lyric had done everything they could to calm her down. Her nervousness caused her to be even more shy than she usually was. As they walked into the house, Lyric saw that her father and brothers were all dressed in suits. Jacomo stepped forward, looking at Cody, his brown eyes kind.

"Dad, this is Cody," Lyric said. "Cody, this is my father, Jacomo Falco."

Cody extended a hand that shook like a leaf in a stiff wind. Jacomo reached out his big hands, enclosing Cody's hand in his. He then leaned down and kissed her on the cheek.

"Pleased to meet you piccolo," he said very softly then.

Cody looked back at him, her eyes wide. "What is a piccolo?" she asked him.

"It's Italian for 'little one,' " he told her.

"You're Italian?" Cody asked Lyric, surprised by that.

Lyric grinned. "Yep, we're Sicilian."

"Which is the best kind of Italian," Mario said, winking at Cody.

Cody grinned, liking Mario immediately.

"That's Mario," Lyric said. "He's the youngest of the boys."

Mario stepped forward, going down to one knee, taking Cody's hand and kissing it gallantly.

"Incantata," he said to her.

Cody widened her eyes "Which means…" she said already recognizing Italian.

"Enchanted," Mario said, winking at her again.

"Incantata," Cody repeated, her accent perfect.

"A Sicilian in the making," Mario said, grinning.

"Move," JJ said then, pushing his brother aside with a laugh. He bent down putting his face close to Cody's. "I'm JJ," he said, smiling at her.

"What do the Js stand for?" Cody asked, already finding her confidence with these men.

"Jacomo Junior," JJ said, winking at her. "But you can call me uncle."

"Uncle?" Cody queried, looking back at Lyric.

Lyric nodded. "Yeah, these three will be your uncles, Code."

Cody looked back at them as JJ stepped back. It was obvious she was trying to assimilate this information. Then her eyes fell on Saldino and she stared at him, blinking a couple of times. She could see that he was less excited about the prospect of a niece. She'd heard Lyric and Savanna talking about one of Lyric's brothers being more difficult than the others, she imagined that this was the one.

Gathering her courage, she took a couple of steps to walk up to Saldino, and extended her hand to him. "I'm Cody," she said, her eyes looking directly up into his, searching his face.

Saldino looked surprised by her action then he looked down at her extended hand, and saw how it was shaking, even though she was trying to be brave. Looking back at her eyes then, he could see the fear of rejection in them, it screamed out at him and touched his heart in a way he'd never thought was possible. He shook his head slowly, and actually saw Lyric tense, then he leaned down, and took the girl into his arms gently, hugging her to him.

"I'm your uncle Sal," he said softly to her, feeling her arms wrap around his neck.

In that moment, Sal became her favorite uncle.

"Cody," Sal called to her from the door to the atrium. He nodded toward the waiting room.

She nodded, stubbing out her cigarette and walked toward him. Sal looked at this girl that had been his niece for eight years; he'd seen a lot of changes in her. She'd grown into a confident, strong young woman, and he didn't think he could be more proud of her. He was worried that she was so calm at that point, knowing how desperately she loved Lyric. He stayed close to her as they walked into the waiting room. The doctor was just coming out.

Cody moved to stand with Savanna, her arm around her mother's shoulders. She felt Savanna leaning heavily on her. Gritting her teeth she forced herself to stay calm, she needed to be here for Savanna, she knew that was what Lyric would want.

"Your wife is out of surgery, we did the best we could to repair the damage caused by the bullets. There was severe damage, I'm afraid," he said, his tone somber. "And your wife has slipped into a coma." He shook his head. "I'm sorry to say that I don't believe she will recover."

Savanna collapsed then, and Cody caught her as she passed out. JJ picked her up and carried her over to one of the couches, even as the doctor called a nurse.

He looked at Cody as she turned back to him. "I'm really sorry," he told her. "I wish I had better news."

Cody nodded, feeling like her world was spinning off its axis and there was nothing she could do to stop it. She stumbled blindly to the main hospital door, panting with the effort to control her emotions. She got outside and remembered that she didn't have her car with her. She ran out to the street and hailed a cab.

An hour later, a frantic McKenna walked into the house calling Cody's name. Jet had called her when Cody left the hospital.

She found Cody sitting on her bed; the room was dead silent, it was eerie. Cody was sitting with her knees up to her chest, her arms draped over them. It was obvious she had been drinking; there was an empty bottle of tequila on the floor.

"Cody?" McKenna queried softly.

Cody was staring at a spot on the bed, but McKenna was pretty sure she wasn't seeing anything. She climbed onto the bed and knelt in front of Cody's knees. She then moved closer, between Cody's parted legs, taking Cody's face in her hands. Cody's eyes shifted to hers then, and suddenly it was like she was seeing her for the first time. In what seemed like slow motioned, Cody crumpled against her and started sobbing. McKenna held her, her heart breaking as Cody cried hysterically, holding onto her like she was drowning in her sorrow. McKenna did everything she could to calm her.

Cody suddenly began panting, gasping for breath, and McKenna knew she was having a panic attack.

"Breathe, babe, you have to breathe..." McKenna told her, her lips to Cody's ear. "You have to breathe, baby... You have to take it slow..."

Cody shook her head, still breathing in shallow breaths.

McKenna took her face in her hands again. "Baby, listen to me," she said, her face an inch from Cody's. "You have to breathe slow," she said, her tone stern. "Slow down, Cody, slow down..." she said, over and over again until she saw Cody's breathing easing.

"They killed her," Cody said, her tone devastated. "They killed her..." she said, her breath becoming ragged again. "Oh God... they killed her...." she said, fresh tears starting again.

McKenna spent hours that night going between holding Cody and trying to calm her down. Cody finally fell into an exhausted sleep, and McKenna lay on the bed holding her, with her own tears sliding down her temples.

The next morning, McKenna got out of bed carefully, trying not to wake Cody. She called and talked to Jet who had stayed at the hospital.

"How is Savanna?" McKenna asked.

"Catatonic," Jet said. "This is so awful, McKenna," she said, her tone sad. "If Lyric dies, we'll lose Cody, you have to know that."

"That's what I'm afraid of, yes," McKenna said, knowing it was true. "What do they think Lyric's chances are?"

"Slim to none," Jet said, the answer making her sick to her stomach.

"Oh God…" McKenna said. "What can I do?"

"Just hold onto Cody tight," Jet said. "That's all you can do right now."

"Should I bring her there?" McKenna asked.

"If she's up to it," Jet said. "If nothing else, she needs to say goodbye," Jet said, her voice breaking on the last word.

McKenna had tears in her eyes immediately at hearing it. She hung up with Jet a few moments later. Walking back into the bedroom, she looked at Cody lying on the bed. Tears slid silently down her cheeks as she imagined how Cody would react if Lyric died. She knew beyond a shadow of a doubt that they'd lose Cody too.

At the hospital, Jet was busy texting every contact she had. She wanted to know who had pulled the trigger on Lyric Falco, and she was leaning hard on every informant she had, threatening everything she could think of to get the information she needed. She was damned if someone was going to take out someone like Lyric Falco and get away with it. She looked over to where Savanna sat, she was leaning against

Lyric's father staring unseeing at the floor. Her father, Edward, finally made it to the hospital, having been in New York when he'd heard the news about his daughter-in-law. He walked over to where Savanna sat, took her into his arms and she began crying hysterically again.

Savanna was sure she was living in a nightmare and that eventually she'd wake up to Lyric's face telling her it was just a bad dream. This couldn't really be happening, Lyric was fine, she was just not home yet... No they were at the hospital... Why were they here again? No, it wasn't for Lyric, it was for something else... It couldn't be for Lyric... They were going on vacation... They were going to Sicily, Lyric was taking her there...

A little while later, they told Lyric's family that they could see her. She was still in a coma with no signs of recovery. Jacomo Falco supported Savanna on one side and Edward supported her on the other as they walked to the room where Lyric lay hooked up to machines. Savanna stumbled when she saw Lyric, reaching out blindly as Mario caught her. He helped her over to the chair near the bed and sat her down. Savanna was breathing heavily, her eyes glassy.

Mario, Saldino, and JJ all leaned down, one by one and kissed their baby sister's cheek. Savanna had begun crying softly, tears sliding down her cheeks. The men left, they couldn't handle seeing their sister so broken. Edward hugged Savanna, telling her he'd be just outside. Jacomo was the last to leave. He leaned down to kiss both of Lyric's cheeks, talking to her softly in Italian, tears on his own cheeks as he hugged Savanna.

Savanna sat in the room, looking at Lyric and feeling like she was dying inside with every beep of the monitors. She cried until there just weren't anymore tears, then she sat, concentrating on her breathing, knowing she needed to breathe. Every so often she would close her eyes slowly and a tear would escape Then she would open them again and stare at the floor, just trying to remember to breathe.

When Cody woke up that morning, she saw McKenna lying on the bed next to her. For a second she forgot about what was happening, and then it hit her again and she closed her eyes against the agony that crashed back in.

McKenna reached her hand out, touching Cody's cheek, wanting desperately to take the pain away for her, but knowing there was no way to do that.

"I need to go back to the hospital," Cody said after a few minutes. "I need to go…" she said, moving to sit up.

"Okay," McKenna said, "but you need to eat something, Cody."

"No," Cody said, shaking her head as she got up and pulled her jeans on. "I need to go now."

"Cody…" McKenna said, her voice tentative.

Cody whirled around. "I'm going, so either you're coming or you're not," she said, and headed for the door, picking up her keys as she did.

"Cody!" McKenna exclaimed, jumping up and trying to throw on pants and go after Cody at the same time.

She got to the garage just as Cody's Ninja screeched out of the driveway.

"Damnit!" McKenna yelled.

After closing the garage door, she walked back into the house and called for a Lyft driver. It took her another hour to get to the hospital.

As she walked through the hospital door, a man approached her and grabbed her arm, she felt something hard stuck against her side.

"Just come with me, juerita…" he said, his Mexican accent clear.

McKenna glanced around at the people in the hospital.

"Say anything and you'll be the next one dead," he told her in a growl.

McKenna nodded and walked with the man. They got into a car that sped off.

Cody walked into the room Lyric was in, seeing Savanna sitting in the chair looking completely spaced out. She walked over to Savanna and leaned down to hug her.

"Mom?" she queried.

Savanna's eyes suddenly focused on Cody. She drew in a deep breath and the tears started all over again. Cody held her in her arms, feeling her heart torn out by her mother's complete devastation.

"I can't live without her…" Savanna said. "She's my life, Cody… She's my life… I can't live without her… Oh God, Cody…" she exclaimed, crying harder. "I can't, I can't…"

In the end, Cody stayed with Savanna the entire day, holding her when she cried, or just sitting on the floor next to her holding her hand when she wasn't crying. At one point early in the evening, Savanna fell asleep out of pure exhaustion. Cody stood up, leaning down to kiss Savanna on the cheek. She turned to kneel next to Lyric's bed then, taking Lyric's hand in hers.

"I'm going to kill the bastards that did this, Mom…" she said. "I'm going to fucking kill them all…" she said softly, her tone determined. Moving to stand, she leaned down to kiss Lyric's forehead, as Lyric had kissed hers so often over the years. "Thank you for everything," she said, her tears starting again. "Thank you for my life, for everything you taught me, and for loving me no matter what stupid shit I did... I love you Lyric, I love you so much... If you can make it back here for Mom, that would be good... She needs you... I love you so much... I'm sorry, but I have to do this... I can't let them get away with this... Not with this... I love you... I love you... Thank you..." she said, her tears falling continuously.

She walked out of the room and down the hall, leaving by the back door. Getting onto her bike, she drove home. There she took a shower, and pulled on jeans, boots, and a black shirt. She loaded her gun and put it into her holster, then loaded her backup weapon and put it into the ankle holster above her boot. She then picked up the Kaybar that Lyric had given her, and slid it into the sheath at her thigh. She pulled on her jacket and turned to pick up her keys. Her phone pinged then, and she picked it up. It was a text message from Jet.

"Cody they have McKenna! They're at the ETown. Do not do anything until I get there!"

Cody looked at the message, gritting her teeth at the image of McKenna in the Sureños' hands. She tossed her phone on the bed and left the room. She got into her car and drove in a direction she knew so well. It was ironic to her that this show down was going to happen in the same place Lyric had killed Churro over eight years before. Almost poetic, Cody thought.

She parked her car, she got out and looked around. There were plenty of Sureños in evidence, but they all just looked at her with varied degrees of malice and bravado.

She was hailed with comments like, "How's the family?" and, "Como esta tu madre?" Asking her how her mother was. Cody gritted her teeth, wanting desperately to shoot each and every one of them, but knowing she needed to get to McKenna first. Walking up the stairs, she looked ahead of her.

"Jesus, the same room even?" she muttered to herself. "Not very original."

When she got to the room she was stopped by two Sureños who frisked her and took her weapons. She'd half expected that. They pushed her into the room then, and she saw McKenna huddled on the bed. She had a flash of Lyric walking into the room over eight years before and remembered that flash of hope that had started in her that night.

"Cody!" McKenna cried.

"It's okay," Cody told her, her voice completely calm.

"Is it, puta?" drawled Martin, who sat in a chair next to the bed.

Suddenly a man grabbed Cody from behind, yanking her arms back behind her. Cody struggled against his hold, but he only tightened his hold further, until Cody had no choice but to subside.

"This is between you and me, Martin," Cody said. "Let her go."

"Right...." Martin said. "It's like the movies, I'm gonna just let her go, right?" he sneered. "Nah, this ain't the movies, Cody, and what I'm gonna do is fuck her right here in front of you and then I'm gonna kill her slow so you can watch that too. And then when I'm done I'm gonna fuck you and kill you too. How's that for a movie, eh?" he asked, laughing raucously. "Maybe like a hot porno, huh?" he asked, with a ribald laugh.

"Don't make me kill you, Martin," Cody said, her tone a low growl.

"Shit… You think you can do that puta? Let's see you try," he said, moving toward her and leveling a punch at her mid-section. Then he punched her in the face and continued punching her until she sagged to the ground.

She was shaken back into consciousness when McKenna screamed. As she opened her eyes, she saw that Martin was yanking at McKenna's jeans, and she was fighting him. He slapped her hard and she subsided, recoiling away from him.

Cody became aware of the man holding her; she could feel his breath on her cheek, so she knew he was close. Without warning she rammed her head into his face as hard as she possibly could, seeing stars for her effort, but he also loosened his grip enough to grab at his face. She turned around kicking him in the knee, hearing it pop and he screamed in pain. She then launched herself at Martin, grabbing him by a handful of hair and ramming his head into the wall above the bed.

He threw her off of him with surprising strength, and Cody hit the floor in a heap, but quickly shifted backwards to get away from him as he advanced on her, blood dripping from a cut above his eye.

"Fucking bitch! You fucking cunt, I'm going to fucking kill you!" he screamed. "Then I'm gonna keep that cunt over there and let all the guys gang bang her till she's fucking dead!"

Cody had moved into a crouch, and hearing what he'd just said she knew she had no choice. Giving a banshee-like scream, she launched herself at him, ramming into his mid-section with all the force she had, driving him backwards. She heard McKenna scream her name as she broke the barrier of the open doorway, and she kept moving, driving Martin straight over the low rail of the balcony. Then they were both falling.

Cody hit the ground and everything went black.

Chapter 9

Lyric woke to the sound of machines beeping. She stared up at the ceiling trying to gather her thoughts and wondering why she felt so heavy. With all the effort she could muster, she turned her head to the right and saw Savanna sitting in the chair. Her eyes were open, but she didn't seem to be conscious.

"Van?" Lyric queried, her voice coming out as the barest whisper.

Savanna didn't move.

"Van?" Lyric said again, forcing more sound into her voice. It was barely audible, but it was enough.

Savanna blinked, and looked over at her. Her mouth dropped open slowly, and she reached up to rub her eyes, sure she was seeing things.

"Lyric?" she cried. "Lyric!" she exclaimed again, moving forward to touch Lyric's face. "My God, my God, babe… Thank God…" she breathed, the tears in her eyes spilling over as she leaned down to kiss Lyric's lips, cheeks, and forehead.

Lyric blinked a couple of times, trying to gather her strength enough to ask questions.

"What… happened?" she asked.

Savanna nodded, assuring herself that Lyric really was awake and talking, she wasn't dreaming it.

"You were shot, babe, but you're okay now… You're okay now…" she said, her tone wondrous.

Lyric's blue eyes searched Savanna's face, she could see the strain on her face and she suspected that she'd been hurt worse than Savanna was saying. She wanted to ask about Cody, but she already felt herself sinking back into sleep, she felt so heavy…

"Love you, honey…" Lyric whispered.

"I love you, Lyric, I love you…" Savanna said, her voice a desperate whisper next to her ear. "Rest now honey, just rest…"

Lyric nodded slightly and was asleep a moment later.

Savanna jumped up and strode out the waiting room where Lyric's family and some of their friends were still holding vigil. Savanna skidded to a halt, her eyes scanning all the people there that loved Lyric so much and she smiled. She walked over to Jacomo, who was looking very old and very tired suddenly. She knelt in front of him, taking his hands in hers looking up into his face.

"Daddy Falco," she said, smiling. "She woke up… She woke up…" she said, her voice reflecting the awe she was feeling.

Jacomo stared back at her for a long moment as if not understanding her. In truth, he was so far away in his mind at that point he didn't understand her.

"Lei è papà sveglia!" Mario told his father, saying in Italian that she was awake.

"Sì?" Jacomo queried, looking at Savanna.

"Sì, papa, sì!" Savanna said, nodding.

"Oh my girl…" Jacomo said then, grabbing Savanna up in a hug and crying at the same time.

The waiting room was filled with tears at hearing the news.

Cody regained consciousness slowly and groaned as she tried to move, her entire body protested wildly. She lay in a hospital bed with machines around her beeping and whirring.

"Cody?" McKenna queried, hovering over her.

"Hi…" Cody murmured, her eyes staring up at McKenna.

McKenna smiled. "Hi," she said, her look relieved.

"Martin?" Cody queried.

"Dead," McKenna said, her tone even.

Cody breathed a sigh. "And you're okay?" she asked then.

McKenna nodded slowly. "I'm okay, Cody."

Cody nodded, closing her eyes again, her brow creasing in a frown. It had hit her again, why she'd had to do what she'd done, and she knew that it hadn't changed anything.

"Cody," McKenna said then, reaching out to touch her hand.

Cody opened her eyes and looked over at McKenna, her eyes haunted.

"Lyric woke up," McKenna said then.

Cody's mouth opened as joy swept through her, it was almost painful the way her heart leapt. "She did?" she finally managed to ask, her heart pounded so hard she almost couldn't breathe.

McKenna nodded, smiling with tears in her eyes.

Cody blew her breath out audibly and her entire body relaxed instantly. Then she started to move to get up off the hospital bed.

"Cody, no," McKenna started to say, but Cody had already discovered that moving at all was really painful.

Cody gasped and lay back down with a grimace.

"Holy shit…" she breathed, gasping in pain.

"Yeah…" McKenna said, her tone teasing and sympathetic at the same time. "A fall from a second story onto pavement tends to really piss a body off…"

Cody grinned. "I kinda hoped he'd break my fall," she said, her tone surly.

"That really didn't work out," McKenna said, her tone wry, but then she grew serious. "You could have died, Cody…" she said.

"He was going to kill you… and me… He'd already killed Lyric, at least that's what I thought… I had to kill him, Kenna… I had to…" Cody said, her voice halting as emotions overwhelmed her.

"Even if it had killed you?" McKenna asked, looking devastated.

Cody shook her head. "I didn't care in that moment," she said, her look lost.

She looked at McKenna then and saw the upset on her face. "I'm sorry," she said sincerely. "I just didn't see any other way. He had to die for what he did, and I had to be the one to do it."

McKenna swallowed convulsively, nodding her head. It had terrified her to watch Cody shoving Martin backwards. When they'd reached the open balcony door McKenna had known what was going to happen. She would never forget the terror that had sent her running to the railing to look down and seeing Cody lying on the pavement with Martin lying a couple of feet away.

Thankfully, Jet had arrived with law enforcement back up just in time. She'd been the first one to get to Cody, calling in the ambulance immediately. It had been a terrifying ride to the hospital, but they'd told her that Cody's pulse was strong and that she would be okay as far as they could tell, she'd been so relieved she'd cried on the EMT's shoulder.

Cody and McKenna were quiet for a few minutes. A nurse came in and gave Cody more pain meds, which put her back to sleep.

When Cody woke again, she turned her head and was surprised to see Lyric sitting there in a wheelchair, her blue eyes looking back at her expectantly.

"Mom?" Cody queried, hoping she wasn't dreaming.

"Yeah?" Lyric replied, grinning as she raised an eyebrow at her daughter.

Cody shifted to try to reach out to Lyric, but winced in pain when she did.

"That's not a good idea, babe," Lyric said, grinning again.

Cody looked back at her, her hazel eyes searching her face. Lyric could see the minute it all clicked in her head. The tears started then, and Lyric moved as best she could to touch her daughter's head.

"They killed you, Mom..." Cody said, tears sliding from her eyes. "I heard them shoot you..." She was crying then, all of the stress, worry, and fear forcing its way out.

Lyric leaned against the side of the bed, still a bit weak herself, but doing everything she could to comfort Cody.

"I'm here, baby, I'm here..." she said, her voice soft. "They didn't kill me, they didn't kill either of us... We won... They lost..."

257

When Cody finally calmed down, she looked up at Lyric.

"And you're really okay?" she asked, as if she wasn't daring to believe it.

"So they tell me," Lyric said, smiling down at her daughter.

Cody drew in a deep breath, blowing it out in a loud sigh as she nodded her head.

"Okay, okay…" she said.

"Now, let's talk about your spectacular dive off a second floor…" Lyric said, her tone even, her eyes reflecting how crazy she thought the action had been.

"He was going to kill her, Mom," Cody said, her tone devastated. "He was going to torture her and kill her… I had to stop him."

Lyric nodded, understanding Cody's motivation. "Can you not do that again, please?" she said her tone light, even as her eyes showed her anxiety.

"Sure," Cody said, nodding. "I think I can avoid that in the future," she said, her tone light as well.

"Good," Lyric said, canting her head at her daughter. "Now you need to get better, 'cause we have a trip to take."

"A trip?" Cody asked, surprised by the change of topic.

"Well, Mom and I missed our flight to Italy," she said, her lips curling in a grin. "So I figure we might as well add a couple of people when we re-book."

"Like?" Cody asked, her eyes shining with hope.

"Like you and McKenna," Lyric said. "I'm thinking we could all use a vacation, what do you think?"

"I think you're the smartest woman I know," Cody said, smiling.

"Good answer, kid, good answer," Lyric said, grinning.

Epilogue

They'd spent days wandering the lush and expansive grounds of La Famiglia Falco, a villa and winery. McKenna had been unable to believe the beauty of the countryside and had spent most of her time staring around her open-mouthed. Cody had never been to the family land either, so she was fairly impressed herself, although she was a bit more circumspect about it.

Lyric and Savanna spent hours sitting on the veranda talking and drinking either coffee or wine. Savanna had spent a lot of time over the last few weeks simply looking at her wife and marveling at the fact that she was still there. They hadn't really talked much about the incident, because Lyric had heard from a lot of people how completely devastated Savanna had been. She didn't want to upset her by talking about it more than necessary.

Two nights into their visit, Cody lay in bed watching McKenna move around their room. She was examining everything and wondering at the paintings and furnishings in the room. Admittedly, it was a beautiful room with murals on the ceiling accented in gold leaf, and antique neoclassical furniture with rich inlaid woods and damask materials.

Cody grinned. "Are you ever coming to bed?" she asked.

McKenna looked over at her, smiling. "I'm sorry, I've just never seen so much incredible art before in my life, and this furniture…" she said, running her hand reverently over a dresser, her eyes alight with excitement.

Cody smiled, enjoying McKenna's excitement. "Worldly rich girl like you, I'd figure this stuff would be blasé for you," Cody said.

"Stop it," McKenna said, sending Cody a narrowed look. "This place is amazing, Cody… Don't you think so?"

"Yes, I think it's amazing, but I think I'd like to lie here with my girl and enjoy her for a few hours…" she said, her tone suggestive.

McKenna looked over at her, seeing Cody lift aside the covers, and pat the bed next to her. She smiled, so glad to see Cody looking relaxed and happy again. She walked over and lay down next to Cody. Cody leaned over her kissing her lips softly. They spent the next hour taking their time making love. Afterwards, Cody held her as they lay on their sides facing each other.

"So you're pretty impressed with La Famiglia Falco, huh?" Cody asked, grinning.

"I'd say so, yes," McKenna said, smiling.

Cody nodded, her grin making her eyes sparkle. "Falco does seem to be a pretty cool name, especially here," she said, gesturing to the area around them.

McKenna chuckled. "Pretty cool," she said, smiling.

Cody looked back at her for a long moment. "Think you might ever want to take the Falco name?"

McKenna looked back at Cody for a long moment, then nodded slowly, her look perplexed. "Cody…" she began, her voice hesitant.

Cody pinned her with a look then, and McKenna found herself holding her breath at the look in Cody's eyes.

"Think you might want to take it with this?" Cody asked, reaching over to the nightstand. She picked up a small box and handed it to McKenna.

"Cody, what is this?" McKenna asked, her voice soft.

Cody smiled softly. "Open it," she said.

McKenna opened the box, and nestled inside was a ring. It was the most beautiful thing McKenna had ever seen. It was antique and in the neoclassic style, designed in white gold, with an intricately carved band, and a large European cut diamond in the center. On the sides of the ring there were carved curled scroll designs. There were also diamond accents on either side of the center diamond.

"Cody, this is incredible…" McKenna breathed, unable to take her eyes off the ring for a long few moments.

"It's a family ring," Cody said. "Lyric's mom wore it, and her mother and her mother before her… It goes back to the 1920s."

"Cody… I can't take this… This is a family heirloom…" McKenna said.

"So are you saying you won't marry me?" Cody asked, her look serious.

McKenna looked back at Cody, not sure why she couldn't breathe for a moment, but then realizing it was because she was holding her breath.

"Are you actually going to ask me to marry you?" McKenna finally said, a grin starting on her lips.

"Gonna make me do it the hard way, huh?" Cody asked.

"At least ask the question the right way," McKenna said, smiling.

Cody looked back at her, her eyes growing very serious. "McKenna Hayden, will you marry me?" she asked reverently.

McKenna smiled softly. "Of course I will marry you Cody Falco," she replied.

"Whew!" Cody said, looking relieved.

"Put it on," McKenna said, handing Cody the ring and holding out her left hand.

Cody slid the ring onto McKenna's finger. It fit perfectly.

"Guess that seals that," Cody said, smiling.

"Guess so," McKenna said, biting her lips and smiling at Cody.

"Cody got the ring?" Savanna asked as she moved to lie down next to Lyric in bed.

"Yep, she got the ring," Lyric said, smiling.

Savanna looked up at Lyric. "And you're really okay with this?"

"Why wouldn't I be?" Lyric asked.

"It's a big step for Cody," Savanna said.

"And you don't think McKenna is the perfect person for our daughter?" Lyric asked, her tone indicating that she thought Savanna was crazy if she said that McKenna wasn't perfect for Cody.

"I think Cody needs someone like McKenna, you're right about that," Savanna said. "But she's still so young…"

"When love hits, it hits, babe," Lyric said. "What's really going on?" she asked sensing an underlying concern in Savanna's words.

Savanna blew her breath out, shaking her head. "I guess I'm afraid of an empty nest," she said, her look sad.

"So, what if it didn't stay empty?" Lyric asked.

Savanna looked back at her. "What do you mean?" she asked, her tone cautious.

Lyric saw the caution in Savanna's eyes. "I mean whatever you want it to mean babe…" she said. "Either that we adopt another kid that needs a good home, or we have a baby of our own."

"You're willing to do that?" Savanna asked, shocked.

"I'm willing to do whatever it takes to make you happy, Savanna," Lyric said, taking Savanna's face in both of her hands. "I love you more than life, and I want you to be happy and fulfilled and to never once have to think about what happened again…"

Savanna's lips trembled at the mention of the incident. "You know if you'd have died, I would have lost Cody too…"

"I know," Lyric said, her voice constricted with emotion.

Savanna's eyes filled with tears and Lyric pulled her into her arms, letting her cry, and feeling grateful to whatever powers that be that had decided it wasn't her time. She'd thought about what would have happened if she'd died, and she knew beyond a shadow of a doubt that Cody would have followed soon after. From what she'd heard, and from what Cody herself had said, she knew that was true. She didn't even want to imagine what that would have done to Savanna. It was terrifying to love someone so much that fear of dying took on a whole other meaning because of how it would affect the person who would lose you.

When Savanna had calmed down, she looked up at Lyric.

"I think I want to have a baby with you," she said, her voice soft.

"Then I think that's what we'll do," Lyric said, kissing her lips, and pulling back to look into her eyes.

She saw a thought cross Savanna's features, and then saw her dismiss it.

"What, honey?" Lyric asked, wanting to give her wife anything and everything she could.

Savanna looked hesitant. Lyric just waited for her to decide to say what she had been thinking.

"Do you think it would be too much to ask one of the boys to do-nate... for a baby?"

"One of my brothers?" Lyric asked.

"Yeah, you know, so a baby would have your DNA too."

"Yeah, and one of my lunk head brothers DNA..." Lyric said, grinning.

Savanna pressed her lips together, her look circumspect.

"I'm kidding, babe," Lyric said. "I think that would be a fair thing to ask. Maybe JJ since he doesn't seem to be interested in settling down anytime soon."

Savannah smiled brilliantly then. "You make me so happy."

"And I plan to for the rest of our lives," Lyric replied.

Back in Los Angeles, things at The Club were in their usual swing. Jet made her way through the crowd, with beers for her and Skyler, a Baileys for Devin and a soda for Fadiyah who finally had a free evening to spend with her wife. Jericho and Zoey were there, as were Quinn and Xandy. There'd been the usual flurry of excitement about Xandy Blue being at The Club when they'd arrived but it had finally calmed down which mean Quinn could relax. Natalia and Raine were there as well. Natalia had met a friend there that wanted to talk about putting together a dance studio.

The bois in the group had admired the newcomer, a redhead with green eyes and a body that was definitely worth the time to admire if nothing else. At five four, Jazmine Collette was a definite showstopper with waist-length red hair that fell in loose curls, a sweetheart-shaped face with a perfect California tan and smooth skin, and wide green eyes that sparkled when she talked. She was a professional dancer and had danced in hip-hop videos and the like, and had been rumored to have dated a number of hip-hop stars. It was for that reason that everyone was shocked when the girl had no problem dancing with the random butches that asked her or moved up to her out on the floor. She was definitely a party girl.

Tyler and Shenin arrived at The Club shortly after everyone else and rounds of hugs were exchanged. Shenin joined the girls on the dance floor, and Tyler took her beer and stood with Quinn, Jericho, Jet and Skyler who were all leaning on the raised bar that surrounded the dance floor, watching their girls dance. Even Fadiyah had been persuaded to dance, and Natalia was showing her how.

"So what do you think of the new girl?" Quinn asked Tyler.

"The redhead?" Tyler asked.

"Yeah, not your redhead, the other one," Quinn said, winking.

Tyler chuckled, then took a good long look. "Nice…" She looks… ah… friendly…" she stammered. "Who's she here with?"

"Well, she came to meet Nat," Jericho said, "but she didn't show up with anyone."

Tyler nodded, her look considering. "Looks like she'll have lots of options when she leaves…" she said, as yet another woman moved in on the girl.

As the song ended, the DJ said she was taking a break, and put on regular music. The girls all headed for the group, except for Natalia and Jazmine, who headed to the bathroom.

Everyone was standing and talking, when Natalia came running back to the group.

"Raine! Jericho! It's Jazmine! Hurry!"

Raine, Tyler, Jericho, Quinn, Jet, and Skyler all followed Natalia to the back of The Club where there was a scuffle going on. As they stopped to figure out what was happening, the girls all spread out to partially surround the two men and the woman.

There was a black guy yelling at Jazmine who was backing away from him with her hands up in front her.

"Hey!" Jericho yelled, distracting the guy for a moment.

Jazmine saw her opportunity and started to walk away but another black man, bigger than the first appeared and grabbed her. She screamed.

Quinn was about to react when a woman from behind stepped in. She was every bit as tall as the man, standing about six foot, and she snatched him up by two handfuls of his jacket and threw him a good three feet from Jazmine. Jazmine had fallen to the floor in the melee. As the group watched, the woman took a knee leaning down to Jazmine and saying something.

Everyone was shocked when Jazmine looked up at the woman and promptly fainted. The woman was close enough to cradle her head, then moved to pick her up easily. Turning around, her eyes scanned the crowd.

"Ray?" Tyler queried, suddenly.

The woman's eyes moved to Tyler.

"Ty," the woman said, nodding. "Good to see ya, where can I put her down?" she asked, a grin on her lips.

"Ah." Tyler looked over at Jet, who nodded for the woman to follow her.

The rest of the group trailed after, having to know what the story.

In the office, the woman strode over to the couch and once again went down to one knee to lay Jazmine down gently. She stood then, turning to look at the women who were all watching her with fascination. The woman was tall, but the two inch heeled boots she wore made her seem taller. , with a strong handsome face that was tanned with black brows and lashes. Her hair, pulled back in a long thick braid, hung half way down her back and was jet black. She had the look of an American Indian, which was confirmed a minute later when she introduced herself.

She grinned showing a set of very white, very straight teeth, her dark eyes sparkling with a knowing look.

"Rayden Black Wolf, at your service," she said inclining her head as her grin widened.

www.ingramcontent.com/pod-product-compliance
Lightning Source LLC
Chambersburg PA
CBHW050718180626
46814CB00002B/500